The Bingo Long
Traveling All-Stars
and Motor Kings

The Bingo Long Traveling All-Stars and Motor Kings

WILLIAM BRASHLER

HARPER & ROW, PUBLISHERS
New York • Evanston • San Francisco • London

FIRST EDITION

Designed by C. Linda Dingler

Library of Congress Cataloging in Publication Data

Brashler, William.
  The Bingo Long Traveling All-Stars and Motor Kings.
  I. Title
PZ4.B82273Bi ⁰PS3552.R33¼   813'5'4   72-R104
ISBN 0-06-010449-X

For Cindy—

And for Josh, Satchel,
Cool Papa, and the Others

The Bingo Long
Traveling All-Stars
and Motor Kings

Chapter 1

MAY 1939   When Leon Carter got to the mound the fans of the Louisville Ebony Aces applauded lightly. It was tradition for Leon to throw his first pitch without a team behind him. It would be a fastball, screaming down the center of the plate from a straight overhand motion after Leon had pawed and kicked his leg in the air like a stallion.

The lead-off hitter was a skinny second baseman, Cool Papa Blue. Cool Papa hit almost .400 last year and led his team, the Memphis Shots, to second place in the Southern Colored League. He would get Leon Carter's fastball invitation like anybody else. The home crowd stamped their feet on the wooden bleachers. The old men yelled, "C'mon, Cool Papa, hit the *in*vite pitch."

Bingo Long crouched behind the plate. He watched Cool Papa Blue step into the batter's box, Blue's baggy pants blowing slightly against his legs, the green script letters spelling "Shots" spread from one arm to the other. "Whatayasay, Blue," Bingo said, and Cool Papa winked without looking down at him. Leon Carter waited on the mound, looking blankly at Bingo and Blue. Then the umpire motioned him on. Bingo gave no sign. He just raised his thick catcher's mitt, held it like a plate at Cool Papa's knees, and waited for Leon's kick.

The pitcher touched his cap, rubbed his hand across his chest, and grabbed the ball from his mitt to begin the pendulum motion of his windup. His left leg began to rise. Bingo dug in on his haunches behind the plate. Cool Papa drummed his fingers against the handle of the bat. Then Leon's right foot pushed against the pitching rubber, his right arm rose like a snake's head and spit out the white pellet. Cool Papa lashed at it, Bingo caught it like a pistol shot in the wet pocket of his mitt. A cheer went up from the fans. The game had begun. And the rest of the Ebony Aces trotted out to their positions.

Sallie Potter wheeled the black bus in front of his restaurant, left it running, and went in to get his team. Inside, Bingo sat at a table with Louis Keystone and a waitress named Cleo. Bingo drank beer from a bottle; the others finished their steaks. Sallie's Ebony Aces were turning a nice profit for him this year, so the food came freely. Sallie had a lot of ways of making money. He ran a few horses, a few numbers banks, and his restaurants were the best for colored people in all of Louisville. He had a reputation for having the best: the best ball players, the best steaks, and between the two, the best entertainment for the money. He paid Bingo and Leon Carter four hundred dollars a month to keep them playing with the Ebony Aces. No colored team paid better than that.

"This bus is leaving," Sallie shouted.

Bingo swallowed his beer and leaned over to give Cleo a kiss. "You be a good old girl and I'll bring you back something pretty from Philly," he said to her.

"Something big," she said, and Bingo put some cash on the table in front of her.

The bus was a '39 Mack. Sallie Potter had had reclining seats put in it just for his team. They piled their luggage on top, eighteen players, and logged from town to town in the Southern Colored League as well as playing exhibition games with teams in the North. The bus had SALLIE POTTER'S LOUISVILLE

EBONY ACES, THE WORLD CHAMPIONS OF COLORED BASEBALL painted on its sides. Though his stomach barely fit behind the wheel, Sallie had bought himself a chauffeur's cap and appointed himself the head driver. He pulled the bus around the corners and through the streets, waving at policemen and kids who yelled, "Hey, Aces, where you all going to?" Sallie shot them a smile and kept on wheeling.

Bingo opened a window and hung out of the bus as it left Louisville. The kids in baggy jeans ran alongside, their hound dogs yelping and nipping, while Bingo held out his big hands for the kids to shake and pull. But the bus rolled on, gaining speed and losing the kids. Bingo hung out until the last, when Louis Keystone pulled him back into the bus. "Those kids is going to vote for me someday, Louis," Bingo said.

"You be the colored man's dream," Louis said.

"You just said it," said Bingo.

They drove all night, into Ohio and then Pennsylvania. Church Russell, the Aces' manager, spelled Sallie at the wheel for a few hours. He was the only other person Sallie trusted to head the big bus. Bingo and the others played blackjack and nickel-dime poker on equipment trunks in the back. Bingo had taken off his suit and draped it over the seats. Only a thin cotton T-shirt stretched over his massive chest and a stomach still hard but showing signs of softening. At thirty-four he felt young and loose, and refused to consider that his body could ever get away from him. His arms angled down from his shoulders, his round face and the stump he called his neck reluctantly tapered to his wrists and fingers, where he held his cards. He would rather play his game in boxer shorts than wrinkle his clothes before hitting the big cities. Each time he shuffled, he snapped the elastic of his garters for emphasis.

"Pick them up and believe them," he jabbered. He had a complete set of chips he had picked up in New Orleans. Each one had a golden *B* on it.

"I can draw those B's to me like flies on a cat's ass," he said.

"You talk it but you can't play it," said Sam Popper as he shoveled in a pile from the center.

"Diamond Jim will take your chips every time," said Louis, looking at Bingo and chuckling.

Bingo sneered at them and looked over his new hand. They called him "Telegraph" because he couldn't keep a bluff. When his cards were bad they just watched for his eyes to shoot around the table like a Ping-Pong ball. When they were good, he licked his tongue over his front teeth and glowed as if he were crossing home plate. His wide eyes and smooth, deep black features came alive. Not a single Ebony Ace hadn't won money off of Bingo at one time or another, even though he owned the chips and was the first to bring out the deck.

"I learned my game from the Mississippi riverboat boys. The hand is quicker than both eyes," he said. He wiped his fingers on his T-shirt and shuffled the deck.

Bingo's bad cards had landed him on the Ebony Aces five years before. Bingo was jumping his team in Mobile to join the Pittsburgh Elite Giants when Sallie Potter intercepted him in a game in the backroom of his restaurant. In a couple of hours Bingo was into Sallie for a hundred and twenty bucks. Sallie said he would match that and top it with two hundred fifty more a month if Bingo would stay on in Louisville. The Aces had only Leon Carter then, and not much of a name, but Bingo couldn't pass up a chance to pay his debts and make two hundred and fifty bucks at the same time. Sallie stopped the cards at the very moment of Bingo's decision and introduced his customers to his new catcher. "We're going to play some classy smoke ball around Louisville from now on," Sallie said.

They arrived in Pittsburgh at ten the next morning. Sallie was driving again, the players were drowsy and stiff from the night of half-sleeping in their seats. After dumping twenty bucks in the game, Bingo had leaned back and slept in his underwear.

In the morning he dressed, spat on his hands, and slapped himself in the face. "I hope this town is ready for me," he said. They were playing the Elite Giants at three o'clock, so Bingo had a few hours to see some friends. Only Louis Keystone was fully awake and ready to go with him. Bingo picked a dandelion for his lapel and headed for Lionel Foster's Pittsburgh Chop House.

"Hey, Henry Bingo Long hisself," the man shouted. "Right here in Pittsburgh." Lionel Foster got up from his table and his pork chops and held out his hand to Bingo. "Now how you doing, boy?" Lionel was a small and slightly built man with a white head of hair and a mouth full of gold. He and Sallie Potter had been friends in Pittsburgh until Sallie learned enough from Lionel to do his own hustling. They both knew baseball and restaurants. Lionel always had had some kind of ball team in town for as long as anyone could remember.

"I'm doing fine. And you, Lionel?" Bingo sat down at the table and looked around at the empty restaurant. Lionel called to a shirt-sleeved bartender for a couple of beers for Bingo and Louis. The Chop House was dimly lit and still a mess from the night before. Lionel kept it open until three in the morning with both the food and the drinks going and a band hitting it in the corner.

"You know this place don't never shut down. Hey, you hungry for something? Put some more pork chops on for these boys, Richard." Lionel dug at his food. "Things is pretty good around here. Looking up. People is getting some money in their pockets and this is the first place they comes. I ain't complaining. How about you, Bingo? You looking good."

Bingo chewed on a chop, holding it in his hands, and nodded. "Still hitting the long ball," he said.

"You know I ain't forgave you yet for not coming here to play with me. You know I could a matched any money Sallie give you. You know that, Bingo." Lionel leaned back and picked at his teeth. "How's Sallie treating you lately?"

"He's still on top," Bingo answered. "Sallie's cool about the money."

"You into him for some, Bingo?"

"Some."

"Knew it," said Lionel. "Sallie's always good for keeping his boys around the eight ball long enough to get them on their knees. You broke now, Bingo?"

"Didn't say that," returned Bingo. "Long as I can hit the ball I'm a rich man." He smiled and drank his beer. Louis Keystone kept his head in his food.

"You getting to be an old man and you ain't learned nothing yet. You want some more chops? They good this morning, ain't they?" said Lionel, and he called his bartender over again. "We having some good music tonight. You coming around, ain't you? Win or lose."

"I'll turn out the lights with you, Lionel," Bingo said.

The Ebony Aces enjoyed playing in Pittsburgh. It was a big town with a lot of colored people and plenty of noise. Lionel Foster put them up at the Burleigh Hotel, a far cry from the fleabag colored people's hotels in the South. The Burleigh had clean sheets and hot water, and it was only a two-block walk from the Chop House.

But Lionel's Elite Giants were another thing. A lot of sharp Northern boys played on the Giants, hardheads from New York and the Pennsylvania coal towns. Judy Gilliams was one of the loosest left-handed first basemen around, "Shoe" Jonal Pryor could hit the ball with anybody. The Elite Giants didn't get around much; they played mostly against teams in the Eastern Colored League. But they were always tough, and Lionel liked nothing better than to see Sallie Potter's boys come up from Louisville.

Carleton Simpson, who had just left the Memphis Shots,

6

threw against the Aces that afternoon. The Aces treated Simpson and the Pittsburgh people to some power. Fat Sam Popper connected, Mungo Redd connected, and Bingo leaned into a pair of Simpson's fastballs so hard the people strained to watch them go. Sallie Potter sat in the stands eating hot dogs. His suit coat could barely contain the bulging fat which rimmed his belt and pushed tightly against his white shirt. Only a single button held his vest closed. Sallie's fat face, his generous wattles, and his pudgy body made it obvious that he had always been the farthest thing from an athlete. As Sallie chewed, Ace pitcher Turkey Travis eased nonchalantly through the Elite Giants for a 9–5 win. At the hotel that night, before the players had left for Lionel's place, Sallie said to them, "Boys, just remember who you play for." Then he left to see his own part of Pittsburgh.

The door was open, the purple neons blinked and hummed. Lionel had all the glasses washed, the bottles shined, and the tables pulled back. Bingo stepped into the Chop House in his double-breasted pin stripe, a fresh carnation in the buttonhole, his white buck shoes. Louis Keystone followed in white on white; Popper, Mungo, Splinter Tommy, and the other Aces were just as turned out. "Hey, Aces! Hey, Bingo! Abbadab-badabba, slugger!" Whistles and shouts, a tip of the hat. "Hey, Mr. Lionel! Set up the house on me!" The place was crowded and ready to jump. A combo tuned and flexed in the corner. Bingo sifted through the people to say hi to Lucille and Virginia and some of the other yallers Lionel had decorating the floor.

Herman on sax was feeling into "Baby, Don't Tell on Me," biting the reed, twisting. Cab on trombone tapped the boards with his heel, slid the slide, half-step, syncopate, his eyes into it. Glide and exchange, take it to Weaver on the bass, pulling, pull it. Cymbal fuzz from Coon, boards tapping, then rim shot and hit it. Lenny, Little Jazz, cracked his lip into his golden cornet. The house was on fire.

Louis Keystone grabbed Lucille and they flew into the center, swinging the jitterbug from Little Jazz. They stepped and whirled, Louis in white smiled and moved like a butterfly, Lucille twisted under his arm and kicked her heels. Bingo latched onto Morgana and they joined the swing. Coon took the beat on the skins and blew the foam off the beer. Lionel watched the lights outside flutter, steam on the windows, drumming fingertips. Bingo felt himself loose and light, Morgana was laughing and brushing him with her silk. But skinny Louis took the show, dipping around and over Lucille, skipping on the air above the boards. Louis connected for a line shot, it rose over short, Louis a snake threw it through the water. "Pow," said Little Jazz, and Louis spun around first. "Tut," said Little Jazz, and Louis hummed into second, white bucks clicking. "Zip," said Little Jazz, and Louis was tiptoe on third, Lucille, the people whistling, skinny Louis wrapping it up.

The combo did not quit through the night. Herman took it from Little Jazz, Cab went from there, Coon mopped up. "Grievin'," "Frankie and Johnny," "Stompin' at the Savoy," "Strange Fruit." One more once. Louis hopped with Morgana, Virginia, back to Lucille, giving no rest to his soles, the people still with him. Bingo bought round after round. He talked baseball with Lionel Foster and Carleton Simpson. He talked trash with Morgana. "Bingo, why ain't you got no lady to keep house for you?" Outside the sidewalks shook and people looked in to see what Lionel had going on. One more once.

By two in the morning the crowd had thinned even though Louis continued to work out some lindy hop and big apple with the ladies. Bingo was feeling a little hazy. When Lionel invited him to the back office he went gladly and sank into an overstuffed chair. The office was small and poorly lit. Lionel had trophies and pictures of the Elite Giants clustered everywhere.

"You boys is got a fine outfit," he said. He leaned his small frame against his desk and lit a cigar. "The man Sallie has got himself another crackerjack ball club."

"We as good as the best," Bingo said, sitting back and closing his eyes.

"I bet you better when old Leon pitches," said Lionel.

Bingo sucked on a cigarette. He talked slowly.

"You fixing to make some deals, Lionel? That what you got up your sleeve?"

"Man like me always looking for deals."

"How much you got?" Bingo said.

"Hah, no amount enough for you. Sallie Potter want all the dough in Pittsburgh for you."

"Then what you talking about?"

Lionel put one leg on the desktop and sat on it.

"I just want to see what kind of gambling man you is nowadays." Bingo sat up and looked him in the eye. "You a big star now, Bingo. You in your salad days. When the people know you in town they come to the park. Lots a people. You with me, Bingo?"

"What you saying, Lionel?"

"I saying you ought to be knowing how important you is. Sallie took a thousand out of that gate today, mostly because of you. And I bet he ain't paying you a grand for a month's labor. You got to know how important you is, Bingo."

"You making me a deal?"

"I ain't making no deals just yet. I ain't pushing no contracts. Just remember that times is getting high again. Just remember that. Then when you get ideas you remember old Lionel's door is wide open."

Bingo blew the smoke from his cigarette and saw gold in the little man's smile, the gold in the trophies around the room.

The band was coming down now. Little Jazz was drenched with smoky sweat, his lip about shot for the night. Coon tapped the offbeat and Little Jazz leaned back to squeeze out "Jesus Keep Me Near the Cross." Louis was stretched over a chair, dead asleep. Little Jazz eased the valves, the vibrato quivering in his neck. He handed it to Herman and his sax pushed it up, the sound glazing itself upon the thick air. Then Little Jazz took it back, sliced some time, and put some Dixie into it. The boys followed, a final spurt, sending it back home. Three A.M.

Chapter 2

Bingo crouched, rocked back on the balls of his feet, and swung his butt down until it almost grazed the dirt. Bingo went into the game at about 225, but when his uniform sagged with sweat and the chest protector clung to him, he knew he would be lucky to end the day above 215. He carried most of his weight from his waist up; he had a torso like a boiler. As he crouched he felt umpire Emmett Bodges knee into him. "Now don't crowd me, don't love me, ump," he said to him. Bingo shoved a couple of fingers down for Turkey Travis, his pitcher, and spat into his mitt. "Hum it, Turkey, sing it, Turkey, give me dinner, Turkey." With his right hand in a fist, all the knuckles facing Travis, Bingo planted the mitt and waited for the pitcher to throw. One of Satler's Colored Giants choked up on his bat and waved it quickly over the plate. The sun again brought sweat with the dust, and it streaked Bingo's uniform as he chattered.

The Satler Giant poked at Travis's fork ball and tipped it back into Bingo's fist. The ball stung his fingers, then deadened and dropped. Bingo hissed and held his breath. "Now hot damn!" he screamed. He clenched the fist even tighter as if to suffocate the pain. Then he waved it at the Satler Giant. "Damn," he repeated, rhyming the pain with every shot he had ever taken in the neck, the apple, the crotch.

"Keep pinching. It'll come back to you," said Church Russell when he got out to Bingo. He watched while Bingo paced and circled and spat on his hand. "Now hot damn!" he said again, and some of the fans in Altoona, Pennsylvania's, Calvin Coolidge Park began to chuckle at him. Church Russell even smiled, and sun shone against the wet of his teeth.

. . . Looking up at Mrs. Eustis, he kept his lips in a tight line across his face, not showing a trace of a smile or a frown. She whipped the switch down upon his outstretched knuckles again and again until the skin perked with white blotches. Then she stopped and he continued to look up at her, still not moving his hands. Willie, Willie Sam, and Lemuel looked over from their chairs. "Now git home, Henry Long. I can't stan' ya no mo'." She threw the switch in the corner. He did not move. "You a tough little nigger, Henry. You tougher 'an the devil hisself." Henry ran out of the shack. Willie, Willie Sam, and Lemuel followed after him.

Henry grabbed the hitting stick and the four of them went to the fence behind Thebe's General Store and U.S. Post Office. Henry hit first because he had got them out of school. It wasn't really school, it was Willie Sam's house and Willie Sam's mother trying to teach the four of them how to read and count. But Henry and the others could usually get her so angry she would use the switch and then kick them all outside. Then they lined up behind Thebe's fence and hit line drives with rocks at tin cans.

When Willie whacked his third rock the hitting stick splintered. They picked up the rest of the rocks and heaved them at the cans. The cans pinged and jumped in the air before they fell. In a nearby brush pile the four of them stumbled and sorted through the mess until they found another branch. Then they took it back in front of Thebe's and began working on it, peeling the bark off and honing it with a rock.

As Henry worked, old Steeples Redus, one of the regular sitters at Thebe's, said to him, "What you boys need is a genwine baseball hitting bat."

"Where we get it?" asked Henry.

"Don' know," said Steeples. "I jest said dat's what ya need."

Steeples cackled at his reply and winked at the others, Shap and Aldus Reed, who sat with him along the wooden bench. Henry continued to scrape the rock against the stick, using his bare feet to keep it steady.

"Why don't yuse ask Tebe's to git ya one," said Steeples.

"How much?" said Henry.

"Don't know. Ask 'im."

"What we use for a ball?"

"What yuse usin' now?"

"Rocks."

"Ain' no good ta use rocks," said Steeples.

"You a big help, Steeples," answered Henry.

The four of them sat at the foot of the bench, saying nothing. Only the gnawing of the rock broke the silence of the dusty street and the Alabama sun. Suddenly, from the north end of town, they heard a commotion of barking dogs and a roar of machinery. Henry and the others jumped to look. "It's the circus!" he yelled. They couldn't see anything but dust rising above the shacks. Then a pair of hound dogs raced around the corner, yelping and jumping in circles. Two long black automobiles followed, honking, billowing dust, the noise of their engines booming against the shacks lining the street. The automobiles slowed after they took the corner and glided toward Thebe's place. Each was a sleek Stutz Bearcat convertible with three rows of seats, spoked wheels, and whitewall tires. They were loaded with colored men who laughed and leaned over the sides to grab at the hounds. Henry, Willie Sam, and the others ran into the street and alongside the automobiles. Henry pawed at the men's hands, which were big enough to wrap completely around his own. Each man was dressed in a suit with a thin driving cap pulled down over his eyes. Then Henry jumped on the running board of the first automobile.

"How you doin', boy?" they yelled to him.

He hung onto the side of the auto, his eyes still wide.

"I said how ya doin', boy!"

"Yeah, good, good!" he yelled. "Hey, where you all bin to?"

He stared at their clothes, the white shirts and wide red ties. Rings shone from their fingers like streaks of sun in a mirror.

"All over. Where you bin?" one of them shouted back. The rest laughed and grinned.

"I bin here in Monkey Run alla time," he yelled. By now the car was well past Thebe's store and heading out of town.

"Monkey see, Monkey who?" the same man answered. The others broke up. Henry shook his head and stared again at each of the men and at the shining insides of the car. He licked his lips. Then he looked back for Willie Sam and saw him running with the hounds in the dust.

"C'mon back, Henry!" Willie Sam yelled above the dogs and the engines. Henry jumped from the auto and yelled. The men laughed and waved their hats back at him. The second automobile passed and the men in it waved as well, shooting back white, wide-mouthed grins that sparkled through the dust.

Henry and the others stood and watched the dogs chase the cars down the road and finally out of sight. They waved frantically until they could no longer hear the sounds of the engines.

"Who were they? Who were those men?" he yelled as he ran up to Thebe's.

"Those was the Grays," said Steeples.

"The who?"

"The Grays. They is a baseball team from up Nawth."

"How you know?"

"They comes through here couple years back. They on their way down to Mobile to play the teams down der."

"Is that what they do for their job?"

14

"Yeah. They is a lot a colored teams around. I seen one once in Birmin'ham. Ain't they a classy bunch in those motorcars?"

"They ride like the Gov'nor hisself," said Aldus Reed.

Henry went back to work on the hitting stick. He could still hear the booming automobiles and see the finely dressed Grays. Nothing as grand as they had ever come through Monkey Run before: honking, grabbing, in their own black automobiles, Henry Long on the running board.

"C'mon," said Willie Sam, and the four of them took the new stick and some more rocks and ran back to the fence. They smacked wild, cockeyed drives that missed the cans by a mile. But they were more excited than ever, yelling with each swing of the stick, "I'se a Gray! I'se a Gray man!" And with the crack of a rock they took off running for first base or center field or wherever a Gray would run. . . .

The fans enjoyed Bingo's injury as much as it pained him. They laughed and heckled him as he jumped around home plate.

"You going to have to hold it with the other hand tonight," someone yelled, and the crowd howled.

"You sure you got it in the finger?" said another. The crowd whistled and groaned and held their fingers to their mouths in pain. Bingo by this time was standing still and letting Church Russell examine the knuckles. Bingo then played catch with Turkey to get back the feel of the ball. Then he held up his taped fingers to the crowd.

"They fine. Yes, folks, thanks to you all, they is just *fine,*" he yelled.

The crowd hooted. Then a lady shouted, "You come over tonight and I'll soak those for you, honey!" The crowd whistled and cheered.

"Start warming the water, Peaches," Bingo yelled at her, and the crowd broke up again. "All right, Turkey, hum it. Sing it, Turkey. Give me dinner, Turkey," he chirped. He began throw-

15

ing dirt onto the batter's shoetops. "Yes, ma'am, Georgia, start warming the water."

From Altoona the team traveled to Chester and Scerbyville, and by Friday they were into Philadelphia. The Philadelphia American Stars was another big team in the Eastern Colored League. On Saturday the Aces would play them in Shibe Park, the home of the major league Philadelphia Athletics. With the reputation the Aces were carrying, and if Sallie could promise a performance by Leon Carter along with Bingo, the game was sure to draw around five or six thousand fans. Sallie had asked for a percentage of the gate, an exception to his usual practice of demanding a fixed guarantee for showing. But in a place like Philadelphia and a park as big as Shibe, the money was in the crowd and Sallie knew it. All he had to do was advertise Leon and Bingo, in big black letters on the fences around the neighborhoods, and wait for the people to turn out.

At game time Sallie went to each ticket booth and watched the sales. On a percentage gate he couldn't rely on anyone's word for the take except his own. With his cigar sliding along his lips like a snake, he made peck marks on the back of an old game program with a snub-nosed pencil, marks which meant nothing to anyone except himself and whomever he had to settle with. During the first three innings of the game he would lean over Bollo Rooker's shoulder behind the locked doors of a backroom and watch the Philly owner count out nickels and dimes. Then Sallie would put his hand into the pile, cut his share, shovel it into a paper sack, and give Bollo a gentleman's handshake. Nobody but the two of them ever knew what the actual take was. That was a simple gentlemen's agreement between owners.

After the team checked into the hotel, Bingo unpacked his case and set out in the city alone. He waved a cab and told the driver to take him to the Brown Elementary School. The cabbie

16

was a short, fat-faced colored man who hardly could peer over the steering wheel.

"You ever heard an ol' boy named Scipio Murphy?" Bingo said to him.

"What's he do?" said the cabbie.

"Nothing now. He used to play some ball."

"Colored?"

"Yeah."

"Why you want him?"

"Just want to pay him a visit." The cabbie did not answer.

"You means Furry," he finally said. "I ain't never known him by anything except Furry, if he the man you looking for. He owe you some money or something, huh? That why you going to the school?"

"He works there, that's all."

"Maybe," said the cabbie. "I ain't never seen him but in a bar. He about dead now. He can't hardly see no more."

At Brown School Bingo walked to an office and was told to go to the boiler room. He followed the dim corridors down a flight of stairs and into the basement of the building. He stopped at a door marked "Furnace." The room was large and dark; a single light bulb shone in a far corner.

A dry, stale smell hung in the air. Bingo paused for a moment to let his eyes adjust to the darkened room, then he stepped down the concrete steps to the floor. Noise from a blower motor covered his footsteps. Passing a coalbin, Bingo stepped into the light of the single bulb. An old gray-headed colored man sat slouched on a stool in the corner. He was asleep, with his head lying in the pocket of his left shoulder. A fat spotted hound lay curled beneath the stool. The dog slept as soundly as the man, each with a lazy, guttural snore. Bingo eyed the pair for a moment, then he spoke.

"Mister Murphy?" His words echoed in the darkness.

The old man's head did not lift, nor did his eyes open.

"No, suh," he said. The dog continued to snore.

"You Scipio Murphy, the ball player?" Bingo asked and walked closer to where the old man sat. The man looked up at him, squinting his eyes because of the light. Bingo could see he hadn't a tooth in his head.

"Nope. Name's Furry." He talked slowly. "What you want?" Bingo sensed the old man's suspicion of him.

"My name's Bingo Long. I play ball for the Louisville Aces. Man told me the ball player Scipio Murphy had a job in this here school."

The old man scratched his chest. The dog was now awake and looking blankly at Bingo.

"Well, that's me. People call me Furry now. It's my dog's name. He go where I go all the time so people be calling us both Furry."

He pointed to a metal chair a few feet away. "Sit down, boy. So you is Bingo Long. I read your name on the signs by the house. They say you the best hitter around. So that's you."

Bingo nodded and smiled. He sat down on the folding chair. The old man stretched and crossed his legs. A white sock dropped around the left ankle as it hung over the right shin. The thin shinbone stretched upward like a broom handle.

"So you is today's crowd pleaser." He paused and pulled out a chaw from his shirt pocket. "You big—how big are you? I'se tall, but I never as big as you. What you play?"

"Catch."

"That all?"

"That's enough."

"I play everything one time or another. Back for the Chattanooga Bees I play every position except left field and that was my ordinary position in the first place. That's why I lasted so long, I was *ver*satile."

Furry rolled his tongue against his gums and spat into a tuna can on the floor. Deadly aim; the can quivered. "I still got the old touch once in a while," he said. "But why you come here? Why you come to see old Furry?"

"People say you was once the best. People say they wasn't a catcher alive could peg you out at second. Lionel Foster says he never saw any man hit the pill like Scipio 'Fox' Murphy. And I told myself I'd like to meet that man Murphy."

"Old Lionel say that because he make some fancy money off Furry whenever I came to Pittsburgh. Scipio 'Fox' Murphy, hah . . . I remember that man Lionel Foster real good. If he still alive he taking money from somebody cause Lionel a fox that don't stay in his den for long. Yeah, if you knows Lionel you be a smart man to stay away from him if he ain't take money from your pocket already."

"Old Lionel?" Bingo asked.

Furry sat up and licked his lips. His eyes widened. "Yeah, him. When I play for Abe Wickling—yeah, it was Abe and the Beantown Clowns around '20, and that was around the time I decide to quit—we ran into Mr. Foster right here in Philly and he set us up two games with his team and I don't even remember what name it had anymore. Lionel guaranteed us a hunerd bucks for the day—hunerd and a quarter for me, Mr. Murphy —or at least that's what he said, for playing his team in two different ball parks on the same day. One on the north side of town and one down there by the can company. Well, we gets a lot of people there for the first game—it was the ABCs was his team, yeah—and we goes to play them again at the other park when Lionel shows up and says, 'Sorry, boys, but the other game's been canceled,' 'cause he can't get the park or something, so he give us all twenty-five dollars and says the big crowd would have been at the other park so we would have to settle for this. We couldn't say nothing 'cause we ain't signed no paper for the game. It was a gentlemen's agreement except Lionel ain't no gentleman. That's what I mean. They all got their angles and he is one of the worst."

"We hit him a couple of days ago."

"Beat him?"

"Bad."

"Then you must have a first-class team yourself. And you a catcher, huh? We had a good catcher for the Bees, old Blue Eyes Nobly Bruce, and he could hit the tomato."

"How about you? They put a valuable man like you in left field with the weeds?" said Bingo.

"Oh, that wasn't until I got old and couldn't move so good. I play everything, some short, some pitch, a lot of third base. But for the Lookouts here in Philadelphia I play left 'cause I was getting on near fifty years old. I quit in '20 when I was fifty-one and I didn't look a day over thirty-five and I wouldn't a quit except my eye started twitching like a butterfly."

"What'd you do then?"

"Anything I could get my hands on. I sing a little, work a little counter, sometimes I sweep 'cause there is always sweeping to do. Like here in this school Mr. Culley an old friend and he been giving me eleven dollars a week to watch the boiler and sweep and see that the kids don't kill theirselves in the place. Nope, I ain't seen a ball for years but I don't mind 'cause it makes me start thinking about the old days like I am doing with you. Old Furry can't bring back the ball games like this old dog can't chase a rabbit no more without killing hisself. And I can't bring back the money I made or the money the bosses or the dealers or the ladies took away from me. Me and this old dog we just sits and stays quiet together like the Lord was around the corner waiting for us to stumble so He could say, 'That's all, Furry,' and call the roll. I can't run around like I used to when I was a young chicken and playing ball like there was no tomorrow and drinking with women who called me Foxy, yeah, that's what they called me, and taking my money 'cause I didn't pay no mind. And what about you, Bingo? You young like me and a star with a sweet-looking suit of clothes. But you must have something in your head or you wouldn't be down wasting time with an old dried-up ball player like Furry."

"I do my game. Like they expect a long ball with a man on third so I do it for them. I ain't saying I don't fool a little or chase the ladies or do a share of dealing from the bottom of the deck. I got a nice life, no complaints, no coming up short." He stopped, and smiled at Furry. "The silkies called you Foxy, huh?"

Furry grinned his pink gums. "The money draws the ladies. But you got to watch for those who is taking it from you more than they is putting out. They don't leave no one alone until you old and worn out."

Furry stopped and fussed with his chaw. The dog crawled from under his chair and stood between the two of them. Then it stretched its front paws ahead and leaned upon them. A slow, whining yawn raised from its chops. Furry spat into the tuna can. The dog sniffed at Bingo's knee, panted long enough for Bingo to smell its swamp breath, then fell back into a heap beneath Furry's chair.

"He getting fatter and I getting leaner," Furry said.

The crowd at Shibe Park was one of the biggest the Aces had played to all year. Bingo craned to find Furry in the stands but he couldn't spot him. Pockets of cotton-headed old men dotted the crowd, some of them hoarse, filmy-eyed, leaning on sticks to watch the game. The people began riding Bingo the minute he took batting practice. A pair of girls behind the Stars' dugout kept calling him "Bubbles" and "Kingfish," two new labels for him. They squealed when he raised his cap and blew them a kiss. A few minutes later he walked all the way to the backstop. From there, with the warm-up pitcher standing on home plate, he swatted some tower blasts out of the park. The crowd hooted at each one of them. Bingo was everything the sidewalk posters said he was, but the crowd wasn't going to admit it to his face.

21

Leon Carter pitched against the Stars. Silently, with his long face expressionless, he laid fastballs into Bingo's mitt. Bingo talked and threw stones and aggravated the batters; the two girls by the dugout kept whistling and winking.

In the fourth inning Raymond Mikes stroked a triple down the right-field line. Mikes hustled over the bases, making wide arcs around first and second. But going into third with a neat fall-away slide, he hooked a spike of the third baseman. He rolled on his back and cried out from the pain. The dust which had swirled with the arrival of the ball and the runner settled slowly on Raymond's sweating, tortured forehead. The foot swelled so fast Church Russell didn't even try to take the shoe off. As they carried Raymond off between their shoulders for want of a stretcher, they could see the foot was broken. And Raymond, an old, dependable regular who played with broken fingers and ribs when it was necessary, grimaced with a sad and fearful look of pain that whitened his lips.

Bingo was sitting in a steaming tub back at the hotel when Isaac Nettles burst in on him.

"C'mon, Bingo. C'mon down and see what the man is doing to Raymond."

"What's happening in heaven ain't important enough to get me out of this tub," Bingo yelled back at him.

"*This* is, man. Sallie has gone and done it to Raymond 'cause of his broken wheel."

"Done what?"

"Let him go. He done given him a one-way ticket back to Louisville and closed the book on him."

"Raymond will be back," said Bingo and he slid down into the water.

"No, man, that ain't it. He's done. Sallie has given him his papers and said he gone and bought a new man. He told Raymond he too old to come back like usual and for him to forget it. And Raymond, with his foot as big as a watermelon, is sitting there in his room and crying like a baby. So, man, Bingo, you has got to come and help us fight the boss!"

Isaac punched his fist into his hand. He was breathing and sweating and swirling the steam from Bingo's bath.

The Aces were standing around the center fielder when Bingo and Isaac got to Raymond's room. Sallie Potter was not there. Raymond sat on the bed, his foot swollen and wrapped with a loose gauze bandage. It was just as crooked as it had been when he got up from third base.

"What's the rub, Raymond?" Bingo asked and tried to force a smile.

"They ain't none no more. That shoe has turned the lights out for me," he said.

"What'd Sallie say?"

"He said that I'd been a fine man for a long time but that since I was thirty-six I was past the repairing age. He got me a ticket back to Kentucky and these here crutches."

"He must a been dealing a new center fielder before Raymond got back to the bench," said Louis Keystone from the corner of the room.

"That's what he told you straight out, Raymond?" Bingo asked. "No promises or conditions? You didn't sign no paper?"

"He said he'd send this month's pay back to me as soon as he could scrape it out of the gate. I didn't sign nothing."

Bingo stood in front of Raymond, looking at his foot. He knew the center fielder was done for the time being, maybe for good. A ball player like Mikes had to be able to run, for he was a poke hitter, a man who pushed singles and doubles where he could get them. Without his speed he could no longer scramble, no longer push pins into opponents' defenses and get away with it. Raymond knew it. Bingo and the rest of the Ebony Aces said it with their silence. Bingo felt the heat push to his forehead.

He stood up. "We going to do something for you, Raymond. We ain't going to let Sallie push you around like a postcard."

"We can't do nothing," said Leon Carter. He stood at the door of the room, picking at his teeth. "Raymond knows he slud hisself right out of the ball game. And nothing we do will help."

"We'll show Sallie who he's dealing with," answered Louis Keystone.

"Sallie knows already. Ain't none of us signed on for steak and eggs when we signed Sallie's paper. He didn't promise nothing for nothing and I ain't saying that 'cause I like him but because we got to know where we at."

"How about you, Leon? When you gets a sore wing will you sing that song? C'mon, Leon. You is getting on as old as Raymond and how can you talk like you do?" Bingo said. He glowered at the pitcher.

"I ain't saying nothing you all don't know. What good are we to Sallie and his wallet when the bones ain't there no more?" he answered.

Bingo fidgeted, searching for an answer. His eyes darted at Leon and the others behind him. Then he shouted his answer.

"A man like Raymond needs some respect, yeah, he can't sit there like an old dog just cause Sallie says good-bye. He is us, and you too, Leon."

The rest of the players nodded and murmured approval. Leon stood unmoved, still chewing his toothpick. Then he took it from his mouth and flicked it on the floor. "When was the last time you hit the ball for Sallie 'cause of respect, Bingo?" and Leon snorted and walked away down the hall.

Bingo hissed loudly behind him; the others said nothing.

"Who's here who is willing to lay it back on Sallie with me?" Bingo said.

"We all is," answered Isaac Nettles. They charged out of Raymond's room behind Bingo. Raymond remained behind sitting on the bed, gazing at his foot.

At Sallie's room Bingo knocked, then entered with the others close on his heels. The room was empty but for Sallie's baggage.

24

They could smell the bath and shaving lotion and knew he had already left for the evening.

"I'll find him," said Isaac. "I'll find him if I got to score at every hop house in this town."

 Chapter 3

"I didn't ask for no one new," Church Russell said. He waved his hands in front of his face as he talked. "I ain't knowed nothing about Raymond except his foot being busted. It ain't like me to be making no deals."

Church stood in front of the players while they dressed for Saturday's game. Isaac Nettles pointed his finger at Church's nose.

"You mean you didn't know that old Raymond got on a Green Line for Louisville this morning with a one-way ticket from Sallie? You didn't know that?" Isaac shouted so loud the brick-walled room echoed his words. He hadn't slept all night and his eyelids hung. He hadn't found Sallie either. Bingo stepped up behind him.

"Who is going to play center today, Church? We going to be asking some honey from the stands to stand out there?" Bingo said.

"I swear I ain't been making no deals. I is for this team the way it was with Raymond in center," Church answered. "I swear on my job, boys."

"Ain't no swearing needed, Church." The voice came from the door. Sallie, in a cool dark suit and vest, sauntered into the middle of the team. He had a white straw hat on his head.

Isaac pushed through to him. "So the man with the knife has showed."

Sallie stood his ground. He pushed his chin out, inches from Isaac's. "Okay, Nettles, tell me your problems real quick so I can get about my business."

"Raymond, he's our business," Bingo said and stood in back of Isaac. "We ain't happy at the way you treated our regular man."

"That's polite of you, Bingo," Sallie said and bit off an end of a fresh cigar. "You saw his foot curled up like it was. He won't do no more than limp on it. What am I supposed to do with a man like that?"

"You treat him like a sucker," Bingo said.

"Raymond ain't no sucker, but he ain't a center fielder no more either." Sallie lit the cigar. He turned to see Leon Carter in full uniform walk out of the dressing room. "Now why don't you all forget it and do what Leon just did."

Sallie blew a cloud of smoke straight up above his head. He took a step for the door. Isaac grabbed his arm and spun him around. Immediately Sallie lashed out with his elbow and pivoted face to face with Nettles.

"You don't touch Sallie like that! You don't muss Sallie like that, boy!"

Isaac scowled, then towered over the chubby owner. A few of the players scrambled to restrain him.

"Now look, Sallie," Bingo said. "We ask a question about Raymond and we want some answers. We don't need no one-way tickets like Raymond got."

A line of perspiration broke out along Sallie's upper lip.

"You just talking, Bingo. You know what the papers say."

"Maybe we be doing some rewriting of those papers."

"Shit, Bingo, what you telling me? You know a man gets injured and he's on his own. We all gambling. Ain't no one gambling bigger craps than me."

27

"We wants some insurance written into those papers—yeah, that's what we want. We just taken a quick vote."

"You get fried chicken from heaven before you get insurance written into my papers."

"I ain't fooling, Sallie. I ain't saying things to amuse you."

"But what you is saying, Bingo, ain't worth my time. You remember Miller Rowe and his bad arm and I don't remember you raising hell over that. I ain't looking out for none of you past what you can do for me and this here team. We got that straight so let's keep our traps shut."

Bingo wiped his hand across his face. Isaac tried to say something but Bingo kept him back. "You be hearing from us, Sallie," he said. "This man ain't nobody's set of craps. You ain't going to have the chance to carry another nigger off the field."

Sallie broke into a big smile. He puffed his cigar and clouded his face with the smoke. "You is some mouth, Bingo." Then he left.

Bingo sat down on the wooden bench and reached for a Lucky Strike. "Well, what you boys think we should be doing now? Raymond is still on that bus with his foot and his wallet busted flat."

Isaac kicked at his satchel. He had argued with Sallie before and got nowhere. The man wasn't boss because of his luck; he had never given his players an inch more than he wanted to give them.

Then Louis Keystone spoke. "I say we form us one of them unions. You know, I been hearing about them unions up in Chicago and around and they been stopping things dead by joining up against the bosses and laying down on the job."

"Shit," said Isaac.

"Them unions has got a million men and we ain't got but sixteen," said Tommy Washington.

Bingo sat up. "But what we going to do with a weasel like Sallie? What we going to do?"

Louis said, "Now this is just me, Louis, talking but I say the union is the trick. I been reading about them in the papers."

"We could call us the Louisville Ebony Aces Union," said Isaac.

"Ain't that shit for a name," said Bingo. Isaac shrugged.

"We communicate our demands to Sallie in the name of the union like we was John H. Lewis hisself," said Louis.

The other players were still listening. No one had even dressed into full uniform yet and game time was less than twenty minutes away. Then the dressing room door burst open in front of Sallie.

"I want a team on the field in cut time or it's *money* from you!" he shouted and slammed the door. The team members hustled back to their benches.

"Some union we going to have," said Bingo.

The bus rolled through Pennsylvania on its way back to Louisville. The Aces had nosed the Stars in twelve innings that afternoon on Mungo Redd's squeeze bunt. They hadn't been beaten now in two weeks; Sallie Potter slept noisily in his reclining seat while Church drove the bus.

Instead of the usual card games, Bingo called the team back for a meeting. They clustered around him, eating baloney sandwiches and sardines packed in jars and cheese. The union idea was still a live issue. Louis Keystone even had an evening paper he was prepared to read which quoted a member of a steel workers' union in Gary, Indiana.

"What I is saying," said Bingo, "is that we got to take the upper hand. We read Sallie what Louis has got here and then we tell him we is a union with a complete constitution of demands."

"What you know about the constitution?" said Isaac.

"Nothing," said Bingo.

"But it sounds good," said Louis and he flicked his fingers against his newspaper.

"We going to ask for insurance. That's our blue tip. A hunerd a month in case we needs it. Then for sauce on the deal we going to ask for a bonus when the seats is full." Bingo rubbed his thumbs along his lapels. He had his suit on even though most of the rest of them were still dressed in their game sweats.

"How much bonus?" asked Mungo between bites of a pickle.

"Twenty-five a man to open." Bingo grabbed the pickle from Mungo and took a bite.

"Ooo-wah," said Louis.

The rest of the team looked at each other and at Bingo. They were tired from the trip and skeptical of any new plans along the way.

Then Leon Carter stood up from the edge of the group. "I don't mean to say it again, but the man is going to laugh and howl until he die." Leon gave a thin, high-pitched moan like a duck call, shook his head, and went up the aisle to his seat.

"We don't need you in the bargaining," said Bingo. "And we ain't going to cut you in either." His eyes darted around to each member of the team. The proposition seemed to totter on their faces in expressions of complete doubt.

"Tell them what you propose if Sallie don't come around, Bingo," Louis said quickly.

Bingo plucked the carnation out of his lapel and smelled it, quivering his nostrils. Then he opened his eyes wide and uncrossed his legs.

"I been on the phone with Lionel Foster. And I got some backing out of him, yessir, on the barrel."

"What'd he say?" said Isaac.

"Just that. He say he put me up if I wants to break and start my own team. Flat out, with no papers."

"What league?" said Mungo.

"None. We be traveling. Hit all over the country and down there in Cuba and Mexico if we got the time."

30

"Who's running the team?" said Isaac.

"Me," said Bingo.

"Shit," Isaac replied.

"From Sallie to Lionel Foster, from the snake to the fox," murmured Fat Sam Popper.

"Hear me now," Bingo insisted. "I saying that if Sallie don't come around with a little gravy we pop this at him and see what he comes up with. We got to have our aces in the hole."

"And if he calls your bluff?" said Isaac.

"Then it ain't no bluff and I wires Lionel to give him the word. Then we in the ball business from the *paying* end."

"Ooo-wah," hissed Louis and he rolled his paper and swung it around like a bat. "No more Sallie between me and the paying fans."

The team fidgeted and talked slowly to each other. Their faces still read nothing but hesitation. Bingo had not sold them like he thought he would. A deck of cards shuffled. Leon began to snore from his seat. Isaac and Mungo finally joined a game, moving away from Bingo and Louis with absent looks in their eyes. Louis looked at Bingo for his next move. Bingo realized he had to come through at this instant or he would lose it.

"Sallie!" he yelled. Everyone froze at the shout, as if it were an umpire's called third strike. "Hey! Boss Potter!"

Church Russell craned his neck to see what the shouting was about. The bus swerved when he leaned. Leon jerked his head up and looked back at Bingo. "Aw, shit, man!" he yelled and glowered at Bingo. But Bingo had the air and looked right past Leon. He stood up to meet Sallie, who had rolled out of his seat and was stumbling toward the back of the bus. His suit was disheveled from sleeping, his face creased where he had been leaning on it.

"Talk, man. Talk fast 'cause I is aroused," he said. Bingo could smell the stale breath from Sallie's dry mouth.

"We was just talking business and we have decided on some propositions to entertain you with."

"I ain't in no mood to be entertained," said Sallie.

"They is propositions just the same."

"Yeah?"

"Yeah. I is the lead man for the Louisville Ebony Aces Union, which is the group responsible."

"What the hell . . ."

"Number one: the union demands two hundred dollars a month for each man for insurance. Put it away in case we need it. Like Raymond did."

"What the hell . . ."

"Number two: the union demands twenty-five bucks a man for every full house. Them is the two propositions but we got more if you decide to be deaf to them."

Bingo smiled and folded his arms in front of him.

Sallie shook his head and yawned. "You tell the union I'm going back to sleep. They can shove those propositions up the ass where they got them in the first place."

"We mean business, Sallie," Bingo said.

"I thought we was done with that shit in the dressing room back there. You signed papers, Bingo, and I stick to those 'cause I ain't a fool. A union, what the hell!"

"You best tear them papers up if you want to have a ball team."

"That big talk, Bingo. Big talk."

"Tell the man, Bingo, go ahead," egged Louis Keystone.

"Yeah, tell me," said Sallie.

"Okay, listen good, boss. We ain't playing cat and mouse no more. You best deal with us or we is going to form a team of our own under me. Just say the word one way or the other, Sallie."

"You drunk even though you ain't been drinking. Listen good, Bingo, and be done with it. There ain't nothing past this team for you colored boys but sweeping and stooping in the fields. I'll blackball everyone who jumps and then you is all done all over. You listen good, Bingo. We going by my rules 'cause I run the farm. I drug you all through the hard times when niggers was starving, unless your memories is short. There ain't going to be no propositions and nothing except what's on the papers. That's all, Bingo."

Sallie wiped the pods of spittle which had formed in the sides of his mouth. His neck bulged from his collar.

"Them words is going to cost you a team, boss. You going to need a new set of niggers for your farm." Bingo sat down in front of Sallie and lit up a Lucky.

"We'll see," said Sallie.

"Check," said Bingo.

They arrived in Louisville at four in the morning. Sallie pulled to a stop in front of his restaurant and the jerking halt aroused the sleeping-dead players. They shuffled off the bus without a word and headed for home. At one in the afternoon they had a league game with the Wheeling Yard Boys. Wheeling wasn't a tough outfit, so Sallie was not worried about the small amount of rest his team would get. He called it tight scheduling, getting the most out of his boys without making them look bad. And since the Aces had fixed salaries, every game Sallie could squeeze in put him that much more in the clear.

Bingo and Louis grabbed their satchels and headed off in Bingo's Auburn Straight-Eight for Chessie Joy's place. Chessie kept the backroom open for selected customers until 6 A.M. When Bingo and Louis stumbled in the place was quiet, the fast traffic had left. A few table games were going and a pair of half-drunk brassies sat slumped around the bar. Bingo rubbed the sleep out of his eyes and tried to smooth his rumpled collar.

"Where you boys in from?" asked Chessie as he pushed them a couple of beers.

"Philly," said Louis.

"Whew! Driving all night?"

"Naw, we was sleeping but the bus was driving all night," said Bingo. One of the brassies pulled a chair up to their table. "Hey,

Charlotte, you looking good." Bingo eased a smile at the lady.

"Yeah, slugger," she whined.

The beer somewhat enlivened the two of them. Bingo put his arm around Charlotte's back and tugged at the zipper on her dress. He licked his lips and made a short popping noise. "Shut up," the lady growled, and Bingo chuckled at her.

"Tell them, Bingo. Tell the people about your new team," Louis said.

Bingo stretched his arms behind his back and yawned. "Just hold on, Louis. Wait until all the strings is worked out." He drank his beer dry.

"What's the story, Bingo? You got something cooking for the Aces?" asked Chessie. He was a long-time fan of the Aces even before Sallie owned the club. For the last two years he set up free beer for the day's top hitter.

"I got something cooking but it ain't with the Aces," Bingo replied.

"Yeah, Bingo told Sallie where to stick his hat," Louis said. "You should a seen it, Chessie, it was red hot."

"Told the fat man off, did you?" said Chessie.

Bingo pushed his glass at Chessie and the little man went to the bar to refill it.

"I thought Sallie was going to start swinging, the way Bingo was lashing on him. You heard about Raymond, Chessie, he been in here with his foot?" said Louis.

"Yeah, I seen him this morning hobbling like a goose. But what you got up, Bingo?"

"You'll see soon enough, Chessie. I got to make some connections yet."

"Yeah, there is big connections to be made," said Louis. He paused and looked into the bottom of his glass. Then he looked up quickly. "What you mean, Bingo, ain't you got it worked out yet?"

"Got to make a few phone calls yet to get through to Lionel. I got to lay this thing out for him."

34

"You mean it weren't all set for you just to give the word? Oh, man, Bingo, you was bluffing all the time. And I thought you had read over Sallie for good," Louis exclaimed. He shook his head incredulously. "Oh, man, Bingo, you a talking fool."

"Keep your lip up, Louis. I made my decision right there in the bus. After today's game I be making those calls and tomorrow we be recruiting for the Bingo Long All-Stars and Motor Kings. We going to do it to Sallie."

Bingo stood up, gave Chessie a bill, and headed for the door. He turned and motioned to Charlotte. "C'mon, darling, I'll take you where you're going."

Louis followed behind.

The Aces continued their sting against the Wheeling Yard Boys. Bingo connected for a line drive homer in the first inning off a fastball he wasn't even sure he saw. Louis stole four bases, two of them with his hesitation steal. He danced off the base trying to draw a throw but ran only after the catcher lobbed the ball back to the pitcher. It was a foolish move against a good team, but the Yard Boys were not sharp, and Louis slid in face first far ahead of the throw. The crowd loved the steal. They whistled at him after each slide as he stood on top of the base with his eyes flashing and his baggy suit red with dirt.

Bingo chattered incessantly even though he was dead tired. He eyed Louis at third each time they threw the ball around the horn. Louis flashed him the traveling look, and Bingo grinned and saw himself driving his Auburn down the highway with his name painted on the side. THE BINGO LONG TRAVELING ALL-STARS AND MOTOR KINGS.

He called Lionel early that night and talked for almost an hour setting up the details. Lionel was more than willing to back Bingo with a little capital until the gates started turning. A couple thousand for equipment and bonuses so Bingo could get the boys he wanted from the Aces. Lionel wanted nothing in return except his front money and the pleasure of seeing Sallie

35

beaten at his own game. He agreed to work out the details when Bingo got the team up to Pittsburgh. They could play their first game against Lionel's Elite Giants. Bingo licked his lips over the phone and asked himself why he hadn't done this years ago. He said he'd have a prime team up at the Chop House by Friday.

The house was a long, white two-story with a wooden-railed porch winding around the side. It was the largest on Pickney Street in Louisville, and at one time belonged to a member of the Kentucky state legislature. Ezell Carter spun the rear tire of his overturned bike, looking carefully for the weak length in its chain. His father, Leon, napped on a sofa pushed out on the porch. Bingo pulled up in his Auburn. He pawed at Ezell, who had run up to him, and poked him in the gut.

"Your daddy dead, Eze?"

"Yep, right there," he said.

Bingo picked up a crab apple and tossed it at Leon. It bounced on the porch boards like a golf ball. The long, six-foot-five-inch pitcher barely opened his eyes to see who it was. Leon was thirty-six now, but only the lean lines of his face showed his age. He had the thin, smooth-boned face of an Indian, a light brown, almost ginger color, with an expression which made him look as if he was constantly brooding. That he seldom smiled made him starkly handsome. Leon opened his eyes and saw Bingo.

"Say, Bingo. What's happening?" he said and closed his eyes again. "You running around on an off day?"

"Doing some setting up. It's all in the works, Leon. I just want you to know that right off."

"Yeah, well, let me know it, then tell me what you talking about."

"I got me a team, I got me a good team in the works. There ain't no more Aces business with me no more. I'se organized and drawed up the plans."

"Okay, boss, lay it on me so I can go back to sleep like I was."

"Listen, Leon, what I told Sallie on the bus is happening now. I quit the Aces and I got me a traveling team. We going to hit the country starting Friday."

"Shit," moaned Leon and he broke into a slow laugh. He crossed his legs, which ran the length of the sofa, and grabbed for his pack of Philip Morris. "You mean a barnstorming outfit this time a year?"

"Yeah, that's it. We going to do it now instead of in winter when everybody else is competing against us. We going to clean up." Bingo leaned forward on the railing he was sitting on.

"Well, good luck, all-star. You going to be needing it."

"That's why I come here, Leon. . . ."

"No, sir," Leon said. "No, sir, right now."

"Hold it, Leon. You know I need you for the kind of people you'll be drawing when they see your name up there. The people maybe can resist one of us when we comes in but they can't turn their backs on the both of us."

"Yeah, that's good. As long as I'm playing for the Aces like I am and the people is from Louisville where I is."

"Damn, Leon, yer Sallie's boy all the way."

"Yep."

"Sallie's sucker, Leon. He's sucking you like a bone."

"Hell, Bingo." Leon sat up and faced him. "I been throwing for Sallie as long as he been here and for the Aces as long as they been here. Before you came around. Thirteen years in July. And they was good years and then thin as soup and now good again. I didn't starve through none of them like a lot of colored right next door did 'cause the Aces kept putting up the uniform and sending me money when they could. Now you saying to forget all that and join you boys like I was some kid with a fishing pole for an arm. I'm getting old and I can feel it and it won't be but time before they be taking the invitation for a ride. I ain't suckering for no one, Bingo. I just know my score and how many innings I got going for me. That's all."

Bingo looked away, out into the yard and Ezell's spinning

tire. He eyed the Auburn, its whitewalled tires and the lines of the chassis.

"I give you five hunerd to start and a flat guarantee after that," he said quickly.

"Shit, where you getting that kind of cash?"

"I got it, you'll see it."

"Who's behind you? You ain't doing it alone with that money."

"Lionel, up in Pittsburgh."

Leon clapped his hands and leaned back. "Oh, yeah now. Big little man Lionel been dangling that carrot in front of your face."

"Three months. That's all you'd have to come along for. Then you could come back to Sallie for the rest of your life."

"And what about my contract I signed until next December?" Leon answered.

"You just jumping the paper for a while. Sallie can't do against you. The law would skin him if he tried. He ain't no threat like he wishes he was."

"Shit."

"Just three months, Leon. You'll make a grand more than you make for Sallie in three months. Easy as butter. Lionel is setting the games up right now."

"Jesus, Bingo. What do I got to say to make it clear? I'm getting old and—"

Bingo jumped to his feet and leaned down to Leon. He looked at him and scowled. *"That's* why I is talking to you. You got to make it while you can, old man. I can give you money you ain't going to see if you don't take it. Short and quick, Leon." He turned his back to him and walked to the edge of the porch. "Make it, man, while the people still know you is the *best.*"

Leon rubbed his long hands together, then pressed his palms

against his forehead. Bingo studied him, his fingers, his eyes. He knew that right now there wasn't a better pitcher alive. Not for any man's money. And Leon could not deny it, not long enough, not hard enough to turn his back to Bingo's offer.

Chapter 4

Bingo and Leon were stooped under the hood of Bingo's Auburn when Louis drove up in front of Chessie Joy's place in his 1938 Lincoln V-12 convertible. Bingo was fingering his spark plug cables, making sure his man at the garage had put them in shape for the road. Louis left his Lincoln idling and hopped out with Mungo Redd, Splinter Tommy Washington, Isaac Nettles, and Fat Sam Popper. Bingo had talked each one of them into jumping the Aces for his All-Stars. The only Ace infielder to balk at the offer was Gerald Purvis, and he was into Sallie for a thousand because of a new La Salle. If Gerald took off and left the La Salle behind, Sallie would grab it and keep what Gerald had already paid him. Gerald was the only player Sallie had comfortably over the barrel. The others had grown wary of Sallie's financial setups long ago. When Bingo approached them with his offer and his sales pitch, they were easily persuaded. He had enough money up front to turn their heads.

Since second-line pitcher Turkey Travis had agreed to come along, Bingo needed only a center fielder and a first baseman to fill out his squad. He let Ezell Carter paint the team's name on the side of his Auburn with whitewash. Ezell messed up "Traveling" and "Motor Kings" pretty bad, but he got Bingo Long spelled right, so Bingo told him it was a good job. Louis had the initials "B.L.T.A.S.M.K. #2" painted on his Lincoln and he added a few five-point stars for class.

Louis was dressed in his custom blue pin-striped suit and vest. But the clothes couldn't begin to disguise that on all of Louis's five feet eleven inches hung only 140 pounds. His neck sprouted out of his collar into a wide, wet smile, giving him a look like he'd just finished his high school graduation. He cocked a skinny-visored touring cap on his head and, for the occasion, he sported a pair of snow white spats.

"Oh, there is a pretty partner!" Bingo howled when he laid eyes on him.

"Dressed up for the leaving," Louis said. He spun around and jerked his hips. "This town is seeing the last of this third baseman for a time."

"My, my, what a dandy," Leon said as he and the others looked Louis over. They were wearing suits as well; Bingo featured his usual carnation in the lapel.

"When you touring you got to do it in fashion," said Bingo. "The people got to know you in town."

Louis's Lincoln was long and spacious, and Bingo's Auburn could easily seat six, so the team had plenty of room for the small satchels they carried with them. Bingo put most of the equipment, the bats and balls he could scrape up, in his trunk. He and Leon drove together since most of the others preferred to go with Louis and sit in the open convertible.

Just before starting off, Isaac Nettles yelled at Bingo and walked over to talk with him. Isaac, who was thirty-eight and showing wisps of gray throughout his scalp, pinched the lines of his brow together as he talked. He was the darkest of all the Aces, with a dour, narrow face. His expression betrayed his age and the fact that he became more concerned about things than did most of the others.

"Hey, what you think about a suggestion I got to make the team complete?" Isaac said.

"Shoot," said Bingo. "I'm open for anything."

"Let's go to Raymond's and take him along. He could be manager or traveling secretary or something like that. Man, it would make it for him."

"Damn, I never thought about that. What you think, Leon?"

Leon looked up at the sky. "Foolish," he said.

"Why? Now just why?" objected Isaac.

"Money," said Leon. "Raymond's dead weight if he can't play. A traveling team can't afford no luxuries."

"Who says?" said Bingo.

Leon shook his head. "Damn, Bingo, common sense says it."

"Shit. Let's show Sallie how to take care of a top-rate ball player. Raymond can manage things like Isaac said, like counting up the take and all, until he gets his wheel back in shape."

"You a good man, Bingo," Isaac said. "Raymond will fly when we shows up."

Isaac ran back to Louis's car and the two autos started out. Leon hung his head off to the side of the seat. Bingo grinned at him. "You got to have understanding when you running a ball team, Leon. That's what it's about." He turned the car onto Raymond's street.

Bingo had not broken the final news of the team's formation to Sallie in person. He preferred instead to get his men together on that Friday morning and quietly leave for Pittsburgh. It was best not to get Sallie into another argument, for then Sallie would let loose with a bunch of threats in desperation just to keep his team. He would have to carry out the threats sooner or later or admit that he was licked. Lionel had told Bingo to break without that kind of fuss. It lacked style but the effect would be just as permanent. Sallie would have to cancel most of his league commitments unless he could assemble a ghost squad in time. Even then, he would lose his gate as soon as the people saw that Bingo, Leon, and most of the rest of the regulars were missing. The timing was also good, for Sallie was in hot water with the local politicians because of a craps operation he was running out of his restaurant. He wouldn't have a prayer in court if he tried to bring Bingo and the others in for breach of contract. He'd have to get back at Bingo on his own, and that gave Bingo the benefit of time. Bingo could have his team halfway across the country before Sallie could do anything to stop him, if he could stop him at all. The only thing Bingo knew for certain was that Sallie, sooner or later, would try.

Lionel Foster stood outside his Chop House eying the automobiles which had just parked in front of him. "So we have the Motor Kings, yes we do," he announced. A pair of his counter girls stepped out onto the sidewalk. They smiled at Bingo and Louis and rubbed the door of Louis's Lincoln as if it were too hot to touch.

"We is made for the open road," yelled Bingo. "Lionel, you ever dream we'd be looking this good?"

Louis got out of his car and clicked his heels. The girls stroked their thighs and purred at him.

"Now we only wonders if you can play some ball," Lionel said and ushered Bingo into the restaurant.

He set the team up with beers and steaks and then sat down at a table with Bingo and Leon.

"Glad to see the old man with you," Lionel said, nodding at Leon. "I thought you was a slave to Sallie's plantation for good, Leon. I did."

Leon looked at Lionel out of the corner of his eye but said nothing.

"I talk faster than Sallie, that's all," Bingo said.

"Or you got to say something different," said Lionel. He shook the ice in his whiskey. "But I'm glad to see you, Leon, because you is another reason why this might turn out to be some good money spent. Just so things don't get away from my man Bingo here. How about it, Bingo? Sallie fight you before you got away?"

"I did it like you said to, Lionel. We played Wednesday some boys from Ranolia and yesterday when we had off I did my packing and this morning we was gone. Sallie couldn't done it better hisself."

"He going to fight you every way. But if you got the odds, you can keep him off you until you rich enough to come back and do anything you want. Them papers ain't worth much to Sallie if he ain't got the boys to go with them. He can't do nothing because them courts is glad to see colored stumble around after themselves. Judge told me I was too rich for any nigger so he wasn't going to help me get more. That's what they going to tell Sallie when he try to get you."

"Funny talk coming from you," Leon said.

"Ain't it though?" Lionel agreed. "Here I is pulling for you boys like you was runaway slaves on the river." Lionel laughed out loud.

"Who says we ain't," said Leon.

"Ain't no slave ever run away with the money you got in your pocket, Leon. Remember that when you feeling like a slave sometime." Lionel finished his drink.

Bingo sawed at his steak. "I just brought Leon along to keep things laughing, Lionel. You know he ain't worth a nickel."

Lionel smiled once again and refilled his glass from the bottle on the table. He had always liked Bingo. Bingo never made trouble, never raised a fuss. He leaned over to him.

"You know what you got to do to make this thing move. You been on the road before so you know. The big cities is easy because the people know you and there is a lot of colored to come out. But when you get to those one-lump towns you is going to have to *sell* the product, you know that, Bingo. They ain't going to be putting out just to see their boys beat by the darkies so you got to show them something they ain't seen before and take your chances. You know you got to show first and win second before you going to take their money."

"Yeah, yeah, I know," said Bingo.

"Good. And watch out for the police because they can cut you when they wants to. There ain't no money sitting in the can."

"What our suits look like? You got them, Lionel?"

"The ladies is going on them. They some Elite suits with some fancy lettering. Don't worry about the outfits," he said.

"Okay, I won't," said Bingo.

Lionel gave Bingo Donus Youngs, a good fielding first baseman, and a kid outfielder by the name of Joe Calloway. Calloway had been a bat boy until he was old enough to try out for the Elite Giants. He was only eighteen, but Lionel thought he might be good enough to travel with Bingo and learn what he could from the Stars. Bingo named him Esquire Joe and told him not to let anything get by him in right field. Joe was tall and bony and Lionel said he had an arm like a rifle.

The uniforms were Elite Giant green and white, with pin stripes and five green stars running across the chest. Bingo had wanted "Bingo's All-Stars" over the numbers in back but Lionel said he didn't have the time for that. Bingo had to admit, though, that the uniforms were top rate, as sharp as any around. In Chicago he would pick up a set of two-tone caps, green bills and white crowns, to complete the outfit.

When they trotted out onto the field for the second game of the Elite Giants doubleheader, the Pittsburgh crowd gave them a loud welcome. Bingo led the team on with his lumbering walk and a smile from ear to ear. When he got to the infield he stopped and bowed to the people. His Stars circled him like elephants in the circus. They had used this entrance on other trips and the crowd loved it. When they stopped running they took out four balls and shuttled them from man to man, criss-cross within the circle. They called it hotball because the ball never stopped changing hands and never touched the ground. Louis Keystone finally ended it by grabbing all four balls and putting them in his back pocket. But that did not stop the motions, and for a minute or so the Stars wildly pantomimed hotball with nothing but fresh air changing hands. The fans laughed and whistled, the kids in the crowd tried to figure out what was going on.

Louis, Mungo Redd, and Splinter Tommy Washington went through their routines in infield practice. As they moved, the three of them in their baggy whites and script letters looked identical even though Louis was twice as skinny and taller than the others and Mungo wore a pair of glasses that all but hid his eyes beneath the bill of his cap and Splinter, for all of his grace and casual nonchalance around the bag, sported a set of teeth so crooked they made him feel awkward and self-conscious off the field. But in the dust of the warm-up, Mungo and Tommy gobbled up double-play balls and skipped through the relay without a bobble. Tommy went across the bag and pivoted in the air with the toss to first. Louis at third took ground balls that skipped at him like stones on cement. After he gloved one, he flipped the ball backhand to a ball boy behind him and then waited for another. To finish up, the infield went through their routine without a ball, jumping and throwing and slapping their gloves in place of it. It was a smooth sight, even better than the hotball act, and the crowd applauded as if the Stars had just pulled one out in the ninth.

Yet there was nothing as sweet as watching Bingo take batting practice. He leaned into each pitch with his huge arms, whipping the bat around and cracking the ball. His usual blast was as high as it was far. At the peak of its ascent it hung in the sky like a dirigible about to burst, and then it lazily fell behind the fence. The kids in blue jeans and barebacks stood behind the backstop and winced each time Bingo smashed one. Some mimicked him, swinging an imaginary bat as he swung his, and then gazed off into the sky following the ball. They could feel the power, the icy connection stinging through them just as if they had swatted the ball like a fat bug and then circled the bases and heard the cheers. Bingo grinned at them, flexed the muscle in his right arm, and then fouled one straight back into the screen about head-high on the kids. It jolted the wires and sent them ducking and yelling.

Over on the sidelines Leon Carter was warming up. He was to pitch four innings and Turkey Travis would follow up. Louis Keystone was standing next to Leon, priming the crowd for a pregame contest. Four or five men leaned on the fence and listened to Louis's proposition.

"A little money against Mr. Leon's arm here. Can I interest a gambling man? Anyone among you all who can take a dollar away from me?"

He waved his hands in front of the men, pointing at Leon's arm as the pitcher warmed up with Sam Popper. Then Louis took out a few one-dollar bills from his back pocket and held them up.

"Right here now. A little money on Mr. Leon's arm. Take no chances, just bet against the man's skill. You win, I'll double your money. Two you take against my one."

Leon threw nonchalantly.

"Popper just holds his glove on a chewing gum wrapper, that's all," Louis said. "He don't move it a half inch, no, sir. And old Leon throws the fastball over the wrapper. If he does I take your dollar, if he don't you take two from me. Ain't no man perfect, and that's the game. C'mon, gentlemen, you be the judge. Just a friendly gamble among us."

He flashed his bills up and fanned them. Three of the men held up a dollar. Fat Sam wadded up a wrapper and tossed it in front of him. Then he held his glove over it. Leon wound up and threw, and he missed the wrapper by a foot on the right.

"Oh, man, you is losing it and costing me money right off," Louis yelped.

He walked in front of the three men and peeled off two bucks for each. He then repeated the challenge. The same three and two more held up a buck. Leon wound and threw; Sam Popper never budged his mitt. The ball streaked into it like a beam of light. Louis hopped down the row of men and took their bills. All five put another in the air. Leon again reached back and threw and Fat Sam's mitt didn't move. Louis quickly grabbed his money. He held the bills up and called the bettors.

"Now it's a man's game, boys. You seen him do it and you seen him miss. Old Louis here is the fool because I plays every time and pays every time. Put your money against the man's arm. Show me what you got."

The first three men flashed bills again. Leon uncorked another fastball over the wrapper. Only two men followed with bills. Leon threw another down the center. Louis took their money. Four in a row. Louis didn't advertise anymore, but stared at Popper's mitt. Five was a good number; four men put their money up. Leon split the wrapper again. Louis hustled to collect. Only one man put up his dollar after that. But Leon hit home once more. Each ball had been thrown the same, like a machine had done it, and Sam never moved his mitt enough to raise a question about it. The man flashed another dollar. He glared at Leon, daring him to throw another strike. Leon threw, Louis took the dollar. Once more, Leon threw a submarine fastball, and Louis snatched the bill.

The man fanned his face with his hat. "You is worse than craps, Carter," he said. He waved Louis away. Louis stuffed the bills into his back pocket and trotted to the bench. Leon split the wrapper a few more times and put his warm-up jacket on. Then he walked to the bench to get his money from Louis.

The All-Stars met little resistance from the Elite Giants. It was the Giants' second game of the day, an "appearance" game as they called it, a game set up for the fans instead of the players. They played nonchalantly, kidding the All-Stars about the routines Bingo made them go through. Leon glided through the line-up with an assortment of experimental pitches, and Bingo's men jumped on three Elite pitchers for nine runs. Only Esquire Joe Calloway showed badly with three swinging strike-outs, but he did bring in a long drive over his shoulder near the right-field fence. Bingo liked him, he liked how the kid galloped along the grass, he liked the kid's arm, and he liked Joe's big, level swing, even though it didn't hit anything that afternoon. Most of all, Bingo liked the way Esquire Joe seemed to enjoy himself while he played. He held a loose, close-mouthed grin on his face as he cradled long flies. There were few things Bingo liked better than watching an outfielder outrun a high blast and then bring it home like a soft peach off a tree.

"You boys doing good, real good," Lionel said to Bingo as they walked from the field after the game. "You got class and you got talent like nobody I seen around. You play it right, Bingo, and you ain't going to be able to keep the people from giving you their money."

Lionel had contacted some of the big promoters in the Midwest and set up a half dozen games in Cleveland, Toledo, and Chicago. These were all league towns, so the All-Stars had to work around schedules to get their games. After Chicago they could hit Milwaukee and then head west across Wisconsin and Iowa.

"You got to watch out for the other barnstormers like Max Helverton's Hooley Speedballers and them white teams from Michigan, them House of David boys with the beards," Lionel told Bingo. "You can't follow them because you lose the edge on the towns. You can play them but when you is done you should go in the opposite direction. It ain't trouble; it's just good business. And remember too, Bingo, that you got to hit those towns when they ain't doing nothing big like harvesting or something because then you lose your crowd. Otherwise they going to welcome you like you was a circus."

Bingo already knew most of what Lionel was telling him, but he listened anyway because Lionel had run almost every kind of traveling show around. Lionel helped him get up some paper for advertising and letters to send to town post offices announcing the All-Stars' arrival. The night before the team took off for Cleveland, Bingo sat down with Lionel and went over possible routines and antics to please the crowds. "Remember," Lionel said, "ain't nothing around pleases more than good ball playing. Better than folks has ever seen. They remember it because it *amazes* them. Yeah, it does."

Bingo called a meeting that night after the players had come in from the Chop House.

"I been doing some talking and some planning and I'm ready to present you with what we going to be doing on this tour. Now you all know how to play and how to look good like we did yesterday with the Giants. And when we be playing the big teams like the Detroit Cubans and the Velvets in Chicago and around in there we won't have no trouble either because they is our own people watching and we know what they likes. But some of you ain't been past Chicago and you don't know what happens out there. In them dog towns we got to play it with our nose. We got to please the people who works them farms. And if they want to see us clown then we clown them until they dead. But if they want to see us play straight then we do and take our chances against what they got. We just can't be looking bad or nonchalant or no good. Because then they be calling us a bunch of shuffles and they ain't going to be throwing their quarters in our socks. So they ain't much we can do until we see what the situation is but we got to be ready. We got to be polite and cheerful all the time even when we ain't feeling it. If we get trouble we just be leaving by the back way and getting on down the road with our hands in our pockets and whistling like we stole the lady's pie. Now that is something I thought I should say right off so you know where this team stands. Lionel say if we play it right we going to take their money. I think he's right because he been around. He takes some lumps too, yes he does. But that's what I got to say."

He stopped and wiped his mouth. Nobody said anything. Then he went on.

"We going to be playing a lot of white outfits too. Some of you ain't played much against white so you got to be prepared. They take what they can out of you if you don't be on your guard. They going to slide into your leg and step on your foot if you leave it out there in plain sight. They going to be saying the same old things to rattle you and get you to forget how to play right. But they ain't nothing. They got to pitch to you when you up to the plate. I hit everything a white pitch can throw and they don't like it but they can't do much but run after it. So that's how we play them. You keep your heads turned behind your back all the time for something sneaking up on you. That's the way you play white."

Bingo stopped again and waited for a reaction. He could feel himself getting excited. The players sat and looked at him, blinking their eyes. Louis Keystone yawned.

"That was a nice speech, Bingo. Real nice," Leon finally said.

"Yeah, thanks, Leon," Bingo said, and he sat down and pulled out a Lucky.

At six the next morning, while the players loaded up the cars for the trip to Cleveland, Bingo was hollered down by a Western Union boy riding a bicycle. Bingo grabbed the telegram; he knew who it was from. It read short and fast.

> DON'T GO NOWHERE. GET BACK BY
> WEDNESDAY OR IT'S THE LAW. I AM
> NOT FOOLING. S.P.

Bingo flipped the boy a dime and crumpled the telegram. He tossed it at Louis, who slapped at it with his open palm and knocked it into the gutter.

"Yeah," snorted Bingo, and he slid into his Auburn.

Chapter 5

Louis Keystone drove his Lincoln like he ran the bases. With one hand on the wheel and the other on the gearshift, with his feet pumping the pedals like a church organist, Louis swiveled the V-12 convertible in and out of traffic. He glided past stop signs and traffic lights, never coming to a full stop but balancing and changing speeds as he would to get a good jump on a pitcher. On the highways he pushed it flat out, regardless of curves or one-lane bridges, like a snake cutting a sound through the grass. All the time he beamed at the controls, running his hands along the knobs, the wind rushing past his face and ears. He changed gears as if they were meshed in soft clay instead of steel, hearing the rhythms, feeling them as cleanly as hooking a slide around the tag in an explosion of dust.

Louis bought the Lincoln with the first chunk of money he made playing for the Ebony Aces. He had first seen the convertible on the back pages of *Sporting News,* then he saw it behind plate glass in downtown Louisville. He weaseled Sallie out of two months' pay, he collected three debts at Chessie Joy's, then he hocked three of his suits, a pair of alligator shoes, two stickpins, and his pearl-handled walking stick. He slapped the cash down in front of the only salesman in the building and jumped into the front seat. In two months he had it paid for and all of his merchandise reclaimed. He glided around Louisville in his top hat and spats, his favorite lady in the front seat. When he parked it he ordered the shine boys to get out their clean rags and gloss it over.

The Lincoln was a natural: fast, shiny, plenty of room, a class machine. Louis had grown up watching fast cars. Every May back in Indianapolis, Louis and his friends dropped their ball bats and haunted the Speedway. They shined shoes, hawked change and butts beneath the stands, but most of the time they gawked at the racers screaming around the track. Back in the neighborhood they jumped the running boards of any auto that gave them the chance. No one Louis knew had a car, his father had never even ridden in one, yet that did not erase the sight and sound of the racetrack. That was speed so close and crazy Louis could almost touch it, each May, when the entire town of Indianapolis turned into a carnival. When Louis was eighteen he put fifty-five dollars, more money than he had ever hustled up at any one time, into a Model T. He drove it for three and a half weeks before it pushed a rod through the engine block.

At eighteen Louis could almost outrun his Model T. There wasn't a soul in Indianapolis who could catch him and his pencil legs. The neighborhood called him "Grease Louis" when he ran Western Union or legged out a drag bunt. He didn't connect that well at the plate, but the dribblers he did lay into the infield were hits because of his speed. He stole on every catcher, he took two bases where anyone else could only see one. When the Indianapolis Dimes signed him in '29, he was known all over the city as the boy with all legs and no stick. They called him "Blur," "Crazylegs," "String," and his old "Grease Louis," but nothing stuck. He was simply Louis Keystone, the slickest runner the Indianapolis Dimes had ever put into a pair of spikes.

After a year with the Dimes he had the money to pay his way into the Speedway to watch the race. He bought himself a Terraplane and took some of his old girl friends where they wanted to go. Then the hard times came and Louis scrambled with any ball team that could make a go of it. By '35 he was with the Ebony Aces, spending what little money he made and going into Sallie Potter for the rest.

Two years later Louis took a razor in the neck from a man whose lady he was entertaining. The man got Louis from behind and would have slit him forever if Bingo had not been there to throw the man across the room. It was the first time Louis had ever bled for a lady, the first time anyone had ever taken him.

On the way to Cleveland that morning Louis punched it as usual. In the early morning there were no patrol cars to shadow him. Only Bingo trailed in his Auburn, madly honking in an effort to get Louis to slow down. Though the morning air was cool and dewy, Louis had the top down. The players who rode with him huddled to keep warm. The angular rays of the sun shot through the trees and raised steam on the road. Louis hung his arm over the side of the door and let the wind play with it.

"You can't be driving like that, Louis. Oh, no, boy, right off you can't be pushing it so hard because that tin of mine has got to keep up. And it ain't got no stomach for it," Bingo fumed at a filling station just outside Cleveland. His Auburn was already steaming. "Man, we got a lot of riding to do before I'm done with my heap."

"This rabbit just loves to scamper," Louis answered. "I feel bad when I got to strap her down."

"You was damn near doing sixty on my clock, Louis!"

"Yeah, mine too."

"Well, hold onto it or I'm going to bust up before we get to Chicago."

"Then you can get yourself a *real* road machine," Louis said, and they drove off into Cleveland.

In the Red Feather Lounge Louis stood with Bingo and Splinter Tommy Washington drinking cold beer and eying the yallers. The Stars had played the Detroit Cubans that afternoon in a preliminary game to the Detroit–Cleveland Bays game. They had the night in Cleveland before getting on to Toledo in the morning. Louis had been to Cleveland only once before, and this was his first appearance in the Red Feather. A Cleveland Bay had recommended it to him. The Red Feather had a loose reputation for homosexuals and an even better one for the white people who stepped in to see what the natives had going. They were the whites, the Bay had said to Louis, who knew how to hop.

Louis jitterbugged with some of the counter girls; he did not hustle but he was loose. Bingo and Tommy mingled at the tables, telling the customers who they were and what the All-Stars could do. Back at the bar, talking with the lady he had just danced with, Louis caught sight of a new entry. She slid lazily up to the bar, not leaning against it but sidling up to it as if it were leather instead of wood. She was blond, platinum and wispy, a Jean Harlow, with arching, thin eyebrows and blood-red lipstick. She lifted her drink, yawning slowly and shaking her hair. Louis eyed her long and coolly, spanning her hips and breasts, which were pouched in a clinging purple evening dress. So this was the class the Bay had told him about, he thought, this was the type of white folk who liked to throw it out at the Feather. The lady stared blankly out at the people. She fingered the rim of her glass, momentarily flinched a shoulder, then ran her hand along her right side to her thigh. Louis lit a cigarette and drew it deep. The lady turned to the bar and caught his eye. She stared at him for a few seconds, then turned casually to the bartender. Louis sauntered over.

She raised the side of her mouth into a slight smile as he approached. Then she looked out into the lounge. Louis uttered a low, almost inaudible hello; she said nothing in reply. He then picked up the change she had lying on the bar, called over the bartender, and paid for his drink with the money. The bartender shook his head and walked away.

The lady did not look at him. "That wasn't a gentlemanly

thing to do," she said. She blew the words over her glass. Louis turned to her and instead of saying anything he slowly moved his eyes down her figure, from her shoulders to her heels, peeling off the dress as he went. He made a gentle smacking sound with his lips. She shifted her weight and gave him a broader view. Then she turned and faced him.

"So what's on your mind, baby?" she said.

Louis smiled and introduced himself. He told the lady what he did and where he came from. She listened and smiled and drank slowly, Louis flashing his eyes about her as he talked, smelling her, easing into her. At the tables Bingo and Tommy took notice. Tommy pursed his lips and wiped his brow, gestures Bingo knew were more a sign of worry than of envy. Louis was not playing with home material, not the dollar brassies at Chessie Joy's place.

They stood for a while. Louis talked and gestured with his hands, the blonde smiled, obviously enjoying his company. She had a way of cocking her head so blond, lazy curls fell over her left eye.

Once on the dance floor, Louis threw her some moves, he spun and went low, and she cocked her hips in approval. She watched him glisten and wheel, keeping a cautious, thin smile on her lips. Louis could smell extra bases.

Just then he was jerked around by a tall, tuxedoed white man. He stood in front of the blonde and glared at Louis. His words were short and quick.

"Hands off, boy. I mean right now," he said.

Louis smoothed his lapels and took out a cigarette. He had run into this kind of situation before.

"I'm just having a time," he said to the man. "I can spot advertising when I see it."

He exhaled a cloud of smoke. The same slight smile returned to the lady's face. The dark-haired man looked at her, then he reached for Louis's glass, which lay on the bar, and slowly overturned it. The Scotch streamed in a thin line toward Louis.

"That's it for the advertising," said the man and he turned away, taking the girl's arm.

Louis squared and faced him. He whistled. The man stopped and turned around. Louis stood with his hand in his suit coat's side pocket. He kept a nail file in it and when he ran his nail along the file it zipped like the short, deadly click of a razor. The man froze and his face reddened. Louis did not move, his hand poised in the pocket.

At that moment Bingo and Splinter Tommy pushed their chairs quickly back and jumped up in front of Louis. They grabbed him by his arms and lifted him into a far corner of the lounge. Louis gave no resistance but laughed as he glided through the air. Bingo glowered at him and threw him into a chair. At this the man in the tuxedo began shouting and threatening Louis. The bartender yelled at the man, but could not be heard above his rantings. In the corner Bingo sat on Louis and faced the cursing white man. The blonde was now trying to pull him away, but he held his ground and shouted even louder, trying to regain what he had lost when Louis zipped him with the file.

"Cool down, man, before you start something," Bingo warned him.

At that the bartender ushered him and the lady out into the street.

Bingo got up off of Louis and shook his finger in his face. Louis was busting up with laughter.

"You going to kill yourself, Louis. You a damn fool!" Bingo thundered.

Louis continued to laugh.

"That man could a had a gun and let you feel it with no sweat from nobody."

Louis kept on laughing. He clutched his sides and stamped his foot despite Bingo.

Bingo rubbed his hands together and looked around the lounge. "Why you have to give him that razor talk? Shit. He

57

almost could have died right there." Then Bingo went over to the bar to get a beer.

Splinter Tommy Washington glanced crookedly down at Louis. Louis looked up, got to his feet, and started for the bar himself.

"She was *ripe* for it, Splinter." He laughed. "My fingers is still warm."

They left Cleveland the next morning and hit Toledo and the Toledo Wolves. Toledo beat them in the ninth by pushing three runs across on Turkey Travis. Bingo felt himself hitching when he swung and failed to connect on anything. He did appreciate the showing of Esquire Joe Calloway though. Joe picked off anything that was even close to him in the outfield and at bat he laced a pair of triples to opposite fields. He had a smooth, effortless style about him that Bingo liked. On tour a player with instant class drew the fans almost as well as a ball player with the reputation of Leon Carter. And Esquire Joe had yet to peg anything but a clothesline in from right field when Bingo called for the throw.

The next day they beat Toledo in a return game and then beat a semipro team out of Michigan in seven innings. Bingo had Mungo Redd and the new first baseman, Donus Youngs, do the pitching against the semipros and they took the game 13–6. That night they left for Chicago and three games with the Chicago Black Velvets.

Lionel had given Bingo a general plan for running the team on the road. Besides traveling light in the two cars, the team would stay in the usual home team hotels as long as they played in big cities or in towns that had a colored ball team of its own. Otherwise they had to play it by ear, finding the hotels they knew would take colored, sleeping in the colored-only hotels regardless of how shabby they were, or just pitching a tent by the side of the road and sleeping on the grass. Lionel had set a dollar-fifty cents a day per man for expenses. That was generous, but it had to go for a lot of things besides food. Finding food would be tough too, for once the team got out of its territory they had to guess where the next open place might be. If none was available, they would have to eat the bread and fish and pickles they brought along.

In the first four games, the team had cleared over two thousand, and it put Bingo comfortably ahead on expenses. Besides the initial bonus Bingo had given each man to sign, each was paid a percentage of the total gate. That way the players would sink or swim with the team. Only Leon Carter did not have that kind of arrangement, and nobody but Bingo knew that. Leon was paid a flat twelve hundred a month for the three months he stayed with the All-Stars. It was twice as much as anyone else would see unless the team constantly played to houses like they got in Pittsburgh or Cleveland. Out west they knew receipts would be much leaner. They would have to play between fifteen and twenty games a week, twice as many as they had played for Sallie, to make good money.

Lionel told them to play as many games as possible. If they hustled the big gates and moved away from the small ones, they could be money ahead in a month and then sail from there. To Bingo it looked like a sure thing. He had barnstormed before and liked the feel of it, even though he had never had anything to do with the money or the promotion angle. Now he was ready for it, he knew Leon's drawing power and he knew his own, and he was certain his boys could put on a moneymaking show wherever they could find someone to play and seven people to watch. The first week convinced him of it. He watched Raymond Mikes pile the bills and tally up. He savored the feeling of knowing Sallie wouldn't be around to skim off the cream from the till. It was nice money and quick money, and Bingo didn't know of two better kinds.

In Chicago they played three close games with the Black Velvets. Chicago was a great town for colored ball. It drew so well the colored leagues played their annual all-star game in

Comiskey Park. Bingo's Stars played the Black Velvets after each of three league games the Chicago team had with the Gary Whips. The Chicago fans had seen Bingo and Leon before and they were anxious to see them with a barnstorming outfit. Boyce Brown, the owner of the Black Velvets, even offered Bingo, Leon, and Mungo Redd a contract to stay on in Chicago with the Velvets. But to Bingo the offer had Sallie Potter written all over it. He laughed at Boyce and told him he was trying to take his gold mine. For the three games against the Black Velvets the All-Stars cleared twenty-six hundred. There was no contract on earth that could make Bingo give up that kind of profit.

In their last night in Chicago, Bingo invited Boyce and three of his Black Velvets up to his room for a game. Bingo hadn't done any real gambling since he had left Louisville, and he was itching to get out his chips. The four of them came up early in the evening and were later joined by Eddie Zollicoffer, a friend of Bingo's in the lending business. Eddie was a short blimp of a man who barely stood five foot five but tipped an easy 240 pounds. He laughed and chewed cigars when he gambled, sweating through his suit coat and dealing with the skinniest set of fingers in town. They played and drank Bingo's Scotch until three in the morning. Bingo chattered and joked for the first few hours, then he got dull and heavy-lipped from the booze. He shoveled his chips, played bad leads, and watched Eddie Zollicoffer manipulate the game. In all, he lost eight hundred, most of it to Eddie, who left dripping wet and with a promise to catch Bingo the next time he came through Chicago. Bingo never saw Brown and his players take off; he slept with his head on the table in the middle of his chips. In the morning he told Raymond Mikes to give him twenty bucks from the bankroll. He would get the money back in Milwaukee.

Wisconsin territory was wide open for the All-Stars. A barnstorming outfit had not been through there all summer. After

Milwaukee Bingo had planned on hitting about a dozen small towns before heading down into Illinois and Iowa. He sent a handbill ahead to all the towns he thought the team had a possibility of getting to. Lionel and Louis had helped him compose it.

GET READY, NEIGHBORS!!! WE WILL SOON
BE IN YOUR NECK OF THE WOODS.

THE BINGO LONG TRAVELING ALL-STARS AND MOTOR KINGS

THE WORLD CHAMPIONS OF COLORED BASEBALL
FEATURING:
HENRY BINGO LONG,
THE GREATEST POWER HITTER ALIVE TODAY
WHO WILL PERSONALLY GUARANTEE A HOME RUN BALL
IN YOUR HOME PARK
AND:
LEON CARTER,
THE GREATEST FASTBALL PITCHER IN THE WORLD OVER,
WHO WILL STRIKE OUT ANY HITTER ALIVE UPON
INVITATION
PLUS:
AN ASSORTMENT OF BALL PLAYERS FROM THE CREAM OF
THE COLORED LEAGUES
TAKING ON ALL COMERS IN AN EXHIBITION BEFORE YOUR
VERY EYES.

COMING SOON TO YOUR TOWN TO PLAY YOUR HOME TEAM
OR ANYONE WHO WILL TAKE THE FIELD.

SATISFACTION GUARANTEED OR YOUR MONEY BACK.
NO CONDITIONS.

The roads which led out of Milwaukee into the middle of the state kept Louis from cruising like he wanted to. Only a few were paved, and then only for a couple of miles at a time. They wound through the farmland like trails, grooved with drainage ruts of hardened clay. The two cars limped over them, gaining speed on a flat straightaway, then crawling over bumpy inclines. They hit the town of Wilsie early in the morning and paraded slowly through its business district. Louis leaned on his horn and whistled while the rest of the players stood up in the car and waved at anyone who stopped to watch. Bingo smiled and threw kisses to the people, Mungo Redd leaned over the side and wailed on his mouth organ. The town stretched only two blocks, so Louis and Bingo had to turn around and make a return entry. The people read the team name painted on the side of Bingo's car, a few of them waved absently back at the players, but most of them just shook their heads.

Bingo went into Freeland's Hardware and Post Office and talked to Wilbur Freeland. Wilbur told him the town's team could play them at four o'clock that afternoon. He also told Bingo of a team in a nearby town so Bingo called there and managed to get a game for six-thirty.

"How many people you got living here in Wilsie?" Bingo asked Freeland.

"Maybe a thousand, maybe twelve hunerd with all the farms around," he answered. He walked to the door of his store and looked at the team.

"Can you boys do what this here letter says you can?"

He pointed at Bingo's flier hanging next to the door.

"All of it and more upon request," said Bingo.

"Well, maybe you can get the people out if they get the word. One of you colored teams came through two years ago and played some nice baseball."

"Where we going to play?"

"There's a field in back with a backstop and all."

"Good. How's your own outfit?"

"Just a bunch of farm kids from around. But they play good. Pinky Mercer, used to play for the Philadelphia Athletics in the big leagues, came out of here about fifteen years back. You ever heard of him, Pinky Mercer?"

62

"Yeah, I heard of him," Bingo said. He walked toward the door. "Four o'clock on the nose we'll be ready. Now we got to drum up some business."

"Yeah, okay," Wilbur said. "The folks will be glad to see you on account of there ain't much else to do nowadays."

Bingo returned to the others out in the street.

"Okay, we got a game for four and another at six-thirty up the road. But we got to get the people out, we got to make the rounds."

They grabbed some lunch at a diner and then drove to the field. It was nothing but a pasture with a pair of wooden benches, a chickenwire backstop, and a dirt infield streaked with crab grass. They changed into their uniforms and headed back into town. Raymond limped behind on his crutches, posting large red-and-white bills wherever he could sink a nail. At Freeland's Hardware Bingo got the okay from Wilbur and he and Sam Popper jumped on a pair of bicycles parked out front. They rode the bicycles in circles around Louis's Lincoln as he drove slowly through town. Esquire Joe Calloway stood up in the Lincoln and read from the team's flier.

"Ladies and gentlemen of Wilsie, Wisconsin!" he screamed. "Now appearing in flesh and blood, the Bingo Long Traveling All-Stars and Motor Kings!"

Louis laid on the horn. Bingo and Sam Popper stood up on their bikes. The rest of the players walked behind the Lincoln, bowing and waving to the people.

". . . The World Champions of colored baseball. No team on earth can match it for talent and beauty at the art of the game!"

Esquire Joe sang the words.

"Featuring Henry Bingo Long—"

Louis honked and Bingo waved his right hand.

"—the greatest power hitter alive today. And also featuring Leon Carter—"

Louis honked once more and Leon, walking, gave a wide, majestic bow.

"—the greatest pitcher in the world today. Yessir, all part of the Bingo Long Traveling All-Stars and Motor Kings!"

Esquire Joe paused as Louis and the parade came to a halt at what they thought was the center of town. Bingo and Sam Popper pedaled around the car. They kicked their legs and wobbled the bikes, smiling and waving their hats.

"Yes, folks," Esquire Joe went on, "at four o'clock in the afternoon at that field you got out there we going to be playing your own team in a challenge game. We guarantee your enjoyment and your amazement or your money back!"

A small crowd of farmers and storekeepers gathered around. They laughed and pointed at the All-Stars. Bingo let a little kid jump up on his handlebars and ride between his arms. Next to the car Mungo started up "Swanee River" on his mouth organ and Donus Youngs, Esquire Joe, and Splinter Tommy Washington joined in trio. Tommy slapped his hands on his knees to keep time. Donus leaned out and caught the bass, Esquire Joe crooned the melody in a smooth tenor that arched up from the three of them, over the whining mouth organ, and hung in the air. They mixed the tones, merging with each other like steam over water.

Tommy kept up the beat. Mungo pinched the organ and squeezed the sound through the hollows of his hands. "All the world is sad and dreary . . ." They floated it out and above the people who listened, into the sideboards and the gutters of the buildings, in the dust which rose like flour from the walks. The three of them sang it, Mungo played, Bingo and Sam cradled the kids who laughed and teetered on the handlebars.

The cords in Esquire Joe's neck tightened, then quivered with every move of his jaw. He pulled the sounds from his throat and poured them over his lips. His face perspired from the sun, his eyes shone beneath his tight, carved forehead. The

64

sound and the feel of the harmony seeped from him and melted over the people.

The rest of the team leaned up against the car and hummed behind the trio. Their green-and-white uniforms were reflected in the deep black shine of the Lincoln. The five green stars dipped across their chests as they moved with the music. Each man had his two-tone hat perched back on his head so the visor pointed upward. Louis jumped from the driver's seat and started doing some of his steps in front of the trio. They picked up the tempo for him, gently, like a breeze on a fire, and he clicked his heels and spun his hips. The people standing around bobbed their heads to the harmony, the little kids crawled on their knees through the crowd to get a better look at Louis and Mungo and the finely tuned trio.

"Why don't you boys get on radio?" a fellow yelled.

"Yeah, you could get on 'Amos 'n' Andy,' " added another. He pointed to Louis's car. "That could be your fresh air taxicab."

The crowd laughed at the man's remark. Bingo wheeled his bike into the center of the group. The boy jumped off the handlebars.

"You folks all come out to the game now. Four o'clock right out there on your ball diamond. You'll all see a better show than 'Amos 'n' Andy,' I guarantee. And bring your friends."

He handed the bike to one of the boys and climbed into the Lincoln. The rest of the players followed and Louis started up the engine. They waved and whistled at the people until they were out of town and into the countryside. They had about an hour to advertise to the farmers.

They drove in and out of farmyards, stopping to talk to a farmer or make faces at his cows. At two o'clock they rode into the village of Stocker, where they had the six-thirty game. They paraded and sang to whoever would pay attention, but Stocker was even smaller than Wilsie so they drew a scant gathering. Mungo soloed on his mouth organ and was joined by an old porch sitter in a chorus of "Sweet Georgia Brown." A boy about ten told Bingo they had better watch out for Stocker's team because it was the best around. Bingo told the kid to come by at six-thirty and see how good the Stocker boys really were. In an hour the All-Stars were back in Wilsie, lounging in the sun before the game.

Raymond Mikes leaned against the Lincoln he had parked near the backstop. He tried to collect twenty-five cents from the adults and a nickel from the kids as they walked up to the field. The pregame promotion brought out a good number of Wilsie. By game time almost six hundred people crowded around the infield. They sat on horses and hay carts; some stood on the hoods of cars they had driven near the baselines. The Wilsie people were loud and good-natured. They joked with Bingo and Louis and coaxed an encore out of Esquire Joe's trio. The All-Stars responded by going through the hotball routines and the infield pantomime. The people cheered and applauded each move. Their own team, the Wilsie Wildcats, watched just as bug-eyed as the townsfolk. A few minutes before they were to begin the game, Bingo nodded at Leon and walked to the center of the infield.

"Ladies and gentlemen of Wilsie, Wisconsin," he yelled. He could throw out a good baritone for his barker routines. "Mr. Leon 'Bullet Ball' Carter will put on for you a pitching show unmatched by any man alive or dead. Standing right here on this here pitching mound he going to drive a nail into that there pole in the backstop. Just watch Mr. Wilbur start it, and watch Leon end it."

He waved on Wilbur Freeland and the hardware man drove a spike a half inch into one of the poles in the middle of the backstop. Leon sauntered to the pitching mound with a ball hanging on his fingertips.

"Now keep your eyes glued on the nail Mr. Wilbur put there. That little shiny paper will make you see it better while it goes into the pole. Okay, Leon."

66

Bingo stepped in back of Leon. The pitcher wound up and threw at the nail and its head of wadded tin foil. Leon's fastball conked against the spike, pushing it farther into the wood. The people cheered and clapped their hands. A boy threw the ball back to Leon. He threw again and rapped the spike. The pole quivered from the impact. Leon fired again and again at the spike, driving it slowly but steadily into the pole. The crowd applauded with each hit. With ten throws he had all but flattened the spike, and the ball was lumpy and misshapen. He tossed it to the kid who had been chasing it down for him. He bowed and doffed his cap to the crowd while they cheered and whistled for him.

"The human hammer, yessir, folks," Bingo thundered. "Now you know why our man is the most expensive piece of pitching arm around. Show him how you like him by dropping that money in the hat we be passing around. We need money for them nails."

Raymond Mikes pushed a hat among the spectators before they had even stopped clapping. On the mound, Leon perspired heavy blotches through his uniform. His long right arm hung from his shoulder; he shook it gently. His blank expression showed none of the effort he had put into the pregame show; his eyes hung, he breathed quickly. He could still throw a fastball so straight and hard that it hissed. His long arm and high kick had the whip action of a slingshot. A young, tight-lipped Wilsie Wildcat stepped into the batter's box to receive the invitation pitch and begin the game. Bingo and an umpire crouched behind the plate. Leon, with his tireless arm, prepared to drive yet another of the countless spikes into the wood.

The All-Stars toyed with the Wilsie team. Leon pitched only an inning, then Bingo let Donus Youngs, Turkey Travis, and finaly Esquire Joe Calloway pitch. On one hard-hit ground ball to Louis at third, they pegged around the horn before finally getting the man by a step at first. Bingo sent a fastball soaring out of the outfield into a knee-high cornfield which surrounded the diamond. The left fielder turned his back to the infield and started galloping after the blast. When he hit the corn he stumbled and flopped headfirst into the stalks, out of sight, like a swimmer into a sea of green.

The crowd howled as Bingo plodded around the bases. A posse of kids took off into the corn to find the ball. After that, Louis, Esquire Joe, and Splinter Tommy Washington showed the people some speed on the bases. Louis stole home on the Wilsie pitcher after telling him he was going to do it. With a big lead-off, he outran the ball and swished across the plate before the catcher could lay down the tag.

At the last out they jumped into the cars and drove off to Stocker. They got there five minutes before game time. A fair crowd had shown, about two to three hundred. The field was in better shape than the one at Wilsie; they had even built a set of wooden bleachers along the first-base side. The Stocker Braves were older and more polished than the Wilsie Wildcats. They boasted an unbeaten string of eleven straight against local competition and took on the All-Stars with a serious, peppery attitude. When Louis Keystone struck out to start the game against the short, chunky Stocker left-hander, the crowd cheered vigorously. The All-Stars could sense a completely different mood here in Stocker, a defensive, proud atmosphere. The kid who warned Bingo of the Braves earlier in the afternoon had not been kidding. They were set to knock off the All-Stars. There would be no showboating this game. Just straight baseball and victory to the best outfit.

The All-Stars tightened up against the little left-hander. They bunted and used the hit and run. Turkey Travis pitched wisely to each hitter as if he were facing a member of the Pittsburgh Elite Giants or the Chicago Black Velvets. The Stocker team was as good as any semipro team the All-Stars had faced. Fat Sam Popper hit one out in the fourth, Donus Youngs doubled in a pair of runs in the seventh. Just before darkness set in, Turkey struck out the last Brave for a 5–3 All-Star win. But they had not been able to relax throughout the game, and they dragged themselves back to the cars.

The manager of the Stocker team brought the All-Stars to a small diner to get something to eat. A single grease cook operated the place. Without a word he shoveled hash brown potatoes and a thin piece of Salisbury steak in front of the players. He said it was the only thing he had left in the house. They ate slowly, drinking cup after cup of the weak, filmy coffee the man gave them. Outside, as the cool air of the night closed around them, the Stocker manager told Bingo he hadn't found a place to put them up for the night. He said the town's only hotel was full and that there was nothing else around. The All-Stars drove back to the ball field. They ate the pickles and crackers they had and then flipped coins for the car seats. The losers stretched out beneath the bleachers and slept in the grass. At dawn, after the sun became too bright to sleep, they got up and drove off down the road.

 Chapter 6

They traveled straight west across Wisconsin, zigzagging a few miles here and there to catch another town or village. They averaged three games a day, one in the morning if they could get a crowd, two in the afternoon. A few hours were spent putting up the paper which announced their arrival and parading for anyone they could catch on the streets. They hit Lawton, Birdsall, Rock Valley, Newton, Landusky, Beaver Crossing, and Fort Calhoun. They played on sandlots, cow pastures, a main street, and carefully clipped public diamonds. They played the prison team in Allamuchy, a girls' softball team with a thick-armed windmill pitcher in Smithville. It was off the field and into the cars, grabbing sleep at forty-five miles per hour, eating on the bench between innings. Whenever they could, they set up a makeshift admissions stand for Raymond Mikes; otherwise they passed the hat.

Louis's Lincoln soon became covered with a heavy layer of dust. His tires were low and his oil was black and thick. The players had spilled food and ground cracker crumbs into the upholstery. Bingo's Auburn was in worse shape. It was missing and steaming and had a bum headlight. Yet after each game, Louis and Bingo turned the engines over and drove on, through the rutted roads and up the hills, driving for spells so long that the players' ankles began to swell. They averaged one hotel every three days, a bath once a week. The sweat and dust worked its way into every player's skin, and the sun stained and dried it.

After two weeks, the team began to drag. They had played thirty-eight games since Milwaukee and had lost only three of them. Bingo's knees ached worse than ever before, his knuckles were swollen from the foul tips he had taken. He had managed to hit the long ball whenever he wished, for the teams they were playing were seldom very tough. Matching the claims made on their handbills was the least of their problems. Against most, the Stars could get by with a good inning at bat and a little razzmatazz in the field. For an extraordinary crowd Leon would repeat the spike routine or call in his outfield. Louis easily pulled off his hesitation steals and Esquire Joe Calloway pegged in line shots to Bingo from the fence in right field. As long as the sun shone they performed unerringly, stopping only to eat or sleep or to advertise.

At Madison Bingo and Raymond checked over the books. There hadn't been a day when they didn't clear over three hundred, so Bingo easily met his bills. He had talked the players into cutting expense money from a dollar-fifty to one dollar a day, so that was another corner he did not have to worry about. So far they were pulling in more money than Lionel had predicted they would. But the strain and the drudgery of the road was beginning to show. When it rained the first day in Madison, Bingo welcomed the relief. The team slept through the day on the cool sheets of hotel beds.

"The damn trouble with the road is always the same, man. You is just out in the wilderness and they ain't nothing to keep you alive." Louis lounged at the foot of his bed drinking a bottle of beer. "There ain't no times, man, no ladies, no music, no hours. And you wonder if the sun don't shine better back in Louisville even though something like Sallie is on your back."

"You got a point," Bingo said. He sat on a chair in his boxer shorts and rubbed his legs with snake oil. The stale odor filled the room. "But that's the price we got to pay for our independence and the cash we been pulling in."

"Well, I ain't long for this kind of treatment because my middle leg is getting out of practice. Yeah, you know, Bingo, I ain't as old as you is so I got to do a lot more dipping. You know what I mean?"

He cupped a hand over his groin and gave a pained expression to Splinter Tommy Washington, who sat across the room.

"We should a brought Morgana and some of those other queens along in a separate car," Bingo said, laughing. "Now wouldn't that make a fancy parade."

"It'd do wonders for my game," said Louis.

Bingo slapped his thighs and his knees. The greasy oil glistened against his skin. Bingo flexed his knees and pinched the stiff tendons, which tightened against his muscles like battens.

"What you think about changing our plans a little?" he said.

"Like how?" said Louis. "I mean I'm for it right off but I want to know what you thinking of doing."

"For two weeks we been hitting every nickel outfit we come up against and some we got to go out of our way to get to. So I say why don't we just play in the bigger towns. You know, them towns with about ten thousand people in them or more. Then we'll get bigger crowds, yeah, and we'll play less. You know, maybe one or two games a day at the most."

"But then we got to be traveling more."

"Yeah, but once we there, we there. We going to have more time to ourselves in the big towns. You know what I mean, Louis?"

"Like Sallie used to do it."

"Yeah, something like that. We still be going to play the little places we know will give us a good game with a big crowd but we ain't going to be hitting those cow towns with the girls' teams. You know? We'll be aiming for Saint Louis and Kansas City and Minneapolis and joints as big as that."

"I know some *places* in those towns," crowed Louis.

"I'm going to be bringing it up to the rest of the boys. They all as tired as dogs. Damn." Bingo leaned back and stretched his arms.

An hour later the manager of the hotel knocked and told Bingo he had a call on the phone downstairs. The call was from Lionel in Pittsburgh.

"Hey, Bingo, how you doing?" Lionel said. He spoke loudly into the phone and Bingo held the receiver an inch away from his ear. "I just come from a big meeting and Sallie is raising some smoke. He putting the pressure on league owners to blackball you boys from the leagues. He was moaning like a half-dead dog about you jumping and leaving the Aces high and dry."

"Yeah, I can hear that old boy." Bingo laughed.

"Sure, man, he was even blaming you and Leon—get that, *Leon*—for starting the whole thing. Shit, all the years Leon been pitching for him. Anyway, what I is calling about is that the other boys around the league seemed to be halfway soft for Potter. Yeah, I could see it all over 'em as he was talking. He was crying about having to go and pick up those ghost players to fill out his team—yeah, even picked up that old boy Junior Marks, you know him? And he been taking a beating with that team at the gate."

"That's good to hear because you know Sallie like I do. I wonder what the fans thought when they see Junior Marks out there in a wheelchair trying to play shortstop. What a time, huh, Lionel?"

"Yeah, but what I is saying is that the other dogs around the league look like they going to help Sallie out with a blackball. And I ain't going to like that when your boys hear about it."

"Oh, they all right, Lionel. We doing real good out here. We're fine."

"Sure, man, but when they hear about a blackball they going to be running scared about their jobs back here. And I got a idea that Sallie knows that and that's why he's pushing for a black-ball, because he can't do nothing else. Man, the law is on his ass like I didn't know. He never even tried to get the judge to stop you boys. So now he doing this to bluff you boys back here." Lionel continued his agitated tone of voice. Without the sight of his easy, gray head and his gold teeth he came across down-right scared.

"Shit. That's an old book," grumbled Bingo. "He don't think he can pull it on us."

"That all he got, man. But if you let your boys get all scared and worrying about things, they could get away from you and get on back to Sallie. I know how things gets on the road when you ain't doing nothing but hitting it all the time. Damn, you should have seen old Lionel when Sallie points the finger at me and says I is probably the one behind you boys. I put on some smiles as big as my moons to cover up. Oh, I mean that man was hot about things." Lionel blew a low whistle and chuckled.

"Yeah, we must a got him where it hurts and I is glad. He was due for a dive," Bingo answered.

"So how you doing out there, huh, Bingo?"

"Lionel, I never knew what you boys took in until I got out here. I mean we been out almost three weeks now and we been seeing that green. We been hustling the small places and doing good. You know, three or four games a day for good crowds."

"You boys worn out yet?"

"Yeah, we start to dragging a couple days but now we hit some rain an' we all right again. Ain't nobody but Louis complaining and he always complaining. But we going good."

"You know I told you, you know it, Bingo. You just keep hitting it hard and don't let up and you'll do all right. But I want to tell you, Bingo, not to be talking about what I told you about Sallie to the boys. What they don't know will do them some good. I figure the other owners will forget about Sallie if they keep getting the crowds and making money. It's good times for colored ball right now, Bingo, best they been in ten years, yessir. Any boy on your outfit could name his own price if he wanted to come back to the league tomorrow. But you don't tell them nothing, Bingo, and let old Lionel take care of business back here. We got Sallie right where we want him, you know that, Bingo."

"Lionel, you so good you make me wonder," said Bingo. He heard a faint snicker from Lionel.

"Well, just keep hitting the pill and don't worry about nothing. Why don't you send me a check in the mail just for good confidence, Bingo? So then I knows everything is going good."

"I'll check with Raymond to see what I can do, so hang on."

"Yeah, and how's that new boy Calloway doing?"

"Hey, he's a fine ball player. He can do all the things in the field like young Bingo Long could when he was that age. They ain't nothing stopping him, Lionel, so you better treat him good."

"Okay, Bingo. You sound fine and you saying the right things. So remember all the things I been telling you about not telling the boys about Sallie and about sending me that check through the mail to my address here. You doing all right, Bingo."

After he had hung up, Bingo stood by the phone and thought about what Lionel had said. The threat of a blackball was an old trick; any owner using it was at the bottom of the barrel and breathing hard. To Bingo it was a good feeling to have a man like Sallie Potter in that position after the way he had operated through the years. In one way or another Sallie had messed over anyone who threatened to cost him money. Now the tables were turned, for a time anyway. Bingo savored the feeling of it, even though it was tinged with uncertainty. For Sallie the snake had all the angles, no matter how low he had sunk. The Stars would have to keep right on traveling, never turning their heads to see if Sallie was coming up the road from behind.

In the room later that afternoon, Bingo talked to the team. Louis and Splinter Tommy Washington sat on one of the beds,

75

Donus Youngs, Esquire Joe, and Mungo Redd sat on the other. Leon Carter, Fat Sam Popper, and Turkey Travis stood in the corner. Raymond Mikes sat on a folding chair with his foot propped up on the edge of Louis's bed. Isaac Nettles stood behind him. Most of them wore T-shirts and the baggy trousers of their suits. They had slept most of the day.

Bingo began to tell them what he had spoken to Louis about earlier in the day: that he was thinking about changing the team's touring plan. He told them about hitting the bigger towns from now on. In that way they would travel more but play less and in front of bigger crowds.

"My dogs say that's a good idea," said Louis.

"I know what your dogs say before they even say it," answered Bingo. "But what do you other boys think?"

"How you going to guarantee big crowds in the big cities?" asked Raymond.

"That ain't no worry, Raymond. You know how the people been turning out."

"Yeah, we is killing ourselves a slow death the way we been going," said Turkey Travis. "I ain't barnstormed it this hard since I left the Clowns."

"Same for me," said Louis.

"We going to be covering a lot more territory this way, Bingo," added Isaac Nettles. "You sure your car can take it? Ever think of that?"

"That's a risk I got to take," said Bingo. "Either the car goes or I do and that ain't no choice for me." He looked around the room at the team. He didn't expect much opposition to a suggestion which would make the tour easier. "Okay, it's on the books then, huh? Raymond and I'll be calling ahead and making the plans."

"It ain't good, no matter what you say, Bingo," Leon Carter said from the corner. "You talking to a tired ball team about going easier and you bound to get the answer you looking for. But that don't make what you say any good."

"Okay, Leon, talk what you mean," Bingo said.

"I been playing the tour long enough, Bingo, and I know like you know that when a team starts to lose its appetite it starts to lose the profits. First you sit back and say we only going to be playing the big towns because the money will be just as good. Next you going to be saying let's only play one game a day so we'll put on a better show. Then you going to be playing every other day and it goes on until you is sitting on your ass and wondering why you ain't making it no more. Yeah, man, I seen it happen to a lot of teams when they lose they appetite."

"You stretching it, Leon. It won't ever get as bad as you say. Never."

"But I seen it. I seen it when a team ain't hungry no more. And barnstorming is hungry ball more than anything else. It's better food than they got anywhere else so you got to scramble to get it if you want it. And they ain't no food unless you play, yeah, like we been without letting up long enough to say you is tired out. Man, you been seeing hard times for ten years now with coloreds and whites standing in lines and riding freights trying to stay fed. And now you ain't hungry no more because you forgot them things just since we been making a little money and things look good. And you all know that if you don't take that money when you can they is going to be someone else to take it instead. It's just like playing ball nonchalant, man. That's why Sallie always made it, because he never let up, not even when he had everyone on his back to get him to slow down and take it easy. I'se telling you plain, Bingo, that you is losing your appetite and you is convincing these boys that they ain't hungry no more either just at a time when they is tired as dogs. You ought to know, Bingo, like I know. When you ain't hungry no more you ain't worth nothing."

Bingo frowned and tried to reply. He folded and unfolded his arms in front of him; he rubbed his hands together.

"You is always against anything this team decides it's going to do. You know that, Leon?"

"You heard what I said, Bingo. You been around. Try to tell me straight that I'm wrong."

Bingo tried to think of something. At times he resented Carter for pulling the rug from under him. The pitcher could be as uncompromising as his fastball, and he was too often right.

"We'll take a vote on it just 'cause of you, Leon. Anyone against that? All right now, who's in favor of what I proposed?"

Louis Keystone shot up his arm.

"All right, who wants to keep doing what we been doing?"

The arms slowly moved upward; some only raised a couple of fingers, others lifted a loosely clenched hand next to their ears. Leon looked impassively at the floor and bit at a thumbnail. Bingo felt a twinge of doubt hit him, as if he had lost his hold over the team. Maybe he wasn't the born leader that Louis told him he was. He looked at the near unanimous vote against him and decided at that moment not to have the team vote about anything anymore. Then Esquire Joe Calloway laughed and spoke out.

"That's okay, Bingo. You just keep letting us do your thinking for you and you going to keep right on robbing the bank." He cackled and the others laughed with him, drowning Bingo's misgivings beneath their laughter.

It rained the following day, a light but steady drizzle from a thick gray sky. The Stars did not move westward to try to get out of the weather because the Madison Red Sox had a double-header scheduled as soon as they could play it. The team was now rested and ready to play again. They lounged around the hotel playing cards and listening to the radio.

Bingo and Louis went to an Edward G. Robinson movie at a theater down the street. On the way out they met Esquire Joe, who was walking slowly down the street looking in the store windows.

"Hey, Joe," Louis yelled. "You doing some shopping? You got money, huh?"

Joe nodded at them and kept looking at the displays. He had both hands in his pants pockets.

"Maybe going to pick up some attire?" Bingo said as the two of them walked up to him.

"Yeah, Bingo, you know. I ain't got much to show but this suit I got on so I'm looking for something new. Something with some style."

"C'mon, boy, you is in the big leagues now where dudes hang out," said Louis. "Pick up my trail, boy, I'll deck you out."

He put his arm around Joe's shoulder and walked him inside a haberdashery. They went past the salesmen directly to the suit rack. Bingo and Louis began flipping through the suits, sending the metal hangers singing along the bar. Esquire Joe stood behind them with his hands still in his pockets and a puzzled look on his face. Moments later a salesman came up to them and asked to assist but Bingo and Louis ignored him.

"We got some styles in mind," Louis said to the salesman and kept right on flipping the hangers. He finally picked out a navy double-breasted and a black pin stripe. Bingo spotted a dark maroon two-button with a matching vest.

"Try those on and then promenade, Esquire," Bingo said. He turned to the salesman. "This young man is a prince so he got to have the garments. Ain't that right, sir?"

The salesman shook his head quickly and pointed Esquire Joe to the dressing cubicle. When he returned in the black pin stripe Bingo clapped his hands. "You is *smoking*, Joe! Oh, Lord Jesus, have you ever *seen* such a sight?" Louis pinched his face together and skipped behind Joe as he looked at himself in the mirror. Bingo twirled Joe around and pulled at the flaps at the back of the suit.

"This number is growing on you, Joe, it owns you." Bingo whistled.

"What you think, Esquire?"

"Yeah, I like it," said Joe. He rubbed his palms slowly along the fabric. The uncut cuffs flopped over his shoes. "It looks like one of your numbers, Louis."

"You couldn't have spoke better, kid," Louis said.

Esquire Joe continued trying on other suits they selected. Louis and Bingo looked up and uttered words of praise whenever he came out. While he dressed, they sorted through the racks for themselves. The salesman tried to straighten the rumpled pile of suits Joe had already tried on.

Louis finally pulled a pair of suits out for himself and left for the dressing room. He reappeared with a one-button sharkskin.

"This is one I am fond of. Get out your chalk, Mr. Tailor, and do some marking." Louis instructed the salesman on a number of alterations he thought necessary. He wore his suits with shortened sleeves in order to show off plenty of cuff and the red rubies in his cuff links. He insisted on at least twenty-two inches of cloth at the ankles.

Bingo broke his string of dark-colored suits with a gold three-button and matching vest. He laid out $85 for it and bought a pair of shoes. He made sure the lapel could accommodate a carnation.

"You get twice the material for the money, Bingo," Louis said. "Ain't nothing but a circus could get under them shoulders."

Bingo pulled at the lapels and pushed Esquire Joe from in front of the mirror. Joe tried on his sixth suit, a brown one which he had picked out himself and was two sizes too large.

When Louis finished with his fitting, he hurried around the store pulling down shirts and hats from the shelves. He grabbed a light gray derby and propped it on Esquire Joe's head. Joe tilted it slightly to the left and raised his eyebrows quickly up and down.

"Oh, man, Louis," he said. "They going to take me for the boss."

"I'll give you a fat cigar and a stick and you can take over, Joe," Louis answered.

80

"These clothes is going right to my head. I got to calm down, I got to calm down some," Joe said. He turned and posed in front of the mirror. Then he turned sideways and took his batting stance, waving his bat and waiting for a pitch.

After a while they sorted through their merchandise and tallied up.

"You going to have these for us tonight before we go out, ain't you?" Bingo said.

The salesman looked at them, then he looked down at the pile of suits and shirts. He was a short, pudgy man with a thin head of hair. He bit the skin on the inside of his mouth and looked at another salesman standing by the cash register. The other man folded his arms and looked away.

"Cash, straight cash is going to speed delivery, ain't it, Mr. Salesman?" Louis quickly said. He took out his wallet and picked out some bills. "Ain't no reason to hesitate figuring up." He touched a finger to his tongue and fanned the money. The salesman kept his head down and added things up.

"Yeah, Joe," said Bingo. "When you get the new stuff you got to wear it before it cools off."

They paid the man and walked out. For a three-hundred-dollar cash sale over the counter, they had been promised delivery that night.

"I ain't never spent a lump like that before," said Esquire Joe. He walked between Bingo and Louis. "It just shot out of my pocket."

"That probably the first outfit you ever purchased by yourself, huh, Joe?" said Louis.

"Yeah, it is," he answered.

"You'll get used to it until you be buying that stuff like so much butter," said Louis.

Esquire Joe smiled and put his hands in his pockets. "How many suits of clothes you got, Louis? How many you got now?"

Bingo laughed. Louis whistled and put his hand to his chin. "A collection," he said.

Back at the hotel Splinter Tommy Washington met them in the lobby. "Hey, Bingo. Hey, Louis. We got ourselves a *place* for tonight," he said.

"Yeah, what you know," said Louis.

"A man come in and say there is a place in town with everything in it. It's one of them pig places, you know? Them blind pig places. The man say it's the top joint in the city."

"Hey, Tommy, I been itching for something to come up." Louis beamed.

"Who was the man? You get his name?" asked Bingo.

"Don't know. Isaac got the details."

"Yeah, well, we be seeing about them details," Bingo said. "We got to watch our step when some slicker come around."

"Aw, shit, Bingo," said Louis. "I don't care if this thing is crooked as hell. I'm going to light my ass on fire."

At six-thirty that night the suits were delivered to the hotel and by eight-thirty Louis was dressed. He joined Bingo, Tommy Washington, and Isaac Nettles, and the four of them drove off. The man had given an address on Dixon Street, a narrow street which ran through the middle of Colored Town. Louis drove the Lincoln slowly, barely clearing the parked cars on either side, while the others strained to read the house numbers. They finally stopped at a huge white two-story which looked big enough to be an apartment house. Its windows were totally dark.

"This looks like the place," whispered Louis. "There ain't nothing but death from the front."

"If there's life in the back, we in business," said Tommy Washington.

"Yeah," said Bingo. "At least somebody's in business."

Chapter 7

It was a large, open room, dimly lit by small lamps with red bulbs set in the walls. Fifteen to twenty people, colored and white, stood in groups or sat in black leather furniture. A bar was set up on one end; it was also leather and dotted with shining gold tacks. The people chattered and drank from ice-filled glasses. Louis walked behind the man who led them in. The man turned to him and smiled, then he made a sweeping gesture around the room. Louis snapped his fingers and winked in reply. The man moved away into the crowd. A girl walked past Louis and Bingo carrying a tray of drinks. She smiled and Bingo stepped aside to let her pass.

"Hey, man, this place has got it. Look at the class here," Louis said to Bingo. "Man, look at the ladies, look at all the grays."

"Let's find out what we got to pay to drink," said Bingo. They made their way to the bar. Bingo nodded at the bartender and asked for a Scotch.

"You got to order your drinks from the girls," the bartender said. "You catch?"

Louis looked at Bingo. "I got it, Bingo. We has hit a real operation here. We just got to play with them. They come to us."

"Well, as long as we here, we might as well drink some," Bingo said.

"I ain't never seen so much white at a joint like this," said Tommy Washington. He looked quickly at the crowd, not staring or meeting anyone's eyes. "There's some real money talking here."

"That's what mine is going to do," said Louis. He walked from the bar toward a cluster of people. Tommy Washington followed him. Bingo and Isaac wandered back into the center of the room.

The girls carrying trays of drinks were everywhere. They stepped in and out of the various groups, sometimes staying and chatting, always pushing drinks, now and then tucking away a bill. Two of them approached Bingo and Isaac. Bingo was sitting in one of the leather chairs; he dangled his hand over the side and brushed the red carpet. One of the girls sat on the arm of Bingo's chair, brushing her hip against his arm. She was tall and thin; her yellow dress hung lightly across her shoulders and opened to the rise of her breasts. Bingo raised his arm around her. She smiled and blew in his face.

Louis stood near the center of the room and tapped his glass with his pinkie ring. He talked with a colored girl named Adele. She toyed with the drink he had bought her. "Is you one of the fixtures here or can you play your own game?" he said.

"What you mean?" she said. "Don't you like this setup?"

"I like it fine. I just wondering how you set in it."

"I'm just a poor thing looking for spare change." She fluttered her eyelashes and took a sip from her glass.

"Yeah, I know what you mean. Like the shine boys downtown."

She lowered her glass and grazed a fingernail across her cleavage. "Sure, sucker. You want to see my polish box?"

Louis snickered. "I'll take a pass on that for now. I got to take in all you hitters before I skid."

"Okay," she said. "Get your eyes full. What's your name any-ways?"

"Jones. Willie Jones. Call me Willie."

"Sure, Willie."

Louis put his hand on his hip. "Say, all you ladies working together or you on your own?"

"What's it matter? If you got it you ain't got to share it."

"Even the blondes?"

"You take your chances with them. You know that, boy. You got to take your chances. You up for another glass, Willie?"

Louis shook her off and moved through the room. A fine smoke mist hung off the ceiling. The red lights cast a glow against Louis's sharkskin suit. There was no music, no group anywhere, just the light clinking of ice and glass and the hum of the chatter. The clumps of colored were a mixture of young and middle-aged, pimps, Louis thought, or gamblers like Sallie Potter who knew how to blow thick smoke from cigars and laugh louder than anyone else. Girls hung on their arms and pumped drinks. A few of the colored men occasionally mingled with the whites. They patted each other on the back and traded greetings like business partners. The colored girls speckled every group, avoiding their white counterparts, giggling, curling bills around their fingers like ribbons.

Louis spotted Adele, the girl he had just talked with. She sidled over to a thin, brown-haired man who sat alone. The man appeared nervous and self-conscious as he looked at and then away from the girl. She twisted her finger around his ear and leaned down to whisper into it. The man fidgeted and crossed his legs. Adele stood up and took his hand. The man followed her across the room. She led him through a paneled door which closed behind them. Louis smiled slightly and rubbed his palm across his leg. Another girl approached him.

"Say, sugar," he said to her. "Don't miss my friend Splinter Tommy here." He turned to where Tommy was standing but saw him talking to another girl. "Him over there. Jump on him before he gets away."

Louis winked at the girl and nodded in Tommy's direction. She drifted over to him. Louis found Bingo and his girl friend. Bingo had loosened his tie. He finished the drink he was holding and the girl brought him another.

"Yeah, Louis. Where you been? They as thick as bugs in here. How you like it?" Bingo patted the girl on her rump. She held a cigarette between her fingers. It pointed straight up and leaked a thin line of smoke which drifted up and disappeared in the lines of her neck. She hid her bills on the inside of her thigh, tucked in a black silk garter.

"We hit it all right, Bingo." He eyed Bingo's girl then looked past her at a group standing behind them. "And there is some foreign pudding like we ain't run into before."

Bingo looked at Louis and then leaned up to him. "Hey, Louis, keep cool with the white stuff," he hissed into Louis's ear. "Poke what you can handle, man."

Louis smiled and took a swallow from his glass. "Don't worry about what I can handle, Bingo."

"Yeah, don't get your ass shot doing it. Then what do we do for a third base?"

Louis lit himself a cigarette. He puffed deeply on it and released a small, thick bubble of smoke. A piano started up across the room and he shot a palm at Bingo and walked over to it. An old colored man with a bald and shiny head pecked away at the keys. A few of the crowd gathered around and lightly tapped their fingers to "My Blue Heaven."

Louis leaned on the piano like the others. He felt a girl brush against his hips but he did not turn to look. Instead he eyed a blonde standing across from him. She pretended to bob her head to the music, but she was off the beat, occasionally drinking then staring blankly at the piano player. She wore a sleek black evening gown which crisscrossed her breasts and tied around her neck. Her head was full of tight platinum curls

86

packed fuzzily together like cotton. She pursed her red lips, which stood out from her powder-white skin. Louis watched her and blew gusts of smoke across the piano top.

She continued to stare at the old man at the piano. He started in on "Don't Worry 'Bout Me." She rubbed her forehead and lit a cigarette. Louis blew more smoke at her, but the clouds lost momentum halfway across the piano and thinned into a harmless mist before they reached the girl. Louis tapped his nails on the piano top, he plinked his glass, he patted out a few rhythms with his palms. The girl lifted her thin, half-moon eyebrows and turned her back to the piano. The man started "Chew-Chew-Chew." Louis began humming and adding some "yah-yahs." The girl kept her back to him.

Louis picked up his drink and slid around the piano. He moved in and out of couples and a pair of hustlers. Somebody grabbed his sleeve and lightly scratched his hand with a long nail, but he moved on and pretended he hadn't noticed. He stepped around a weaving man doling out bills like paychecks to a pair of giggling brassies. He finally reached the spot at the piano where the girl had been, only to see her standing across the room at the bar. He watched her for a moment while the piano man began "Strange Fruit." The girl played with the bow on the back of her neck. She raised her arm up and revealed the plunging lines of her gown. It fell far below her shoulder, exposing smooth white ribs and the beginning rise of her breast. Her skin was white and powdered. She grimaced and lowered the arm again.

Louis finished his drink, said "Muvah" quietly to himself, and started over to the bar. He knew the girl wasn't hustling. She wasn't escorted by anyone, none of the girls were, but she refilled her glass over and over again at the bar without laying anything down for it. Louis decided to ask her to set him up again. Yet when he reached the bar she started to dance with a paunchy white man who was chewing on an unlit cigar. Louis shoved his glass on the bar and shook his head. He rubbed his hands together and put them on his hips. The girl moved slowly with her partner into the other couples who had joined them. She kept the same listless expression, gazing over the man's shoulder as the two of them shuffled. Louis thought she might have spotted him once and returned his stare, but then he wasn't sure.

"You look too hard and you'll get your fingers burned," she said. Louis turned and faced a tall, buxom redhead. She looked him straight in the eye, almost six feet in the air on her high heels.

"I'd like to be doing something with my fingers," Louis said. The girl handed him his glass, refilled.

"You mean like diddling my sister out there?"

"You got it." He nodded at her and shook his glass back and forth in his hand. He looked out at the blonde.

"It's not hard to spot you boys when your eyes start bugging out. Especially on something strange." She poked her pinkie into Louis's drink and stirred it around the glass. Louis watched her and pursed his lips. She lifted her finger into her mouth and slowly withdrew it, keeping her lips in a bunched, moist circle.

"Now why can't that platinum out there take your attitude?" he said.

"She ain't in the habit of advertising to you boys. Too dangerous."

"What do you mean? What you in business for?" he said.

"The boss won't have it. This place has got a clean reputation for keeping things separate."

"Shit. There's colored girls all over everybody."

"I'm talking about white girls, sonny," she said. "We'd get our brains blown out for dealing you boys."

"Yeah, yeah, I got you," Louis mumbled.

"Anyway, you boys shouldn't be interested. You got your own dark meat."

Louis fidgeted and looked at the redhead. She had a long,

silken green dress which cupped a large bosom and a hefty butt. She had her hair pulled back so it rested on her shoulders.

"Yeah, well, just relax, slugger. I ain't crowding your territory," he said, and he looked out again to where the blond girl was dancing.

"Nobody but Joe Louis gets white girls around here, sonny," she said.

"Joe Louis wouldn't dare step in with me." Louis smirked. "I'd kill him."

"Sure, but until you do, we got the rules. You play on our tables, you drink our booze—"

"And we don't get our black hands on your girls. That the thing with you?" Louis said, his voice taunting and cocky.

"Listen, sucker, I can take this place or leave it," she said. "If you got the dough to shake, I'll take it."

Louis turned his eyes downward and caught a shoreline view of her left breast. She raised her arm and quivered it slightly, then she quickly turned away.

"What's your name, Red?" Louis said. He forgot about the blonde for the time being and surveyed his new acquaintance.

"I'm Sheila. And which one are you, Amos or Andy?" She laughed in a short cackle.

Louis nodded. "Yeah, that's it. I'm Andy."

"You know, I ain't missed that show for years. Isn't that something?"

"Me too," said Louis.

"In my opinion, you people are the *funniest* alive. You know that? It's the way you talk just *kills* me."

"Yeah, me too, Red."

"Call me Sheila."

"Call me Amos."

The girl broke up. She punched Louis on the arm and stamped her foot. "You see what I mean. You coloreds just *kill* me." She laughed even harder.

"Okay, take it easy, Red. I ain't here to do an act for you."

The girl straightened up and fixed her hair. She took a drink. "Yeah, buster, I know," she said. Her smile disappeared. "It's probably hanging down to your knees and just itching to dance."

"You got it, Red. Now maybe you can get me a hot wire to that blonde out there. What's her name?"

"It's Lois. But she don't play for nickels. Especially with spooks."

"Now don't get nasty, Red. I got the dough to play ball with any one of you dollies. You too, if you up to it."

The redhead left her drink on the bar and put her hands to her hair. "Hang onto it, sonny," she said. She walked into the crowd, swinging her hips back at Louis. He watched as she talked to the blonde.

In a few minutes she was back with the blonde at her side. "Lois, Amos here seems to think we might like to take a chance on him."

Louis held out his hand to the girl. She lightly brushed her fingers across it and quickly withdrew them. She peered up at him. "You the one standing by the piano a minute ago and making a lot of noise?" she said. Her voice was deep and raspy.

"Yeah, I was there but I didn't see you," Louis said.

"Like hell you didn't," said the redhead. "They got people in jail for gawking like you did."

"Yeah?" said Louis.

"Yeah," said the blonde. She looked up at her cohort. "What's the deal, Sheila? Has darkstuff here got a proposition?"

"Yeah, Amos, anything behind that big mouth of yours?"

"Name it, girls. I can spot both of you together or separate for an inning or two or for the whole ball game. I pay dough up front just to prove my intentions."

The blonde spoke. "Double money for the risk. We're doing you a favor."

"Same for me," said the redhead.

"Ooo-wah!" said Louis. "How much is that for the both of yuse?"

"Make it an even three hundred," said the blonde. "If you can roll it."

Louis looked at the two of them. He shifted his weight. He looked up at the ceiling and pretended to count with his fingers. The girls stood with their hands on their hips. The blonde opened her mouth slightly and moved her tongue across her lips.

"We got a stiff on our hands, Sheila," she said. "This boy ain't got nothing but a big mouth and sticky pants." She exhaled and turned to the redhead.

"Well, what do you say, sonny?" the redhead said.

"Yeah. Okay," Louis said. He nodded his head and pretended to pick at a tooth with a fingernail.

"What do you want to go?" said the blonde.

"The both of you. We'll shoot it out for a while and then I'll decide if I want to ride all night."

"Fine with me. At the prices I said, you got that?" The blonde spoke in a monotone, like a cashier at the dog races.

"Both together," said Louis. "All three of us going at it."

"For God's sake," complained the blonde.

"Wait a minute. Let's give Amos a chance. Maybe that thing's as long as he thinks it is." The redhead raised her eyebrows and leaned against Louis. She pushed her huge hip out.

"Yeah, I is damn good at double plays," he said.

The redhead told Louis to follow them in a few minutes. She said they couldn't let anyone see the three of them leaving together. Louis agreed and they left. While he waited he looked for Tommy Washington and Bingo but he didn't see them anywhere. He figured they were probably off making their own transactions. Suddenly an arm grabbed his sleeve and jerked him around. It was Isaac. Louis laughed and was about to tell him of his setup when Isaac started in.

"What in hell you doing, Louis?" Isaac demanded. He was

sweating and nervous. "Where you going with white shit, man?"

"C'mon, Isaac. They is the cream of this place. Hand-picked them myself."

"Damn it, Louis! Leave it alone. We going to be picking you up off the floor." Isaac still clutched Louis's sleeve.

"Oh, man, this joint deals ass, Isaac. There ain't nothing says we got to stay with black."

"Where you been all your life, Louis? White ass hangs you!"

Louis eased a wide grin on his face. He held up his hands to Isaac. "Isaac, boy, find yourself something eager and don't worry about me. I be in and out before they find a tree big enough." He slapped Isaac lightly on the cheek and walked away. He could hear Isaac curse under his breath.

He found them at the end of a hallway which ran to the front of the house. There were two or three doorways on each side, all closed with a trace of light appearing at the floor space. Louis noticed the change in this part of the house. Its flowered wallpaper was stained and curled; a dull smell of stagnant air, even mildew, hung in it. The girls turned into a room, a small bedroom with a lavatory, brightly lit, an oval throw rug over the floorboards. The bed was most prominent, with a large brass frame and a red bedspread. Louis gave it a quick once-over and patted it with the palm of his hand. A puff of dust rose then floated back down.

"The old batter's box," Louis said. The two stood at the door with their hands on their hips. Louis reached in his pocket and pulled out a clip of bills. The blonde nodded.

"Well, he's got his library card," she said.

"Sure he does," the redhead said. "We don't entertain panhandlers."

"Good. So start entertaining," Louis said. He took off his coat and laid it on a chair.

The redhead turned and opened the door.

"Where you going?" said Louis.

"I've got to check up on how the party's going. They miss me already."

"But you signed on with me. Remember?"

"You got all you can handle, Amos. Maybe more." She cocked her head at Louis and swiveled out.

"Hey!" he yelled.

"Shut up," the blonde said. "You don't hustle her. She hustled you."

"Yeah, I got it. I just got that," he said slowly.

She turned her back to him and waited. He looked up and finally unzipped her. Her black gown fell from her shoulders and she stepped out of it. She had a sheer black slip beneath. Louis could see the outline of her panties and garter belt.

"I admire that silk," he said. "Always have."

"So do I," she replied. She turned to him and put out her hand. He was sitting on the bed, unbuttoning his shirt.

"For your money you can leave your shirt on," she said. He spotted a light but rounded bulge at her stomach when she took the slip off.

"I forgot your rates." He put his cuff links in his pocket. "Let's go the whole ball game. I don't want to wrinkle my cloth."

He handed her four or five bills and they disappeared inside her thigh. "My name's Anita," she said, suddenly becoming friendlier. She sat down next to him.

"I'm Sam Lewis," Louis said. "That's French."

She gave a small laugh and ran her hand through her hair. He got up and neatly folded his trousers across the chair. He turned to her in nothing but his underwear—a pair of polka dot boxer shorts and a baggy undershirt—and his long Argyle stockings.

She giggled at him. "You're sure skinny, Sammy." Louis smiled from ear to ear and wiggled his knees together.

She stood up and pulled the spread off, bending down and offering a tantalizing view of her rear end. The black panties and garter straps made her skin look even more white than it was. Louis eyed her thick, molded thighs, rounded slightly and smooth. He reached out and patted them firmly with the palm of his hand, making a slapping noise as if he were clopping the shanks of a horse. She whirled around and faced him.

"Get your black hands off me!" she hissed. "You ain't bought that!"

Louis winced and rubbed the straps of his undershirt. "Ooo-wah," he sighed. "You is one of them prima donnas."

"You bet your ass," she snapped.

He backed off and walked over to a small dresser. He bent down and smiled in the mirror. He pinched his cheeks and brushed his eyebrows. Then he pulled down his lower lip and inspected his gums. He had long considered a ruby inset for one of his front teeth. A pimp back in Pittsburgh had one and when he smiled it shone halfway across the room.

"What are you, a queen or something?" the blonde said. Louis turned his head to one side and admired the razored part.

"I'm just seeing if things is in top shape. And they is."

He faced her and slapped his hip. He reached down and plucked the carnation out of the lapel of his coat. With a deep breath he smelled the flower, then he stepped over to the bed where the girl was sitting and placed it on her crotch. Its whiteness stood out nicely against the black panties.

"Now you got your own private garden spot."

"Sure. I knew a stripper who finished off her act like this." She grabbed the flower and flipped it back to Louis. He put it behind his ear. He wiggled his hips.

"C'mon, Sam, we're wasting time."

"Look, blondie, when you been starving as long as I has, you got to do it right."

"Then get me something to smoke. I've got to do something while you go through your act." She looked at him for a moment. "You sure are skinny," she said.

Without replying he moved to the bed. He lightly catapulted over her to the wall, grabbing the inside of her thigh as he went. She slapped at him, he pulled her down, and they scuffled.

94

She kicked him and kneed him and dug her nails into his back. Louis pinned her, pushing her shoulders into the sheet. He bent over the base of her neck and bit her, a nip like a beagle. He could smell her and she squealed. She reached her hand between them and goosed him. He shoved his knee between her legs. She was almost panting, defiantly clenching her teeth and hissing into his ear. He pressed his knee against her crotch and she grunted. Then she bit him on the shoulder.

"C'mon, jungle ass! C'mon, boy!" she sneered. He could feel her strength relenting, her moves changing mission. He wrestled the twisted slip from her waist, where it had bunched, and raised it over her head. He heard the elastic snap of her garters; her fingers were nimbly unhooking them. When the belt hit the floor, slightly damp and its pouch full with Louis's wadded bills, she was clawing for every ounce of infielder she could get.

It wasn't five minutes when the door banged open and the redheaded woman charged in. "Get out, Anita! Get out!" she shouted. "Jack's found out and he's coming up!"

The blonde scrambled out from beneath Louis. She was sweating and her hair was matted to one side of her head. She furiously searched for her underwear, crawling on her hands and knees and reaching under the bed. Louis sat upright. "Hey, what's going on, Red? What's happening?" He was stark naked with the sheets wound around his feet.

"You better get your ass out the back door, smoke. The house is coming."

The redhead was breathing quickly. She tried to help the blonde dress. The girl had just pulled on her brassiere when a short, greasy-haired white man came into the room. He pushed by the redhead and grabbed the arm of Louis's companion. She yelped as he pulled her up and sent her struggling across the room. "Bitch!" he snarled. He had thin gold casings around his teeth. "Sucking tar ass on my time!"

"He made me do it, Jack! He forced me," the girl protested. The little man, sweating in a white shirt and tie loosened at the

95

neck, scowled at her. He started for her and stopped. She cowered against the dresser in a half crouch, twisting her slip in her hands.

Louis grabbed his shorts and started shoving his feet through them.

"You broke the rules, nigger," the little man shouted at Louis. He was chewing a small chaw and it speckled his bottom row of teeth. Then he spat loudly and a pod of juice splattered on the floorboards. "Nobody crosses this house, nigger."

He turned to a pair of colored men who were standing at the doorway. Louis had not seen them before. One was huge, at least as big as Bingo, with head completely shaved and glistening. He smiled at Louis, a wide, malevolent grin, and Louis spotted a ruby, red and polished with spit, shining in the middle of his mouth.

The little man threw Louis's clothes at him and he grabbed the blonde by her hair.

"He dragged me here, Jack, I swear it. He's got a razor, Jack, so help me," she screamed. He pushed her through the door and down the hall. Louis could hear her whimper as the man turned and followed her. Without looking back at Louis, the redhead followed. Only the two colored men, the larger one still smiling, remained within the room with Louis.

They stood watching Louis, saying nothing. By now he had his boxer shorts on and was hopping across the room after his socks.

"I can't say I got my money's worth out of that, you know what I mean, friends?" The two said nothing.

"That little pussy bit me like I was her Sunday dinner. Look at these here marks on my shoulders."

He looked up at the two. The shorter one pointed at Louis's clothes.

"Maybe you boys can see about getting me something else. Damn. You know what I laid out for that little blondie?" He

96

buttoned his shirt and slipped the cuff links in. "Hey, who was that short guy? He own this place?"

The large man no longer was smiling.

"Hey, I like that rock, man. I got to fix me up with something like that." Louis tied his shoes and pulled on his suit coat. The carnation lay crushed on the floor, a few feet away from the pool of tobacco juice.

He bent down in front of the mirror and then stepped for the door. "I can find my way back to the action, boys. I'd appreciate it if you could see about hustling my cash back from that little girl." As he stepped between the two, they reached beneath his armpits and hoisted him in the air. He shouted in protest as they carried him down the hall. He skipped and peddled in midair as the two of them walked. The huge man to Louis's right again had the smile on his face.

They carried him to a small stairway which wound almost straight down the side of the house. Louis tried to kick and twist away, realizing as they went down that he was being more than escorted out of the place. He raised an elbow and tried to clip the smaller man's face, but the man leaned away and responded with a sharp knee to the side of Louis's thigh. The blow stung his entire left leg and he went limp trying to clutch it. At the bottom of the stairs one of the men kicked open a thin, grimy door and suddenly they were outside, in the narrow space between houses.

"Hey, brothers, you can ease on me now," Louis said. "C'mon with the rough stuff now."

They spun him around and pinned him to the side of the house. Louis relaxed for a moment. The two of them glared at him, still pressing hard against his shoulders. He eyed the bigger one and waited for him to make a move at him. But the man stood there, as if preparing to cuff him across the mouth or just stand back and sneer at him. The two released their pressure and Louis stood straight. He brushed his lapel and adjusted a cuff link.

"That's better now. You boys read me. I didn't pay no attention to that little girl but what she had me on that bed. I ain't got no hard feelings. I'll be checking with you boys later."

He took a step between them and started for the back stairs. He hadn't taken two steps when his neck was jerked back as if he had been clotheslined. He lost his balance and flipped backward. The big, bald-headed man towered over him, then he raised Louis by his collar and threw him back against the house. Louis landed heavily against the wood, knocking his head with a dull clunk. He instantly bolted out to escape, poking a hard elbow into the ribs of the smaller one. The man jackknifed, but the larger of the two managed to grab Louis again and pull him back. The small man straightened up, still breathing heavily from Louis's pointed elbow, and he smashed him in the ribs. Louis lost his breath and tried to brace himself, but the man's blows followed one after another. They were short and heavy, like the butt of a rifle, cracking against each side of Louis's rib cage, never once landing in the soft of his stomach.

Louis slumped, his knees buckling. The figures before him went gray and started to swim.

"C'mon, man," he moaned.

The small man stepped back. Louis was nauseous, almost out, when he heard the larger of the two, who held him from behind, mumble something. Then he saw it, through the black, numbed glaze before him, lying there across the palm of the small man. It had an ivory handle, smooth and polished. Louis forced two shrill, pinched cries; he squirmed with whatever he had left, like a calf with its feet bound. The huge arms behind him locked him in place.

The ivory handle inched closer and clipped Louis's buttons from his coat. Louis grimaced, summoning strength to clench his teeth and wishing he might black out and freeze the white-hot slashes of the blade. The ivory handle rose once more and severed his tie from the collar in a clean, soundless stroke. The handle lingered before opening up Louis's shirt, then his undershirt, which tore with the whine of a bedsheet. Louis breathed quickly as the handle lightly lifted the tattered material and exposed his chest. He could feel the breath of the man behind him, he caught a glance of the ivory handle before it blinded him and laced him with grooves.

Bingo had taken a bottle in with him and the girl.

"Hey. Hey, Alice, girl," he whispered, shaking her. Once in the room, she had drunk with him, and now she lay spent and sleeping in the mess of sheets. Bingo got out of the bed. Its springs groaned and the thin brass ends straightened up. It was 3 A.M. according to his watch. He rinsed himself off with a wet cloth from the lavatory. It was cool against his face and his eyes. He went for his trousers and kicked a shoe against the wall. Alice turned over and moaned.

"Don't touch my stuff," she rasped.

"That you, Alice? You come back to life?" He went over and patted her on her bare butt. She turned her head on the pillow away from him.

"You heard what I said, ace."

"Yeah, okay. You done the grand slam as good as I ever seen it," Bingo said. He swung his hands as if to hit a fastball. Then he cupped his crotch. "Your prices is high but your aim is dead."

He whistled slightly and squirted under his arms with a tiny bottle of perfume he found on the dresser. On the way out he turned out the light, but not before he gave the girl's foot a tug and saw her gently raise her palm in reply.

The crowd in the lounge had thinned considerably when he returned. Bingo saw hardly any of the girls. Isaac and Tommy Washington were sitting in a corner and they got up to meet him.

"Man, what took you?" Isaac said.

Bingo grinned and started to talk when Tommy cut him off.

"Louis ain't around, Bingo. He left before you and he still ain't come back."

"Yeah," added Isaac. "And he went out with a pair of gray girls. I mean real gray ladies, Bingo."

Bingo looked at them both and shook his head. "Now we don't know nothing about what Louis been doing, do we? You boys seen him before; how you know what he's up to?"

"You said we wasn't going to pull all-night shit," said Tommy.

"That won't stop Louis," said Bingo.

"Hot damn, just like nothing," fumed Isaac. "I don't like these joints."

Bingo laughed and lit a cigarette. "Didn't you get nothing, boy?"

"Yeah, but I got it and left it so long ago I can't even remember it no more."

"You got to learn, Isaac, that you ain't running out a drag bunt when you get in those little rooms."

"I ain't one to linger," Isaac said. He smiled slightly and looked about to add something but stopped and folded his arms across his chest.

"Isaac said Louis left with *two* of them girls," Tommy said. "One a blonde and another redheaded one who was *taller* than he is."

"Jesus," said Bingo. "Two-tone! Louis got hisself an eye, don't he?" He slapped Isaac on the shoulder.

"Dark meat on white bread," added Tommy Washington, and Bingo slapped him as well.

They waited fifteen minutes longer before Bingo decided to step out. Isaac stayed behind in case Louis should show. Bingo and Splinter Tommy found their way down the back stairs and around the house. Bingo said something about how bad it looked on the outside. It needed a paint job; its gutters were barely hanging from the roof.

"They got to have camouflage for a joint like this," said Tommy.

On the street they ambled over to Louis's car. Bingo nonchalantly walked around to the driver's side, thinking he might find some cigarettes on the seat. He swung open the door. And he saw Louis.

"Goddamn!" Bingo hissed. Louis lay across the seat with his knees pulled up to his chest. His entire front was bathed in blood, from the base of his chin to his groin. Bingo reached down and lifted Louis's shoulder and tried to roll him on his back. Louis exhaled loudly at Bingo's touch. The smooth felt cloth of the seat was soaked with blood and smudged with dirt.

"He been razored," said Tommy. He pawed at the shreds of Louis's coat and shirt. "Sliced bad," he said.

The back of Louis's clothing had been slit down the center just like the front. The skin was slashed in a dozen vertical stripes, the blood now congealed and riddled with dirt and grime. The grooves were no deeper than an eighth of an inch.

Bingo slapped him lightly on the cheek. But Louis only groaned and clutched his chest and stomach, still laying in his crouched position. Then Bingo lifted Louis's arms and touched his ribs. He held his breath at what he felt there. It was nothing but a spongy, swelling mush.

"He ain't got a rib left down there." Bingo paused. He felt Louis's smooth forehead. "Get Isaac and let's go," he finally said, and Tommy bounded off toward the house. Bingo bent over Louis and whispered to him.

"We going to fix you up, Louis, we going to fix you up," he said slowly and tried to move him gently across the seat to the right side. He got a blanket from the back of the car and laid it across the stained area behind the steering wheel.

Isaac ran up with Tommy and cursed out loud. "We got to go back up there and get somebody for doing this," he said.

Bingo told him to get in the car.

"We got to get him to a doctor. We got to go," he said.

He drove slowly, trying to keep the car from lurching and jolting Louis. The three of them could smell a dank, sour odor from his breathing and his flesh.

Chapter 8

The sun was shining the next morning so the team was up early and ready to work out. Leon and Esquire Joe piled equipment into the trunk of Bingo's Auburn. They had slept the entire night before and were eager to loosen up after the two-day layoff. Mungo Redd, Fat Sam Popper, and Donus Youngs followed on their heels. The three of them had started out the night before, heading in the same direction as Bingo and Louis. But Mungo forgot the address and they ended up in a bar, returning to the hotel before midnight.

"Go see what Bingo's doing," Leon yelled at Mungo. Mungo nodded and was about to hop up the stairway when he spotted Bingo coming in the front door. Splinter Tommy and Isaac followed him. The three of them were looking haggard and sluggish. Bingo had lost his tie and the tails of his shirt hung out like limp feathers.

"Hey," drawled Leon when he saw them. "What's up with you?"

Bingo stopped and fumbled for a chair. Isaac and Tommy walked past them all and plodded up the stairs to their rooms. Bingo clapped his hands together in a single dull thumping noise. He looked up at Raymond Mikes, who had come into the lobby.

"You got a cigarette, Raymond?" he said.

His hand shook noticeably when he lit it. The smoke flooded from his mouth as he exhaled.

"Louis got cut up and every one of his ribs broke," he finally said. "We left him in a hospital back there."

The players crowded quickly around and began shooting questions. Bingo smoked quickly and tried to tell them what he knew. Mostly he described what Louis looked like when they found him in the front seat. The team talked hurriedly among themselves, speculating about what Louis had met up with.

"Why don't we go back there and clean up the place?" Fat Sam Popper said.

Leon hissed at him and spoke. "Louis was messing white, huh, Bingo? Same as always?"

No one said a word until Bingo replied, "Yeah, that's it, Leon." Bingo got up and went to his room to catch some sleep.

The rest of the players stood around the lobby until Leon walked out to the car and headed for the ball field.

By one that afternoon, Bingo, Isaac, and Tommy Washington were up and in uniform for the day's doubleheader with the Madison Red Sox. The Stars had but nine players to field so Turkey Travis had to play the outfield when Leon pitched. They switched for the second game even though Raymond volunteered to play, despite his cast and his crutches. The Red Sox were only a fair outfit so Leon cruised through the first game and the Stars took it 3–1. Esquire Joe got four hits, half of the team's total, while Bingo, Isaac, and Tommy Washington stood up at the plate dewy-eyed and fanned at the ball.

It was a lackluster showing and Bingo couldn't help but notice a number of people wander away from the ball park. In the first inning of the second game he did manage to slam a liner back through the middle and out in the field he tried to chatter things up. But he was sore and dead on his feet, and only because the rest of the players took up the slack the Stars pulled out a 9–6 win. It was seven-thirty that night when he collected their share of the gate—sixty percent of a fair-sized crowd, so he didn't complain.

They ate quickly back at the hotel and drove to the hospital. Bingo had given a boy a dollar to clean up the front seat of Louis's car and even though he spent a couple of hours on it, large reddish blotches stood out in the fabric and Bingo had to cover it with newspaper.

Nobody said anything about the house or the possibility of looking into Louis's beating. They understood the ground rules for such places, the unspoken risks a customer took if he chose to buy. They had all seen it before in Louisville, Pittsburgh, any town they could name. If they were to go back there they would get nothing but blank stares, stares that told them they had so much time to forget they had ever seen the place before.

Louis's bed was in the middle of a long open room. As the players filed in they waved and nodded at some of the patients who were sitting up in their beds. Louis lay flat on his back in the colored section near a hallway. It had taken Bingo fifty dollars in cash to get him a bed at that time of the night. The going rate for colored in the daytime was thirty-five.

Louis had his eyes wide open and he grinned when he spotted Bingo and Leon and the others. He did not raise his arms; they lay motionless by his sides against a gray blanket and a white sheet. Bingo lifted the blanket slightly and showed the others. Louis was taped solid from his neck to his waist. The players stepped to the front of the bed and each took a look, offered a "How you doing, man?" Louis wiggled his head slightly and didn't move a muscle. Leon stood at the end of the bed and looked at the clipboard, which had Keystone, Louis P., at the top of it.

"Says here you just got scratched by a bottletop, Louis," he said, and the others laughed quickly.

"How long you been up?" Isaac asked.

"A few hours," said Louis. "You play today?"

"Yeah, but they didn't have no team," Mungo Redd answered.

Bingo stepped back and watched a nurse walk by. She stopped at a few of the beds, she marked some of the clipboards, then she walked on. Bingo wrinkled his nose at the pervasive smell of antiseptic, like the snake oil Turkey Travis put on his arm. "They treat you all right here, Louis?" he finally said.

"Yeah," Louis said. He stared up at them. "But I'm burning up, man."

"Well, c'mon, Louis," Tommy Washington blurted out. "Tell us what happened to you. Who did it?"

The others shook their heads and leaned closer. This was the first time Louis had been fully conscious and alert since they brought him in last night.

"I just got me a girl friend and they cut me up," he replied.

"Shit, Louis. Start from the beginning. Give us the story like it happened to you," said Tommy.

"The girl fixed it up. A redhead with a big ass, right?" said Isaac.

"Yeah," said Louis. He spoke stiffly, still not moving his arms or shaking his head. He shifted his eyes quickly from man to man. "She was big as hell. But she got me this blonde—you see her, Tommy?"

"Didn't see nothing. I was busy," Tommy said.

Louis went on, scowling and screwing up his face with each detail, grimacing whenever he rocked himself. He described the blonde and exaggerated some of the things he did with her before being interrupted by the short white man and his two friends.

"White man own that joint?" said Bingo. "Thought it was colored."

"White man cut you like that?" added Isaac.

"No, sir, they was colored. Two of them."

"Colored? Shit, Louis, you sure?"

"Yeah, one big one and one little one. Damn. That boy had him a stone in his mouth red like a cherry."

"Colored working for white." Isaac scowled. "Don't that beat it."

"Give me three, four days," said Louis. "I pay me a return visit to those boys and show them some real cutting."

He bent his arm at the elbow and zipped his nail across the sheet. He grunted and they could see the pain on his face. He laid his arm slowly back down on the bed.

The players stood around his bed with lifeless, gaunt expressions. They could feel his pain, they sensed the foreignness of the hospital with its smells and bottles. They were unsure of themselves in this place, wondering within themselves about how to react, who to blame, what to say. Getting cut up was common enough, a thing you could run with, but Louis lay there, their own Louis Keystone, third baseman, with his sharp, cocky eyes, and his body as useless as a broken bat. They searched for something to do, like reaching for dirt or stealing a base to start a rally, somehow to control the game, to put it back in hand. Bingo sensed it the sharpest. He had felt few things in life as delicate, as frustrating as Louis and the whiteness of his bandages, and the burning muddle of splintered ribs beneath.

After twenty minutes of chatter and nonsense, they left the hospital and went back to the hotel. There they sat around the lobby.

"How about tomorrow?" asked Raymond Mikes. "Anybody got some ideas?"

"We only got nine guys. How we going to travel?" said Mungo Redd.

They looked at Bingo. "We'll stick around here," he said. "Play some punk teams around until Louis can go with us."

"But we got games scheduled, Bingo. We got to be in Iowa next week—Davenport, Iowa. We can't skip those games," Raymond said.

"We got to. We a team and we can't leave Louis on his back here. What you think, Leon?" Bingo passed it to Leon before the big pitcher could come out with anything, certain Leon had an opinion.

"The lady at the hospital say that Louis is bad but he can walk around if he want. It's just going to be pain for him," Leon said.

"When you talk to a lady?" said Bingo.

"While you boys was standing with Louis I caught one of them nurses."

"Shit. I didn't see you."

"Yeah, well, since Louis can get out of bed if we tell him to, I figure we can just go." Leon leaned far back against his chair and yawned.

"Take him with us?" said Raymond Mikes.

"No, Raymond, send him back to Louisville or Pittsburgh or some place. We get someone else until he's ready," Leon said.

"Shit. No. We can't do it to him," Bingo said loudly.

"We got Raymond for a cripple already; we don't need two," Leon replied.

"Goddamn it, Leon! You going to kill this team. We got to take Louis."

"Who going to pay for him? Who going to pay for his bills up there in that hospital? Start thinking money, Bingo."

"Damn! Damn! Louis and his white ass!" Bingo said.

They argued over the problem, each player offering his own solution. Most of them wanted to keep Louis on but they didn't want to pay his way. Leon said nothing further. He listened to each argument arrive at the same conclusion. Bingo overheated and bellowed over everyone. He puffed and pounded his meaty hands together.

"A traveling team's got to go light or it ain't a traveling team no more," Leon finally said. "You boys ought to know that by now."

His smugness infuriated Bingo.

"How about it, Bingo?" Leon said.

108

Bingo stood up and paced across the lobby. He puckered his lips, then he mumbled something to himself.

"I got to clear my mind from you boys. There's too much yelling and shit for me to think," he said.

"Hell, Bingo," Isaac said.

"Yeah, that's right, I just decided I got to think this thing over in my mind. I'll catch you all later," Bingo said.

He walked over to the desk and bought a cigar. Without removing the wrapper, he stuck it in his mouth and went up to his room.

Only five minutes later Leon walked in on him. Bingo was sitting in a straight-backed wooden chair drinking from his bottle of Old Forester.

"Why you got to deck me in front of the boys all the time, Leon? You make me look bad every time we got to make a decision."

Leon sat down on the bed. "Just like you catching me, Bingo. You don't miss nothing but when it gets tight I call my own pitches."

"What's that mean?"

"Means you got to use your head more."

Bingo grunted and took a short drink. "Man, I buy the boys beer and steak and I show them a good time when they with me. They like that, Leon, and they got respect for me out of that. And you can't shove that back at me like you do. I got to save face with those boys."

"That your problem, is it?"

"So I'm going to appoint you assistant promoter of this ball team, Leon."

"Good, that means more money."

"No, it don't. It mean you come to me in private whenever you got an idea. Then I'll take it to the team in a proper fashion. And I give credit to my assistant promoter."

Leon whistled through his teeth. "Boy, that sound good, Bingo. Make me feel important."

"Yeah. So what's your first idea?"

"Right off the bat, huh?"

"Yup."

"Okay, boss. First, you got to learn how to mix business and pleasure."

"I do. I mix a lot of business with a lot of pleasure," Bingo said.

"Business Man says you got to get Louis out of the hospital and quit paying his bills. Got it?"

"Keep going, Leon."

"Business Man says get out of this town and start playing ball again. The team is getting smelly."

"And what does the Business Man say if I want Louis with the team?"

"He say that's *dumb.*"

"Good. We going to take him. We going to get him tomorrow and lay him on the seat and go."

"Yeah. One more thing. The Business Man say that if you want to keep the boys paying off you got to keep them *tired.* Push from one town to the next town and let them sleep just enough to play some more. Then they too tired to go out sporting and getting cut up. That the number one rule from the Business Man."

"How about the Pleasure Man?" Bingo said.

"He had his turn last night," Leon replied. He leaned back and stretched out on the bed. Bingo poured more Old Forester. He took a slow look around the small room, yawned, and said, "Shit."

They left the hotel at seven the next morning after grabbing a quick breakfast at a diner and appointing Esquire Joe official driver of Louis's Lincoln. Esquire Joe beamed at the wheel and squealed away from the curb. He assured everyone that they had not made a mistake by giving him the wheel, but he didn't mention that he had never had a driver's license in his life. He had learned everything about the Lincoln by sitting next to

Louis and taking pointers. Driving the automobile was a natural once he let her go.

At the hospital they stepped quickly up to Louis's ward and helped him out of bed. Bingo had made certain about Louis's condition and his release earlier that morning. He told the people he wasn't going to pay any more so they might just as well let him go. Louis was the only one who put up a fuss. He groaned loudly and held his body as rigid as a bound mummy when they put him on his feet.

"Check my bandages, man!" he wailed as they pushed him through the hospital corridors. "You ain't dealing with a well man here."

He shuffled and winced at every corner. At the stairs he took one at a time, straining his legs as if they were broken instead of his ribs. The players could not keep from laughing and making cracks.

Esquire Joe leaned over his shoulder and repeated, "Hey, Louis, guess who's driving now. Guess who's driving now, Louis? Can you guess? Huh, Louis?"

"Shut up, man. No one drives that car except myself," Louis said.

At the desk Bingo paid the nurse in cash. He took the money from a clip, gave it to her, and walked away before she could give him a receipt. Out front he watched Mungo and Isaac try to ease Louis into the back seat of his Lincoln. "Now watch it there, damn, watch it!" he said. "Don't touch my back, damn! Shit, man."

Esquire Joe slid in beind the wheel and revved the engine. He added his own sound effects and looked back to see if Louis was noticing him. Louis said nothing until he was settled and reasonably comfortable. Then he looked over to Joe. "Dammit, shofer! Drive this thing like a cloud or I'll break your ass!"

Joe eased the car out into the street slowly and deliberately, smiling from ear to ear. Louis crossed his arms over his ribs and scowled.

"You going to teach me how to get the girls someday, boss?" Joe said.

Louis stared straight ahead. "Drive, boy," he said.

The two-day layoff had permitted Raymond to set up a few games in the towns between Madison and the state of Iowa. In a week they planned to be in Davenport, where they would pick up two more players. There were plenty of small-town teams the farther west they drove. Bingo and Leon had played against some of them with all-star teams years back. Raymond also kept a check on where the House of David team was traveling. If the two teams crossed paths in a good-sized town, it could be a big attraction and a good gate. The white Davids swung out west a few times a year and played colored teams whenever possible. But usually they stayed back home in Michigan, so meeting them in Iowa was strictly chance.

The two cars cruised onto the two-lane highway. Bingo stayed out in front and ordered Esquire Joe to keep his distance. They had not been on the road for some time, or so it seemed to the players, and they rode comfortably. They talked and joked instead of sleeping or reading newspapers. By noon they were in Chinoot, Wisconsin, and ready to stand off the Chinoot Four Baggers. The people of Chinoot were ready and waiting as soon as they saw the letters on the side of Bingo's Auburn.

"Hey, Motor Kings! Hey, hey! We're going to lick yuse guys!"

The Four Baggers were little better than a fair nonprofessional team, but their fans turned out in droves to see them. The mayor, three-hundred-pound Lloyd "Jelly Belly" Umthun, stood on the back end of a tractor parked behind the backstop and announced the line-ups with a huge cardboard megaphone. The Stars joined in the fun and went through all of their routines—the hotball warm-up, infield practice with a ghost ball. Mungo even juggled, an act he had perfected since the tour started. Bingo hustled around, joking and picking up bets with the fans. Then he stepped up to the plate and hit a practice pitch so far over the fence it landed in a pasture and just missed a Guernsey.

At the start of the game, the outfield—Esquire Joe, Sam Popper, and Turkey Travis—sat down behind the pitcher's mound and brought out a deck of cards. While they shuffled the cards and dealt them out Leon whipped the first of nine fastballs past a Chinoot Four Bagger. The fans screamed at Leon and the batters, Bingo chattered back at the fans, mocking their team and repeating his bets. The outfielders thumbed over their cards and played a hand. Bingo finally offered fifty dollars to any batter who could line one through the middle and break up the poker game. Leon blurred fastballs down the pipe.

They kept up the clowning with the Four Baggers and their fans throughout the game. Bingo blasted one out of the park and ran the bases backward. Donus Youngs at first base sat on a rocking chair and didn't move from it to take a throw. Esquire Joe caught a flyball behind his back in right field. The kids in the stands ran up and down the Stars bench asking for autographs on their own gloves and bats. After nine innings the Stars had run up a 14–4 lead, but the fans were still hollering and carrying on. Jelly Belly Umthun was shouting as loud as ever behind his megaphone.

Bingo had planned to load up and take off as quickly as possible after the game. They had another game thirty miles down the road at six. But Jelly Belly and a few others approached him after the game and invited the team into town for dinner. They all but pushed the Stars into coming.

When the Stars drove back into Chinoot they found Main Street closed off and filled with tables. Heavy-set farm women were bumping each other with platters full of food—bread, pork chops, green beans, beef stew, potato salad—and the team hustled behind the tables in full uniform and started loading up. In no time the street was filled with people eating and passing food as furiously as the Stars. Some of the kids crept up behind

Bingo and offered him a leg of chicken or another pork chop. With his cheeks bulging he shook his head and showed them the three he already had on his plate. Everywhere the Stars turned there was a lady offering them something more—another pork chop or a pitcher of milk. A little later on Jelly Belly Umthun took his megaphone and announced how happy the town was to have the Stars with them. Bingo stood up and waved a pair of chicken legs over his head in agreement.

Over at the cars Louis sat alone, gingerly eating from a plate on his lap. It was too painful for him to move in and out of the car; even the slight pressure against his back from sitting began to burn. Once in a while Splinter Tommy came over to check on him. A few kids followed him and peered at Louis. He unbuttoned a few of his shirt buttons and showed off the bandages. They stared wordlessly and then ran away. Louis tried to maneuver himself into a comfortable position, but nothing was comfortable except sitting upright and touching nothing. He grimaced and grunted continually, and he couldn't get up much of an appetite.

To show their appreciation for the feast, Esquire Joe and his trio joined Mungo Redd on his mouth organ and gave a serenade. The people cheered loudly and applauded for more after each number.

Finally Bingo hustled up and grabbed Jelly Belly's megaphone. "Chinoot's sure the best town we ever been to," he hollered. "We took a vote and voted it the first place we coming back to if we ever need a home town." The people applauded once more and laughed when a couple of the Four Baggers stood up and shook their fists.

From Chinoot they traveled to Manton and Onionville, then Wahlert, Glenville, and What Cheer. The constant riding and bumping was rough on Louis. He was pale and weak and ate little. It was almost impossible for him to sleep in any position, and he became drowsy and nauseous on the road. Every five days he was supposed to have his bandages rewrapped, and

Bingo had no idea how they were going to work that out. After four days on the road, Leon ordered Bingo to get Louis off the tour and back to Louisville. Bingo fussed and tried to think of an excuse to say no. But he and everyone else knew Louis's misery. Bingo agreed to put Louis on a bus when they got to Dubuque the next day.

Louis was tired and wobbly when they drove him to the terminal. The long ride to Louisville would be hard on him, but not as bad as traveling with the team had been. Bingo helped him with his bag and paid for his ticket. He made sure Louis had enough money to get by.

"Get your skinny ass back when you can throw the ball," he said.

Louis smiled weakly and raised a hand to wave at the rest of the players. Raymond tottered on his crutches, then he waved one in the air when Louis stuck his head out the bus window. "I know how you feel, Louis," Raymond said, and Bingo gave him a dirty look.

"You be back, boy. You got us for friends so you be back," Bingo shouted. The bus started off and left the players standing and giving short waves. Louis pulled his head back in the window and was gone.

In Davenport they picked up two new boys, Earl Sibley, a short, bowlegged infielder with no neck who would take Louis's place on third, and Parnell "Big Juice" Johnson, a pitcher and outfielder Bingo had once seen in Texas. Sibley was young, about twenty-four, and almost bald, but he was a tough hitter and a quick base runner who ran with short, jerky motions and always slid in headfirst. Sibley's only problem was his temper. He had been thrown off the Chattanooga Baynell Braves when he went after a hometown umpire and bit him.

Big Juice Johnson was much older, up with Leon around thirty-five or thirty-six, but he was a smart pitcher who was known for the things he put on the ball. His favorite pitch was

115

his nickname pitch, the juice ball, which he threw with the help of a streak of tobacco juice on the seams. The ball dipped in and down on a right-hand hitter, and was very heavy to hit. Big Juice threw anything else he could think of along with it. He used bottle caps to throw his cut ball, he used Vaseline for his shine ball. He could throw any one of those pitches any time, for he kept most of his supplies—a dab of Vaseline, a bottle cap, an emery cloth—in his back pocket.

After Davenport they decided to stay with the Mississippi River and head for Saint Louis. They went through Botlow and Blue Grass, swinging in and out with the wide, brown river, honking at barges and pleasure boats. As they drove, Bingo became more and more anxious to stop and buy a fishing pole and a bucket of minnows. Shacks with bait signs advertising "Fresh Catfish" lined the highway and turned his eye.

"Damn, we got to stop and do us some fishing," he yelled. "The Mississip is the best river in the world for them catfishes and them walleyes."

Leon looked at him and tried not to show any interest. But he was a veteran fisherman himself and there wasn't anything he would like better than sitting on a dock waiting for a cane pole to jerk.

"Where we playing at?" he asked.

"We going to Beedle. You remember that town?" Bingo said.

"So step on it, Bingo, so we can get there round noon and get us some poles," Leon replied.

"You talking now, Leon. Oh, my, you coming around." Bingo laughed and pushed the Auburn up to fifty-five.

"I can smell those big ones spitting in the grease. Mmmm, mmm!" said Leon, leaning down in the seat.

At Beedle they pulled into the ball field just before noon and unloaded. Five minutes later Bingo, Leon, and five other Stars —Isaac, Mungo, Sam Popper, Donus Youngs, and Turkey Travis —headed for the river. Near the town's grain elevator they found a bait shack and bought cane poles, hooks, a bucket of minnows and a can of worms, and a case of Burgy beer. They fished off a small breakwater levee for almost an hour, but the sun was too hot and the fish weren't biting. Bingo finally leaned back and pulled the wide straw hat he had picked up over his face and dozed off. Isaac and Sam Popper drank the beer and flipped pebbles in the water. Turkey caught a little bullhead and Leon snagged a wide-mouthed bass; otherwise their lines just caught the lazy ripples of the river and stayed limp.

They returned to the ball field two hours later and went through the motions, and afterward the Beedle manager let them dress and sponge off in the girls' half of the washrooms. Then he showed them a prime spot on the river for channel catfish. The plaçe was a small half-moon cove. This time the entire team accompanied Bingo and Leon. They brought along a couple more cases of beer and another bucket of minnows.

"Now we going to see some big-league fishing," said Bingo, and he put on his straw hat and stabbed a minnow. Esquire Joe and a couple of others went crashing off into the woods nearby. They said they were going to hunt for firewood so they could have themselves a fish fry. By five the sun began to cool and Leon pulled in his first cat. He smiled and held it up to the others.

"Take my picture, mama. I got me a big one," he drawled.

Then he threw it in the sand. A while later Mungo pulled one in, and more followed.

Bingo talked to his line, put a little English on his pole.

"You c'mon now, boys. Shoo home to Bingo, give me the kingfish now," he chattered.

In a couple of hours they had caught over a dozen, and Esquire Joe had a campfire going. He grabbed a couple of skillets out of the car and a can of lard.

"You know how to clean them fish, boy?" Leon asked him.

"What you think, old man?" flashed Esquire Joe. "I could clean fish before I could clean my ass."

"And you ain't learned that very good," added Bingo.

117

In a few minutes Joe was flipping cats over the flame and the grease sizzled and pinged into the fire. Bingo and Leon kept catching more and throwing them into the supply pile. They caught catfish and bass, hungry, good-sized fish.

Just as it began to get dark, a car drove up on the dirt road nearby. A pair of white men got out and started for the campfire. One of them wore a badge on a green-and-blue plaid shirt.

"You niggers got a license to fish here?" he barked. The players didn't move, looking up sideways at the two and chewing on fish.

"We guests, boss," Bingo said. "The ball team in town said we could fish here."

The shorter of the two men stepped forward and looked at Bingo.

"Oh, hey, Billy, these guys are that colored ball team that played this afternoon over to the park," he said.

"Yeah, that's us. We the All-Stars," Bingo said.

"But you ain't got no licenses to fish, I bet," the man with the badge said.

Bingo laid his pole down and shoved his straw hat to the back of his head.

"Aw, we ain't caught much. Just little bitty things."

"Which one of you boys is Long? The big hitter," asked the short man.

"You looking at him in person," said Bingo.

"Oh, yeah? I read about you somewhere. You ever play against Dizzy Dean and Martin and the Cards?"

"Yeah, we played those boys couple times."

"Say, Billy, these guys are the real McCoys. They play big-league teams. How about that, Billy?" he said and nudged his partner and looked around at the rest of the team. "They say these boys are fine ball players."

The man with the badge put his hands on his hips. "Dizzy Dean, huh? You hit him?"

Bingo chuckled. "Aw, shit, boss—"

"No, sir," Leon quickly interrupted. "Dean is too tough for us. We can't touch him. Can't even see him."

The man with the badge smiled slightly. "Yeah, old Dizzy's *good.*"

He pulled the last word across his lips.

"He too fast for us boys," Leon repeated.

At that the first man turned to Bingo. "Okay, boys, just don't catch no more fish tonight. Leave some for us."

"Yessir, yessir," said Bingo.

The two men started walking back to their car. The shorter man paused.

"Nice to meet you guys now," he said. "You stop by Beedle sometime again." He waved and walked away. The team watched as the car's taillights disappeared.

"That Dizzy Dean, he too fast for me," said Bingo. He slapped Leon on the shoulder.

"Yessir, boss." Leon nodded and dropped his line back into the water. "He's goo-o-o-d."

"Can't touch him, boss," repeated Bingo. "Can't even *see* him."

Chapter 9

Leon returned from the post office the next morning with a bundle of newspapers his wife had sent him from Louisville. It was the first batch he had received since Chicago. He slipped off the twine and started sorting through them, handing a few to Isaac and Donus Youngs, who had gathered around. Besides the Louisville *Tracer,* Leon's wife had sent along copies of the Pittsburgh *Courier,* a newspaper that always printed the news of the colored teams.

Bingo quickly ran over when he saw the papers.

"Hey, Leon, you got the press?" he said. "What they saying about me? Let's see, man."

Bingo edged between Isaac and Donus, who had spread a copy of the *Tracer* out on the hood of the Lincoln. Most of the sports page carried stories of the Cincinnati Redlegs and the Louisville Thoroughbreds, a minor-league team in the Washington Senator chain. Only a small column was given to the Ebony Aces and its split of a doubleheader with the Wheeling Yard Boys. "Shit, they got Meltnor Gaines playing for them. Where they get him?" said Isaac.

Bingo grunted and sorted through some of the other copies. "I got to find my name somewhere in here," he said. He looked up at Leon. "Hey, what you got, Leon, the *Courier?*"

He quickly moved behind him. "Listen up to this," Leon said. "Sallie's spreading some story about us. Oh, damn, he say we going to start us a league of our own out here. Oh, man!"

"Let's see," said Bingo, and he followed Leon's finger down the page. He pointed at a column by the paper's sports editor, Robert J. T. Campbell.

The ever volatile Sallie Potter, owner and general manager of the Louisville Ebony Aces, is not relenting in his crusade against his runaway players, better known as the Bingo Long Traveling All-Stars. Potter is hot about it. And he's got more news for Eastern League owners the next time they get together.

I talked to him the other night, and old Sallie had a mouthful to report. He says Long and Leon Carter are trying to organize a new league out in Iowa and Nebraska. And he claims some of his new boys, who Sallie signed on in desperation when Long, Carter, and ten other Aces jumped the team last month, are getting offers from Long to come out west and play with him.

"Long will try anything," Potter told me. "He's as crafty as a fox when it comes to taking my ball players." Potter said a few more things but I cannot print them here, if you know what I mean.

What's Sallie got up his sleeve? (And you can trust me when I say that Sallie knows all the tricks.) He says he'll threaten to suspend any of his own players for a permanent time if they jump. Other owners are liable to bend an ear to such talk. They don't like what Long and his partners in crime did either.

From this corner, I can only say that Long's and Carter's departure was everybody's loss. Potter also reports that his gate receipts have hit the sag recently. And that could make the paunchy owner just a little more red in the gums.

Lionel Foster of the Elite Giants in Pittsburgh phoned in to tell me not to worry about Potter, however. Lionel says he'll come up with something that will make the league owners—and Sallie Potter included, I take him to mean—smile once again. Could he have something brewing under the boards with Bingo Long and his buddies? Your guess is as good as mine.

"What that man say we in crime?" bellowed Bingo when he had finished reading. "Why he write that for?"

"He don't know nothing," said Leon.

"Yeah, but he's sucking Sallie's ass. Read that—'He's as crafty as a fox when it comes to taking my ball players.' He don't know the half of it, man," Bingo fumed, and he studied the article.

"Looks like Lionel taking care of everything for us," Leon said.

"Starting a *league*. Shit. Ain't enough towns out here to start a *team*, much less a league!"

"Aw, take it easy, Bingo. Sallie's just talking so he can start something. You know the man."

"Yeah, I know him." Bingo grabbed another copy of the *Courier*. He searched through it until he came to an article circled with a black crayon.

"Hey, catch this piece. 'The All-Stars, headed by Bingo Long and Leon Carter. ɹ team of barnstormers who were once the starting nine for the Louisville Ebony Aces, beat the Chicago Black Velvets three in a row over the weekend. They must be some kind of sterling outfit'—oh, say it, brother! sterling is the word!—'what with Carter polishing the apple on the mound and Bingo slugging it at the plate.' That's right, man! That's just right. 'It's a shame they have run off and disgraced organized Colored Baseball—' "

Bingo slammed the paper shut. "What the shit! They smearing us back there, Leon!" he shouted.

Leon stared impassively at the paper he was holding. Isaac and Donus handed Bingo a couple of *Tracer*s and spread another out on the hood.

"Oh-oh! Look at this. Right here in the Louisville paper," said Isaac. Bingo looked over his shoulder. "It says that it looks for certain that a 'inter-league suspension will be slapped on Bingo Long and his traveling teammates.' " Isaac read out loud in slow, deliberate sentences. " 'Sallison Potter, owner of the colored Ebony Aces, announced today that the Eastern Colored

League will soon suspend Long and his traveling team, which includes Leon Carter and most of what once was the starting line-up for Colored League teams. "We got to start somewhere," Potter said today. "And it's got to be at the center of the trouble." The exit of Long last month nearly pushed the Ebony Aces into bankruptcy. The team now has a full roster and will finish out its League schedule, according to Potter.' "

Isaac stopped reading and looked up at Bingo. "What that mean, Bingo?"

"Shit. Don't mean shit," Bingo replied.

"That's right," added Leon. "Don't mean shit."

"Damn Sallie. He's getting the people against us. I ought to light his ass on fire," Bingo said.

Leon closed his paper and opened up the letter from his wife. He read for a while then looked up at Isaac and Donus. "Don't you boys show that paper to the rest of the team."

"Why not?" asked Donus. "If it don't mean shit."

"Yeah, that's right what Leon says. Sallie's telling stories and we know it. Ain't no good to show the boys and make them jumpy," said Bingo.

"That's what I mean," said Leon. "That ain't good news for some of the boys."

Donus and Isaac looked at him for a moment, then checked Bingo, who nodded in agreement. Bingo grabbed the copy of the *Tracer* and tossed it into a basket near the front of the post office. They got into the car and drove back to the café where the rest of the team was finishing breakfast.

They swung away from the Mississippi River and went across Iowa. Bingo wanted to move west across the state and then hop down to Kansas City. There they could get a series with the Monarchs, one of the top teams in the Western Colored League. As they traveled, the Iowa farm towns became smaller and farther apart. Long stretches of the road were gravel and Bingo drove alongside Esquire Joe so he would not cover the Lincoln with his cloud of thick brown dust. Yet even that did not keep the cars and the players from being covered with the brown powder. They didn't open their mouths to talk because of it. To pass the time they tried to count the cows in the pastures. The corn was almost waist high, stretching as far as they could see and boring them so that they tried not to look at it.

After two days they had played only four games and had covered 250 miles. But they kept on, deciding to stick it out until they could reach Kansas City. On the third day Earl Sibley, one of the new ball players, began complaining. He hadn't toured much before and wasn't used to the traveling. He got on Bingo's nerves, and Bingo found himself pushing the Auburn, trying to hustle it to Kansas City and more games.

In the middle of the dust and the heat of the afternoon, the Auburn began to struggle. It lost power and coughed, as if it were trying to burn the dust instead of its gasoline. Bingo pumped the accelerator and shouted at the car, but it only lurched and backfired for a few hundred yards and then stopped altogether. The team jumped out and leaned over the steaming motor.

"She's done," said Bingo. "She don't want to play for the team no more."

"Just the damn carburetor," said Mungo Redd, the mechanic of the team and the one with first say on such things. "She choking to death on dust and dirt."

"I bet it's the generator. My uncle put three generators in his Auburn before he threw it away," commented Esquire Joe.

"Like we going to do you if you don't shut up," Bingo said.

Mungo had a set of hand wrenches and a screwdriver and he began working on the carburetor. He puttered with it for five minutes, ignoring advice from Bingo, then he asked for a rag and the spare can of gasoline. For another five minutes he dabbed at the carburetor with the gasoline-soaked rag. Then he lifted his head out.

"That should do something," he said. "Fire her up, Bingo."

Bingo hopped in and pushed the ignition button, but he got nothing. The engine sputtered but wouldn't run.

"See, I told you it was the generator," said Esquire Joe.

Mungo scowled and leaned back under the hood.

"Maybe I throwed a valve. How's that sound, Mungo?" Bingo said.

"Damn thing's got a thousand things wrong with it. Just a matter of which is worst," Mungo replied.

"Ain't nothing wrong with it a rope can't fix," Leon said. "Let's tow her in someplace."

"Yeah, okay," agreed Bingo. "Hot as hell out here."

They found some clothesline they had taken along to tie on the luggage and wrapped it around the cars' bumpers.

"Going to break, you watch," said Mungo.

"We'll push the damn thing and get it going," said Leon. "Then jump on the Lincoln."

"I'll drive, Joe. You go back there and push," Bingo said, and he climbed into the Lincoln. "Need some experience at the controls in this."

"Shit!" returned Esquire. "Your car breaks down and *I* got to push it."

They lined up in back of the Auburn and began to push. When they had it moving at a good speed, the Lincoln pulled it without too much strain on the rope. They ran around the Auburn and jumped into the Lincoln. Bingo slowly increased the speed. The two cars drove easily along the road for about a mile until they started up a long grade. The rope tightened between the bumpers; Bingo could feel the full weight of the Auburn as he accelerated. Then one of the ropes broke with a snap. They were just barely two-thirds up the grade when the entire bunch went. Mungo quickly braked the Auburn and the Lincoln lurched forward.

"Damn!" said Bingo. "What a job we got now."

The team slowly got out of the Lincoln and walked back to Mungo. They decided to push it to the top of the grade, and it took all of them to do it. Bingo drove beside them and shouted encouragement. He received nothing but sneers in return. They puffed and grunted and sweated through their shirts. Once at the top they retied the ropes and started coasting down the other side of the grade. About halfway down Bingo spotted something on the side of the road and put on his brakes. The Auburn slammed into his bumper and jerked him forward. He madly waved his arms over his head trying to get Mungo to stop.

"What the hell, Bingo? We just got her going good!" Mungo screamed.

Bingo pointed over to a fence. "We'll get us some wire!" he shouted and walked over to the field.

"Can't steal the man's fence!"

"We'll borrow some of this," Bingo said and pointed to a coil of barbed wire dangling from a post. He got Mungo's pliers and struggled with the wire, bending and twisting it with the pliers until it snapped off.

"Stuff is got little bitty prickers all over it," he said. "Like to killed me."

He brought the wire over to the Auburn and gingerly wound it around the bumper.

"Them cows got patches on their ass from rubbing against this," he said. He had cut enough to wind four lengths of it between the cars.

"I ought to have some of that for my dogs," Leon said. "Teach them something."

The wire held and the Lincoln pulled Bingo's car grudgingly down the road. The players were squeezed in on top of each other, since they wanted to get as much weight out of the Auburn as possible. By now they were drenched with sweat and catching some of the dust that swirled around the car.

"I saved you boys a lot of work finding that wire," Bingo said, but he got no reply except a chorus of heavy breathing.

In a half hour they crossed the tracks bordering Pelton Junction, Iowa, and limped into its lone Mobil Oil station. The gravel drive was thick with oil and scattered tractor parts. Mungo spotted a pair of legs stretched beneath a pickup parked in the station's single stall. He whistled in its direction.

"Just a second," a voice echoed. After a few minutes the legs slid from under the truck and a tall, lean man with a grease cap on his head came over.

"What you colored boys want?" he said. He looked at the wire connecting the two cars.

"Car won't run," said Mungo.

"What's wrong with it?" the man said. He spoke with a slight drawl.

"Don't know. Just quit."

The attendant read the painting on Bingo's car. He moved his head with each word. "What that mean?"

"Nothing," Mungo replied. The others found a water pump next to the station and started drinking and dousing themselves. Esquire Joe took off his shirt and soaked it, then he wrung it out and put it back on. The attendant leaned under the hood of the Auburn. He put his hand to his mouth and rubbed a smudge of grease across it, then he took out a huge red hanky and wiped his brow. "Ain't never seen one of these before," he finally said.

"That ain't good," Mungo said.

Bingo came over by them. "The man here found the trouble?" he said.

"He say he ain't never seen a Auburn before."

"Good," said Bingo. "He in for a treat."

An old farmer in bib overalls came over from the post office across the street. He stopped and stared for a minute at some of the players who were still splashing water by the pump. Then he walked over to the Auburn.

"What you got, Lester? What these niggers, some pickers?"

"Naw, they ain't pickers," Lester said. "You ever seen one of these, Jimmy?" He motioned at the motor.

"What kind—Auburn? Oh, yeah, I heard of these cars. Where

127

you niggers get it?" The old man spat a pod of chaw on his shoe.

"Kentucky," said Bingo. "Best they got down there."

"That one up there is what you mean. That's one of them Lincolns. Blow me down, *that's* a car," the farmer said. "Where you niggers get that kind of car?"

Lester returned with a long-handle wrench and pulled out a spark plug. "This one's done," he said and tossed it over his shoulder into the dirt. He went down the line, shaking his head and dropping each plug into the dirt with the first one. He left only two in. Then he looked at the distributor cap. "Yer points is gone too."

"Just what I thought," said Mungo. "Just what I thought back there."

"Bet you ain't got no power left in that battery either," Lester said. He started wrenching the cables from the battery posts. Bingo grabbed Mungo by the arm and pulled him aside.

"Hey, what the hell? We can't let the man pull the car apart! You see him throw those plugs. Damn, he ruined them!"

"Yeah, okay. I know what you mean," Mungo said and he hurried back to the attendant, who was now holding the battery and was about to toss it on the drive.

"Hold it, man," Mungo yelled.

"Yeah, put that back!" added Bingo.

Lester lifted the battery back on its platform. "That thing ain't no good, ain't got enough juice in it to buzz a dog's ass."

"We'll jump it with the Lincoln," said Mungo. "You got to give it a chance before you kill it."

He motioned to Esquire Joe and the two of them started to unwind the barbed wire from the bumpers. Then Joe drove the Lincoln around and edged it up to the front of the Auburn.

"You got plugs for it?" Mungo asked Lester.

"Wouldn't a thrown them away if I didn't," he said.

He walked into the garage and returned with a box of plugs. He put them in and set up a pair of jumper cables from the

Lincoln's battery to the Auburn's. Bingo tried to start it but it wouldn't turn over.

"Your generator don't sound good."

"That the problem?" Mungo asked.

"Nope. Carburetor, more than likely." Lester waved at Bingo to quit grinding on the starter and he disconnected the jumpers. "You probably got an acre of topsoil in it." For five minutes he leaned over the carburetor until he had it off. He held it over his head and looked at it. Then he brought it over to a pail of gas and sloshed it around inside. He put the carburetor to his mouth and blew on the jets, leaving little black circles of grease on his lips. Then he put it back into the pail and left it there.

"Oil's black as pitch," he said, wiping off the dip stick on his sleeve.

"If that thing is so bad, how'd it keep running?" protested Bingo.

"Didn't," said Lester, and he walked back to the pail with the carburetor in it. He fussed with it a little more, blew on it, and carried it to the car again.

"How you know how to take this thing apart if you ain't never seen one before?" Bingo asked him.

"They're all the same," he said and leaned in over the engine. He had a harder time getting the carburetor back into the Auburn than he had taking it out, but he finally did it and then poured a can of gas into it. He hooked up the jumper cables to the Lincoln and told Bingo to try it. It kicked and backfired, popping like an air rifle and belching black smoke out the exhaust. Finally it turned over.

"Keep it going. If you're lucky you can get some of the battery back," Lester yelled. He poured a pail of water into the radiator. Bingo hopped from the front seat with a big smile on his face.

"Hot damn! She's ready for another five thousand!"

The old farmer looked at him and slapped his knee. "I

wouldn't trust that thing to ride out of here." He let go with another mouthful of juice.

Lester the attendant walked into his station with Bingo and Mungo following behind. "Want my advice, boys?" he said. "Get rid of that automobile as soon as you get to the next town. That's Maquota, about forty-five miles. They got a Ford place there."

"She's running, ain't she?" said Bingo. He grabbed a candy bar from the counter.

"She's limping like a jackass. Points is bad, battery, generator, water pump. Got good rubber on it but that's all." He took out a pencil and started marking the cover of a telephone book. "You owe me five dollars and a quarter."

"Car cost me six hundred bucks," said Bingo. "Brand new."

"Give the man some money, Bingo," said Mungo.

They walked out of the station and waited for the team to finish up in the lavatory and stock up on candy bars. The Auburn coughed and backfired a few times when Bingo started out, leaving more black smoke behind. But it smoothed itself out once they were moving again. When the cars were out of sight, Lester ambled onto the drive and picked up the plugs he had removed. Four out of the six were in admirable shape.

By dusk they were in Maquota with enough time for Raymond to schedule a pair of games for the next afternoon. They drove past the Ford garage, a combination tractor-automobile dealer. Bingo circled it a few times, looking it over and seeing if he could spot a likely replacement for the Auburn. Only he and Mungo knew that the Auburn was ready to go. Bingo wasn't sure how he wanted to announce the fact to the rest of the team.

There were no rooms in town for the team to spend the night, but the manager of the Maquota Blues let them bunk down in a pair of hunting cabins he had built on the edge of his farm. A quick-running creek flowed next to them, and looked like a good place to clean up in. The cabins had room enough for eight, so only four men would have to sleep in the cars. Most of the team decided to take advantage of the cool night air and get some sleep. They unraveled their bedrolls and slept on the floor of the cabins. It had hit ninety degrees in the sun that afternoon, most of which they had spent pushing the Auburn.

Bingo persuaded Leon and Raymond Mikes to go into town with him for a drink. They found a rear table in a place called Dollie's Tap, and Bingo bought a round of cold beer.

"Leon, I got trouble with that car," Bingo said, quickly revealing his reason for getting him and Raymond away from the rest of the team.

"Yeah? What the man say about it back there?" Leon replied.

"He said more things was wrong with it than I could count. Made me dizzy." He drummed his knuckles against the tabletop. "She on her last leg and going fast."

"You getting another one?"

"Don't know. Don't know what kind of money we got for that."

Raymond leaned forward. He sat with his right foot stretched out beside his chair. The cast on his ankle was bulky and clumsy. "You want a finance report, Bingo?" he said.

"Yeah, shoot one at me."

"Since yesterday we got four hundred for operating costs. That's still fat from them games in Milwaukee. For salary and capital money we got seven hundred. That's good now, but this week ain't been good. You lucky we didn't give Sibley and Big Juice a bonus; that would a killed us."

Bingo bit a fingernail. He was wearing his usual white shirt and trousers from one of his suits and he had on his soft-billed driving cap.

"Still about a grand for cushion. How 'bout a car? Think we can buy a car out of that, Raymond?"

"Depends. If we hit some crowds in Kansas City you can buy two."

"How about right now while that heap out front is still running?"

"Slim. We going to be eating crackers if you do."

Bingo looked at Leon. The pitcher had ordered another beer and was watching it foam over his glass. "You see what we got, Leon?" Bingo said.

"How about your money, Bingo? You got money. You buy yourself a car and take a cut out of the team's fund. No big deal."

"What you mean, my money! I ain't got no money. Got some here, got some there—I ain't got nothing. What you talking about?" Bingo pushed his hat back on his head. It left a line along his forehead.

"What you do with all the dough you been earning off this tour?" Leon said. "Got to go somewhere."

"Shit! I buy you some beer, I buy me some clothes, I eat some good beefsteak on the way. I don't know where that money goes!"

Leon smiled and belched from a long draft. "Thought I'd ask is all, since you going to be keeping the car when the team is done."

"Damn, Leon! Whose car was it that broke down? Tell me that."

"Okay, don't get nervous. Just thought I had a quick answer to the problem."

"Ain't no solution when it's money I ain't got. Now do some thinking, Leon. What you think I can do?"

"I wash my hands, Bingo. Don't want nothing to do with it."

"Shit. Now what?" Bingo pushed his chair back from the table. He had drawn the attention of the bartender and some of the regulars seated up front. He pulled his hat back over his brow and lowered his eyes.

Leon went on. "You in a fix, right, Bingo? You need another automobile and you ain't got no money to get it with. So you want me here to tell you how to get it out of the team in some way so they won't holler too loud. That right? So I say I don't want nothing to do with it."

Bingo's expression went blank. "Good," he said. "Just when I need your big-sized brain to go to work you take a walk on me." He stared for a minute and turned to Raymond. "What you think? You work for me so you can't bail out."

"If it were up to me," Raymond started, "I'd milk the car you got until Kansas City. Then hit the big ball games and tell the team you need a percentage for travel expenses—say fifty bucks a man. If the gate is big enough they won't kick and scream so hard and you got yourself about six hundred. And buy yourself a car." Raymond leaned back and looked satisfied with himself.

"What if the boys don't want to?" said Leon.

"They got to. I'll kill them," growled Bingo.

"Just tell them it's their car too; they get their money back at the end of the tour when Bingo sells it," Raymond returned.

"Shit!" said Bingo.

"Aw, they don't have to know you going to keep it," Raymond quickly said.

"Good, 'cause I am," said Bingo.

"See why I don't want nothing to do with it?" Leon said.

Bingo liked Raymond's plan. He asked Leon's word not to talk about it to the rest of the team, and the pitcher nodded indifferently.

"Sometime if I should call you Sallie Potter by mistake you'll understand, won't you, Bingo?" Leon said, and he quickly drank his beer and didn't hear Bingo's mutterings.

In the pitch blackness of the night, they had trouble finding their way back to the cabins. Once off the main road they had to follow a pair of ruts almost completely overgrown with weeds. Within fifty yards of the cabins Bingo turned off the headlights so as not to disturb the sleeping players. That made things even more difficult. Bingo slammed the Auburn into a stump before he stopped, and the three of them groped their way in the darkness for the cabin door. "Who there?" someone growled when Leon pushed it open. He lit a match and saw the cabin floor covered with bodies. It was the same in the other cabin, so Bingo and Raymond stretched out on the seats of the Auburn, Leon crawled into the front of the Lincoln. They slept soundly, bothered by nothing but the gurgling creek and the wheezing of a cicada.

Chapter 10

"Not a dime," he said.

Leroy Hawkins wiped the sweat from the creases in his neck with an oily hanky and looked up at Bingo.

"Wouldn't give you the fat half of a dime for that car, boy," Leroy repeated. He was paunchy and half bald, and the heat brought out gray circles under the arms of his white shirt. He pointed at the Auburn parked out front of his garage.

"Thing looks like hogshit," he said.

"That's why I need a new one," Bingo said. "You got a deal for me, say the man at the bar."

"He did, huh?" Leroy said. He winked at two of his customers who had come up behind him. "That boy was probably on the bottle saying that. All I got cheap is some tractors. Sell you a tractor."

"I ain't no farmer. I got me a ball team and we need a new car," Bingo said. He had driven to the garage alone while the rest of the team was taking some hitting at the town's ball field. They had a doubleheader at one.

"Tell you the truth, boy," said Leroy. "I ain't never sold an automobile to a colored before. I don't know how you work it."

"Yeah, I got it, boss." Bingo laughed. He stood almost a foot taller than each of the three men. "You think I buy it now and pay you tomorrow."

He kept laughing. Leroy Hawkins rubbed his hands with an oil rag.

"I tell you what," Bingo went on. "Give me a good deal. You take my Auburn off my hands—it's still good, good tires and some brand-new spark plugs inside; she runs nice. I'll put up straight cash for a new car. Otherwise we make terms."

"Who's selling the car here?" Leroy said. "Me or you?"

"I'se just telling you how good you got it," Bingo said. "What that Ford out there sell for?" He pointed at a line of three used cars parked in front of Hawkins' place.

They walked out and looked at the cars. There wasn't a price on any one of them. Hawkins told Bingo he didn't like to do business with people he didn't know. Bingo said straight cash for everything, so Hawkins stayed with him. The best Bingo could get out of him was $650 for a '35 Ford V-8. He bargained with Leroy over the Auburn, but Hawkins said he was doing Bingo a favor if he took it off his hands. The price stayed: $650 for the Ford. Finally Bingo shrugged and told Hawkins he'd be back. He took out his wallet, showed Leroy the face of a hundred-dollar bill he had put in that morning, and flashed him a smile.

"That what we talking about, Mr. Hawkins," he said. "That green, ain't it?"

Leroy and his two friends leaned over to get a better look. Then Bingo slid into the Auburn and left them standing there.

He drove down the town's main street on his way back to the ball field. It was a wide, black-topped street with three-story brick buildings towering on each side of it. The din of the traffic and the people echoed between the buildings and reminded Bingo of the streets in Louisville or Pittsburgh. He eyed a tavern and a drugstore and he gave a pair of blond-haired girls a honk. They turned and he smiled and they quickly jerked their heads back again.

He accelerated past a tractor towing a wagon loaded with feed bags, pulling out then back onto his side of the road. He hadn't lifted his foot to the clutch to downshift when the rear end of a pickup loomed in front of him. In a split second he swerved and braked and then his head jerked with the crash. The truck had kept on coming out of an alley and hit him broadside. Bingo held tight to the wheel and strained to balance himself when he felt the car tilt on its side. He whipped the wheel into the tilt and the car rocked back onto all fours with a thump, Bingo still not sure of what had hit him. Then he ducked as a crate of muskmelons slid across his hood, up against the windshield and into the street, melons rolling in all directions like bowling balls.

"Goddamn!" he yelled as he jumped from the Auburn to see what had hit him.

He was met by a woman in bib overalls and a straw hat who had the stub of a cigar wedged in the corner of her mouth. She scowled at Bingo, then bent over in front of him and started to toss melons back into a half-empty crate.

Bingo walked around her and took a look at the Auburn. The side was caved in, both doors and part of the front fender. Orange pieces of melon were splatted against it and a crate was pushed through the back door's window.

"Damn sight clear the road, why don't you?" the woman snarled. She tossed a couple of lumpy melons in the back of the truck.

"Not me, ma'am. You can't be talking to me," Bingo said. He shook his head with a pained look; he squinted his eyes.

"Yeah, doggone. You ruined me a couple crates. All on the street."

"Look at my car!" Bingo said. He tried to open the front door and the hinge snapped off. He held the door in his hand and looked at the woman. "What you going to do about this?"

She flipped another melon in the truck. "Nothing. It's broke already."

Bingo looked around at some of the townspeople who had come up. Then he spotted Leroy Hawkins. Leroy talked first.

"What happened to your car, boy? Leona here hit you?"

"Yeah. She bust it up for good," Bingo said. "You pay for it, lady?" He set the door against the car and wiped his hands.

"I ain't paying you nothing. You drove in front of me," she said in a hurry. "Where you niggers learn to drive?"

"Hold it now. Ease off," Bingo said. "Ain't no way I can drive in front of you when you backing up."

Leroy stepped up to him. "You're okay, boy. This here lady's a friend of mine."

"Good. Now you can pay me for my car," Bingo said.

"Bring it down. We'll talk about it. Go on your way, Leona. And don't hit nobody, you hear me?" Hawkins motioned to the woman. She grabbed the crate that had sailed past Bingo's windshield into the street. A pair of beagles and a little boy with no front teeth were working on the rest of the melons lying in the gutters. The woman slammed the door of the pickup and drove away.

Bingo picked up the Auburn's front door and put it in the back seat. Then he heard a hissing noise and turned to see the front tire go flat. The fender had been pushed into the rubber and punctured it. "Shit," Bingo sighed. He climbed behind the wheel. Leroy and three or four others walked alongside the Auburn as Bingo limped it back to the Ford lot. It jerked and swayed on the flat front tire. Bingo's head bobbed with it.

At Hawkins' garage Leroy pointed out a spot for Bingo to park the Auburn.

"Now you got to come to terms," Leroy said. "That car ain't no good to nobody."

"Turn it around, Mr. Hawkins," Bingo said. "You got to make it up to me for what that lady friend of yours did."

Leroy laughed and looked at his friends. "What lady friend? I don't know who that was who you hit."

Bingo took in all the smiles. He got the setup in a hurry. "Maybe just a minute I'll take a walk down to the sheriff and tell him what happened to my car."

"Go ahead, boy. He wants to know what happened. You tell him we here were all witnesses. We saw the whole thing." Hawkins grinned and took a bottle of Coca-Cola from the man next to him. He took a long swallow and then held the bottle against his forehead.

Bingo stared at the men for a minute and tried to figure out what he could do. Then he turned and started to walk away. "I be back, Mr. Hawkins. Just you wait for me," he said over his shoulder. Leroy smiled and waved his bottle.

It took Bingo only a few minutes to walk to the ball field. He fumed all the way; kicking at the dirt and thinking of ways to get back at Leroy Hawkins and his boys.

"Where you been?" Raymond Mikes yelled at him. "Where the car?"

Bingo shook his head angrily from side to side. "Man, I got hung up back there."

He told them about the wreck and what Hawkins had done. "And he got friends. We got to go back there and face them down."

"Can you get a car out of him?" Leon asked.

"Damn," Bingo said. "We got to, Leon."

The entire team crowded into the Lincoln, four in each seat, and headed back into town. Leroy Hawkins and his friends were still out in front of his garage looking over Bingo's Auburn. Turkey Travis wheeled the Lincoln right in front of them, and the All-Stars piled out.

"Hey there, Mr. Hawkins, sir," Bingo said. "Me and my boys here came to talk about the car. What you say?"

Leroy tossed his pop bottle away and walked up. He looked at the team, dressed in half uniforms and sweat shirts. Their spikes made thin slits in the oily dirt of his drive.

"Can't say nothing, boy. Your car over there ain't in too good of shape," Leroy said. The rest of the team was over looking at the side of the car that the melon woman had rammed.

Hawkins turned and yelled to a kid in the garage. The boy was about ten and had been fussing with a can of gasoline. Leroy bent down and said something to him and the kid took off down the street. Then he looked back at Bingo. "You ready to deal for a car, boy?" he said.

"What you give me for the Auburn?" Bingo said.

"Told you. It's wrecked. Can't give you nothing for a wrecked car."

Bingo motioned to Leon. "Hey, come here and listen to this man."

Leon walked over. Leroy Hawkins looked up at the pitcher. "Now don't make no fuss, boy. You niggers come in here with your car, ain't nothing we can do about it."

"Man says someone hit him," Leon said.

Leroy looked at the two men standing behind him, the same two who had been there before. "We didn't see nobody hit nobody. We just seen that car over there with this here boy driving it. That's all we seen."

Bingo scowled and repeated his story. By now the team was standing behind him and a few townspeople had come over to see what was happening.

Then the kid that Leroy had sent off returned with a skinny, gray-haired man who wore a baseball cap and a gun around his waist.

"What's up, Leroy? Where'd all these niggers come from?" the man said.

"Hey, Gleason," Leroy said to him. "These boys here are trying to tell me I owe them a car. What you think of that, sheriff?" Leroy hit the last word hard. The men behind him grinned.

Leroy repeated his version of Bingo's wreck.

"Ain't right! Ain't right!" Bingo objected.

"Calling Leroy a liar, boy?" the sheriff said.

"No, sir, he just ain't telling the truth," Bingo said. Then he told what happened. "And that lady left when Mr. Hawkins here said he'd fix things up for her. That's what happened, sure as I got two eyes in my head."

He pushed up to Leroy Hawkins and pointed at his nose.

"You making me a fool in front of my team here. You can't be doing that," Bingo warned. He towered over Hawkins like a tree. Hawkins cocked his head and turned to his friends in back of him.

"They saw it like me. So don't be calling me no liar, nigger!" he said quickly.

Bingo moved closer. He could feel the team edging in behind him to get a better look. It gave him more confidence.

"I'm telling you, man," he growled, "you got to square this with me."

At that the sheriff pulled out his gun and stuck it by Bingo's chin.

"Back, boy, back!" he warned. "You clear out now before we got to move you!" He pulled his baseball hat down on his forehead and stuck his jaw out.

Bingo flinched at the sight of the gun. It had a long gray barrel and it smelled like oil. He backed up and stumbled on the feet of Leon and some of the others standing behind him.

"You see? You see this here now?" the sheriff said, nodding at his gun. "It's what we got to keep strangers and niggers out of this town. You see it now?"

Leon grabbed Bingo. "C'mon, man. Fool's got a stick too big for him." He pulled Bingo away from the sheriff and toward the car. The team followed, pushing through the crowd that had formed around them. They piled into the Lincoln and drove back to the ball field.

When they got there Earl Sibley, the new infielder they'd picked up for Louis, spoke. "We can't take that shit, Bingo. Nothing in this weed town but that man and his gun. Give me two minutes and I'll have his gun from him," Sibley said. He took his hat off and stroked his bald head as he talked. He had a tooth missing in front and it made his *s*'s hiss.

"Aw, hold it, Earl. We can handle that man without no fighting," Bingo said.

"No, man!" Sibley returned. "This ain't colored country. We got to get them fast. They aching to pick us off back there."

"Shit," Leon interrupted. "We going to play the game and humor the boys. Then they talk business and we can buy us a car and get on out of here."

Sibley punched his fists together. "Hell, man. We can wait till dark and slash those boys good. Get that garage, or them cars. Get them good. Then we can get out before they know it."

"I hired you on to play ball for me, Earl, not to shoot for me. Take it cool, papa," Bingo said. He offered Sibley a cigarette. Earl declined and let go with a wad of juice from his cheek.

"We got an hour before we play," Leon said. "Let's do some hitting, Bingo." Leon grabbed his glove and a ball and motioned toward the field. Bingo nodded and followed him, but not before he saw Earl Sibley grab a bat and swing it wildly against a post of the backstop. It thwokked against the wood like the cut of an ax and backlashed at Sibley.

The Maquota Blues showed up with half of the town trailing behind them. They wore softball uniforms, with trousers that snapped around their ankles instead of knee-high socks. Their shirts had a large "MB" on the front, and "Hawkins' Ford" on the back. Leroy Hawkins and the boys from the garage sat in the front row of the bleachers. The sheriff sat behind them, with his Blues cap on and his gun still strapped around his waist.

Bingo and the All-Stars dispensed with their normal routines. They played catch and finished up their batting practice. Bingo glared at Hawkins but the fat man laughed and waved at him.

"Hope you boys have a good game today," Leroy yelled. "We come out to cheer for you."

Mungo Redd grinned back at Leroy and rolled a ball up his sleeve. Bingo scowled at Mungo and Mungo trotted to the bench. Leroy saw it all.

"Got your team under control, huh, boy? You the mother dog they suck after?"

Leroy leaned back and bellowed out a laugh. The others took it up with him.

Bingo was about to say something to him when Leon grabbed his sleeve and pulled him over to the bench with the rest of the team. "Just the same old shit, Bingo. Don't mess now," Leon said. He was sweating and loose with that thin, grim look on his face.

The Blues peppered things up the best they could in the infield. They weren't any different from the rest of the teams the All-Stars had hit out here. They had a left-handed second baseman and a right-handed first baseman, and their long pants hung on their ankles. Their pitcher was a blond with a gaping hole in the toe of his right spike. The white of his sock stuck out like an eye.

But Bingo and the All-Stars were too mad about the car and Leroy Hawkins to play their usual game. Hawkins started off in the first inning with a chorus of insults, mostly aimed at Bingo, and the team found it hard to just sit there and take it. Tommy Washington topped one back at the pitcher leading off; Bingo struck out with three mighty swings trying to put one of the Maquota fastballs out of sight. It brought down the house and Leroy with it. They hooted the Stars as they trotted out on defense.

Turkey Travis was on the mound, and he reached back for all the steam he had. Leroy started in on him and his arm. At every remark Hawkins received a loud shout of laughter from his audience, and it primed him for more. His tongue was red hot. "Hey, shine! Got anything on the ball except shoe polish?" Leroy yelled. The sheriff behind him loved that one and whistled with his little fingers in the side of his mouth. Leroy winked at him and turned the wheels for another offering. "Hey, Rastus, I got a watermelon says your daddy was a monkey!" The fans broke up. Turkey threw a fastball over Bingo's head all the way to the backstop.

The Maquota team took it up from Leroy and laughed with him. At the plate their lead-off man smiled and wiggled his rump. Turkey threw four fastballs over his head and walked him. Bingo ran out and told Turkey to calm down and pull in his ears. While they talked a kid stood up in the stands and let out a Tarzan yell, beating on his chest and fluttering his T-shirt. "Watch it, boys, he just called out the elephants!" yelled Leroy, and he had the crowd with him again.

Turkey found the plate and got the next batter to pop up. But he walked the next man on a three-two pitch when Leroy screamed at him as he wound up. Bingo whirled around and glared at the umpire, but the man had a pleased expression on his face. "Turn around, catch. Play ball," he growled behind his mask.

With two men on, the Maquota clean-up hitter walked up to the plate. Leroy screamed at him, the fans stood up and pointed to the fence.

"C'mon, Freddie! Blast it, Freddie boy!" Leroy shouted. Freddie Blake was a tall farmboy with thick wrists and big shoulders. He had the sleeves of his uniform rolled up to show off his biceps. He gritted his teeth at Turkey Travis and pointed the bat at him. The crowd loved it. Once in the batter's box, Freddie Blake dug himself a pair of ruts and planted his feet. Then he waited for his pitch.

On the mound Turkey was sweating and mad. The runners were dancing off first and second and chattering at him. And Leroy kept up the pressure. "Hey, smoke, you give up, smoke?" he yelled. Freddie Blake waved the bat slowly over the plate. Turkey grabbed the ball and spun it in his hand until he felt the seams. He had a pitch for a situation like this and Bingo gave him the sign for it. He wound and let it fly—head-high screwball with as much backspin as Turkey could give it. It came in at Freddie Blake's shoulders and rose toward his ear. Freddie stepped into the pitch and then dove when he saw it coming at him. Hitting the dirt just as the pitch sailed past the button on his cap, he landed on his butt in a heap.

The crowd booed and shook their fists at Turkey. Leroy and his friends jumped out of the stands and leaned over the fence, cursing and spitting and calling for Turkey's head. The sheriff had his gun out again and waved it in front of his face. The manager of the Blues rushed out to the third-base line.

"You don't throw at my boys, nigger!" he screamed. "Throw him out of here, ump!"

The crowd kept it up so loud that the dogs began to howl.

Bingo walked out to the mound and stood with Turkey. He was joined by Leon from the bench and Mungo Redd.

"Nice pitch, Turkey," Bingo said. "You almost gave the boy another eye."

"Shit," muttered Turkey.

The umpire walked toward the four of them and warned Turkey about throwing a beanball.

Leon held his palms up to the umpire and told him things were under control.

"Don't skull these boys," he said when he turned to Turkey. "You'll kill one of them and we'll never get out of here."

"Damn sheriff's got his gun out. Look at the fool," Mungo Redd said.

"Starting a Klan meeting," said Leon. "Take it slow, Turk."

Leon walked back to the bench and Mungo back to short.

Freddie Blake dug his spikes in the dirt of the batter's box. His back foot was trenched in a good inch and a half. He pointed his bat at Turkey again and wiggled his butt. He had a big patch of dust on it from hitting the dirt with Turkey's beanball.

"He's George Herman Ruth here in person looking at you, smoke," Leroy yelled at Turkey.

Turkey wound up and got ready to fan Freddie with a spitter.

He threw it and Freddie swung his club in a roundhouse motion as if he were swinging an oar.

Somehow he connected and the ball cracked out to right field. It was as high as a silo and deep, and Esquire Joe took off with his back to the crowd. Leroy and the rest came alive, screaming and slapping each other on the back while they watched the ball climb. The sheriff swung his gun above his head, lost his balance, and stumbled backward into a clump of schoolgirls, who screamed at Freddie Blake and at the struggling sheriff who pulled at their dresses to get back on his feet. The two runners on base peddled around the bases as soon as the ball was hit. The first one tripped over third as he watched and the second runner had to pull up short to keep from passing him.

All the while Esquire Joe loped like a setter after the drive, keeping his eye on the ball and trying not to stumble over the clods and cow flop as he ran.

Then as Freddie Blake plopped his spike on second base and the second runner stomped on home, as Leroy and the crowd threw their hats and swallowed their chews, Esquire Joe stuck his glove out over his head and caught the ball. It laid in the pocket of his glove like a pearl.

Bingo and Turkey let out a whoop when they saw it. Leroy and the crowd and Freddie Blake did a double take and went quiet. Out in right Esquire Joe stumbled some before stopping his momentum and turning to whip the ball back into the field. The two base runners scrambled to get back to second and first base. They didn't go back around third but hightailed it across the pitcher's mound past Turkey, who had a smile running across his face as big Freddie Blake's bat. Splinter Tommy Washington took Esquire Joe's throw and relayed it over to Mungo to double up the first runner and get the third out of the inning. Mungo flipped it underarm to Donus Youngs to get the other runner and a fourth out just to show the people it could be done.

146

The crowd still wasn't sure if it had seen right. But Bingo's laughter and loud palm slaps along the All-Stars bench brought the catch home to them. It hit Freddie Blake and he stood there staring out to right. Mungo started to trot past him to the bench when the runner he had just doubled up barreled into him and knocked him down. Freddie Blake saw it and joined in; he kicked Mungo in the leg before the other Maquota player jumped on the shortstop with his fists flying.

Mungo got two hard rights to the side of his head before he knew what was going on. In no time the rest of the Maquota team was pushing and shoving to get at him. The Stars rushed up and waded in, throwing players to the ground and starting separate fights. Earl Sibley jumped in the middle of Mungo and Freddie Blake and started uppercutting Blake to the neck. His forehead glistened and he bared his teeth and looked like he was ready to bite.

Leroy and the sheriff were on the field in seconds, pushing and shoving like the rest. Leon caught sight of the sheriff with his gun drawn and grabbed the man's arm. He spun him around and gave him a short cuff to the ear before grabbing the gun out of his hand. Leon heaved it on a line drive out into the grass of center field. Bingo, still in his pads and mask, started throwing Maquota players off his Stars. He lifted a little shortstop up by his collar and propelled him in the air toward home plate. The shortstop's arms and legs flailed in all directions and he looked like a pile of rags caught in a windstorm.

Then Bingo saw Turkey Travis land one on Leroy Hawkins, spinning the fat man around and sending him sprawling into the dirt. Bingo grabbed Leroy by an armpit and pulled him up to him.

"You stop this now or someone's going to get killed!" Bingo shouted at him.

As he said it a Maquota Blue stumbled into them, holding his neck.

"My boys will kill you!" Bingo added.

147

Leroy shook his head and gave Bingo a dazed look. Then he held up his hands and wagged his head in agreement.

"C'mon, hold it now . . ." he mumbled and began pulling people apart.

Bingo turned and spotted Earl Sibley with a bat in his hand. Earl was headed for Freddie Blake with the bat cocked and ready to split the kid's head open between the ears.

Bingo lunged for Earl and caught the bat just as Sibley began to lift it. The bat ripped a fingernail clean off one of Bingo's fingers as he grabbed the barrel. Earl spun around and glared at Bingo.

"You could kill the boy now!" Bingo screamed.

"Aim to!" Sibley shouted back.

Bingo pushed him away. "No way, man! C'mon, cut it!" he yelled.

By this time Leroy had regained composure enough to effectively pull people apart. He was shouting at the top of his lungs for the fight to stop.

"Lay off now, Cletus," he bellowed. Cletus Newbold was the game's umpire, and he had Donus Youngs pinned to the ground while a couple of Maquota schoolkids kicked him in the legs. Leroy threw him off and Donus jumped up and sent the two kids sprawling headfirst into the backstop.

After five or ten minutes more of scuffling and pushing, Leroy finally bellowed above the melee and established order. Bingo was sucking his nail and holding Earl Sibley around the neck. Three Maquota Blues were sitting on Freddie Blake. The sheriff was off in center field looking for his gun.

"Let's everyone lay off now before someone gets hurt bad," Leroy shouted.

"I'll kill me one of those jungle bunnies," Freddie Blake sneered and he squirmed under the weight of the three butts that held him.

"Ain't nobody going to get killed one way or the other," Bingo shouted.

"Yeah," said Leroy. "This game is finished and done with right now. You niggers clear out of here."

Bingo pulled his chest protector off. "We leaving on our own sweet time, mister."

"You mothers mess with us and you going to lose one," Earl Sibley threatened. He snarled at the car lot boys standing by Leroy Hawkins.

"That bastard bit me," said a Maquota player. "Right in the arm."

He held it out and showed the people the red marks.

Bingo and the rest of the Stars started for their bench, walking slowly facing the Maquota team and the rest of the crowd.

Esquire Joe looked down at Freddie Blake and smiled at him. "Nice hit, boy," he said. "You poled it far."

"Eat shit, black fugger," Freddie hissed.

Esquire chuckled and grabbed a ball lying behind third base. He rolled it over his fingers and up his arm and flipped it with his shoulder to one of the kids sitting on Freddie. The kid took it and stuck it in front of Freddie's nose like an apple before Freddie freed a fist and slapped it away.

Bingo sat in the front seat of the Lincoln eating an apple and fussing with one of his spikes. The Blues and their fans, with Leroy and the sheriff bringing up the rear, had left the field over an hour ago. The All-Stars sat on the grass around the car waiting for Bingo to give them the word about moving on. They still had their uniforms on, their white sweat socks with brown spots on the toes and holes in the heels.

"Can't put twelve players in one car. We going to suffocate," Raymond Mikes said. He rested his cast on the flour sack full of bats.

"Shut up, Raymond. I know what we can and can't do," Bingo shot back. "This damn shoe is going without me." He threw the spike on the ground.

"You need a plan, boss?" Earl Sibley said. "You thinking of how to get back that car of yours?"

"That's what I'm thinking," said Bingo. "That's what I been thinking all day now."

"Listen to that boy and we all be in jail with no key," Raymond said, nodding at Sibley.

"We have ourselves a automobile too," Sibley said. "That more than we got now."

Earl rubbed his hands over his bare skull. He had a band running around it from the pressure of his hat.

"What you got in mind, Earl?" Bingo said. He checked to see if Leon was around and saw him sleeping under the bench by third base.

"Them Klan boys got our car and they ain't paid for it, right, Bingo? So we pay the boys a visit and make ourselves a trade. A car for a car. Right, Bingo? Only we work it so they ain't around when we be picking out what we want," Earl said. He bit into a thumbnail and spit out the piece.

"How we going to do that? Nobody here ain't never stole hisself a car."

"Who said?" Earl answered. "This fucker here have hisself five cars already, ain't paid him a dime for none."

"Shit," said Raymond. "What you talking about—stealing a car?"

Raymond sat up and Bingo shushed him. "Hell, Raymond, cut your voice."

"Tell me the word, Bingo, and this boy bag you the best the Kluxers got to lose."

Once the Lincoln was on the road it didn't seem like such a struggle. None of its eleven passengers could move except Bingo, who had to work the pedals. The equipment and their satchels were wedged into any open space they could find. The Lincoln sagged closer to the ground than it ever had. Bingo could feel it strain to pull the load; and every stone they rode over on the gravel road jarred them to their teeth. Bingo grinned and kept saying the farther they got from Maquota the better. He kept up the chatter as they traveled, occasionally eying Raymond Mikes, who was the only person besides Big Juice Johnson who Bingo figured was aware that Earl Sibley had stayed behind.

After twenty miles they came to Crowder, Iowa, and a sign told them they were only fifty miles from the Missouri border. It was almost seven o'clock, not enough time to set up a game, so they looked for a place to camp out for the night. The lady at the general store told Bingo the town didn't have a team anyway, that anybody who wanted baseball went up to Peacock and played. She also said the town didn't have a hotel and that its restaurant wouldn't serve colored. They bought three loaves of bread, a jar of jelly, a ring of baloney, and some honey. In a field of old pear trees they parked the car and had supper.

Leon lay on his back, with his head resting on his satchel, eating a baloney and jelly sandwich. Splinter Tommy had built a fire and the flames crackled and made shadows on Leon's face. He stuffed the last of the sandwich into the side of his mouth, washed it with some soda pop, and looked over to Bingo.

"Why you leave Sibley back in that town, Bingo? What you got him doing for you?"

Bingo jerked his head up at Leon and gave him a look of surprise. Leon looked right through it.

Chapter II

Earl made his way from the ball field to the woods on the other side of the cornfield. He wouldn't check out the town until it got dark. One look at his shiny face would bring Leroy Hawkins and his boys out with the dogs. Earl had his satchel with him, and he ate a couple of candy bars he had stuffed in his underwear. He took his uniform off when the sun went down and put on a pair of black pants and his dark sweat shirt. When he was dressed like that, no one but an owl could run with him. From the bottom of his satchel he pulled out his only tool. It was a doctored ice pick, with a stub-nosed screwdriver set in the end of the handle and heavy wire wound around. With it he could pick a lock, unhook a latch, or undo anything that kept him out of what he wanted to get into.

With the darkness he could feel the ground getting cool and the mosquitoes buzzing him. He slapped at them when they hovered near his ears, deciding he was far enough away from anyone to be heard. The woods were alive with crickets and cicadas and Earl soon figured it was time to get out before he was bitten by something big. He crawled into the cornfield nearby, keeping his head below the three-foot-high stalks. The corn was green and fresh without being dried by the sun as it would be in a month. Earl didn't know a thing about corn except that he liked it creamed with fried chicken.

Glancing around him, he was amazed at how dark everything got in the country. No street lights, no neon, just a spot of light here and there in a window of a farmhouse. From where he stood he could see the road leading into Maquota. Once in a while a farm truck rolled in and stopped at the tavern, where a pair of sitters slouched out front spitting into a cuspidor. Leroy Hawkins' garage was dark as pitch; not even an office light or a window blinker was turned on. It was a beautiful sight. Earl smiled as he looked between the stalks. There was nothing better than night, he thought, as black and heavy as they make it.

He ran his fingers over the tip of his pick. The same pick he had used in Detroit on the used car lots. Good as any man's key, a policeman said while putting the cuffs on him one night. With a little time Earl knew he could have got those cuffs off too.

He sprinted from the cornfield, across a clearing, through an orchard of plum trees, and into the parts yard behind Leroy's. Damn, he thought with a quick sense of confidence. Find me right here in the man's back pocket.

Bingo hardly had time to explain when Leon and Isaac pushed him into the Lincoln and headed him for Maquota.

"Leave that mother there to break the law and he going to be dead," Isaac screamed as the car bumped and leaned down the gravel road.

"His idea, not mine!" Bingo protested. "Earl volunteered with no word from me. Said he wanted to even the score with them boys."

"Shit, Bingo, that boy's dumb as hell about things. He don't know he's a dead man with his nuts cut off first if they so much as find him sneaking around," Leon said.

"He a criminal too," Isaac said. "I know. I know. I never leave my things near him cause he know how to take things."

"Every fucker's a criminal for you, Isaac. Even your old lady," Bingo said.

"Shit, man, just get us back there so we can find him before they does," Leon said.

"You see yourself a fire and smell that tar, you turn this thing around in high gear, Bingo," Isaac said. He rubbed his hands together, looking like a mother worried about her child swimming in the deep water.

Bingo pushed the Lincoln down the dirt road, the headlights cutting through the dark night, the dust flying up in a great gray cloud behind. Giant beetles splattered against the windshield like eggs. Every now and then Bingo swerved around a coon frozen in the light in the middle of the road. Just hearing Leon and Isaac bitch at him made him afraid for Earl.

Earl crouched in the shadows behind a pile of engine blocks. He decided to get a reading on the traffic going by Leroy's before he started in. He waited for what he thought was ten minutes and saw two cars, then another one, or maybe one of the first two going back. He would have liked all or nothing, a busy street with plenty of traffic or none at all. A car every so often like a drop out of a bum faucet made him nervous. It would be just like one of these farmers to spot something moving in Leroy's for no reason at all and call the town out, he thought. From the noise he figured there were ten, maybe fifteen, people inside the saloon, but he hadn't seen any one of them come out on foot and walk past Leroy's.

He got sick of waiting and crawled over to the back door of the building. Bingo had told him just to hot-wire a car and get off, but Earl himself had a few more things in mind. He hadn't hit a place since he broke into his old girl friend's place six months back and took her for a loan without her being around to argue.

154

The back garage door had a greasy padlock on it, no hinge or door lock. Earl found a piece of iron rod in the yard, gave the padlock a quick snap, and it gave. The sound hadn't carried farther than the road, there was no broken glass, no splintering of wood, and Earl was inside.

The place was even darker than the yard outside. Earl could smell the grease from motors split open. He paused to let his eyes adjust to the darkness and his hands searched through his trousers for a toothpick. He finally found it and stuck it between his teeth. He worked it into the gums on the side of his mouth until he could taste the blood. He liked to work when his gums burned.

He moved away from the door toward the front office, feeling his way along the walls as he went. Each sound echoed through the building. Once in the office he crouched so as not to pop his head in front of the window. The neon Ford sign hanging up wasn't working, so the only light in the place came from the half moon or whenever a pair of headlights passed by. Earl looked out into the street and was about to start going through the place when he saw someone coming down the road from the saloon. Earl ducked and bit on his toothpick. He looked again and breathed relief. It was an old farmer staggering like a sick cow from his whiskey. He wore a pair of bib overalls and blew his nose with a red rag of a hanky. He stumbled up to the front drive of Leroy's no more than twenty feet from Earl's head as he peered through the lower corner of the glass, and stopped to lean against the fender of Bingo's Auburn. The car hadn't been moved since Leroy and his boys had pushed it there after it had been hit by the lady in the melon truck.

The farmer stood there tossing his head slowly and wiping his mouth. He spat a cheekful of juice and the leftover saliva dripped down the front of his overalls.

"Get your ass down the road, man," Earl said to himself.

The farmer slumped down on the fender and took out a fat

peach from his pocket. He bit into it and added to the train down his front with the juice.

"Jesus," Earl hissed. "Damn picnic."

The farmer was about to take another bite when the peach fell from his hand, hit the shoe, and rolled across the drive. He stopped to find it, lost his balance, and after two clumsy lurches he lay out flat on the drive.

Earl bit his toothpick in half. "Shit," he said. It echoed through the darkness. "Got to break ass before he brings a crowd."

The farmer breathed heavily on the hard, greasy ground, dead asleep. Earl hustled around the counter, knowing full well that he had precious little time to do his work in peace. He inched over to the candy machine and found the padlock on its backside. He took his pick out, punched in the keyhole and snapped the lock open.

"Damn, still got my feel with these mothers," he said to himself. He swung open the machine and grabbed the coin box and dumped the nickels in his pocket. Then he flipped as many candy bars into his pockets as he could, making them bulge like the pouches of a guinea pig.

After that he rummaged around the counters looking for Leroy's cashbox. He quickly searched through the clutter of tractor manuals, road maps, *Liberty* magazines, calendars, and advertising posters but couldn't find a thing. Then a cigar box fell from one of the shelves and three silver dollars and a five-dollar bill tumbled out.

"Shit," Earl hissed and stuck the money in his pants pocket next to the candy bars.

Crouching like before, he hustled out from behind the counter, took a quick look at the farmer, who was still passed out on the drive, and then headed for the backroom. He moved his hands slowly along the wall, not to guide him but as if he were searching for something. He finally slipped into what he thought was a storage room. A string from a light bulb brushed

156

against his face but he didn't dare pull it and turn the light on. Yet it was so black the darkness seemed to enfold itself around him like a giant pair of arms. He ran his hands along the shelves in the storeroom, along boxes of what felt like spark plugs and gaskets and valves. Then he hit it on the left-hand wall. A board full of nails. He plucked it clean, added to the collection in his pockets, and headed out.

All four of Leroy's new and used cars were parked in front of the building along with Bingo's Auburn, and only yards away from where the drunk farmer lay. Earl grabbed his satchel where he had left it in back and crept quietly around front behind the cars. He could see much better, thanks to the light of the half moon. The crickets in the weeds growing at the base of the building screamed as loud as ever as he crawled among them. He had never had that much sound coverage in a Detroit job, he thought, and for a minute was glad for the noise. He crept up behind the cars, making sure he was out of sight from the road. He would know if anyone came around; he had a good ear for that. It made his game back in Detroit when he was hitting joints regularly because he had no cash.

He would have preferred a convertible, even a replay of Louis's Lincoln, but Leroy had nothing of the kind on the lot. Earl picked out a two-tone black and maroon '36 La Salle sedan and threw his satchel underneath. Stooping, he tried the door handle. It almost surprised him to find it locked so he pulled out his ice pick and went for the front vent window. He worked it past the glass and the metal frame. La Salles had the weakest vent of any car Earl had ever done; couldn't keep a kid from getting through it. With a quick jerk he had the window open and he shot his arm inside the car and opened the door. He grabbed his satchel from underneath, threw it in the back seat, and looked over what he had got into. It would do the trick. Earl took a look down the street at the saloon, then over to the farmer. No problem with either one yet, and he bent down beneath the car's dashboard and searched for the ignition wires.

157

Bingo kept the Lincoln highballing straight down the road into Maquota. Leon and Isaac sat straight up in the front seat with him, peering ahead as far as the headlights cut into the darkness.

"They'd lynch him; those Kluxers will lynch him as quick as they can get all the folks out of bed to make a crowd," said Isaac.

"Who say he caught yet?" argued Bingo. "Earl's a pro at breaking and getting into, from what he says. He pulled off seventeen of them jobs in Detroit, he told me."

"Before he got caught," said Leon. "This time going to be the last time he get caught if he get caught."

"I been reading where Jesse Owens been complaining to the President about all them lynchings down south," said Isaac.

"So what?" said Bingo.

"So that ain't going to stop one more out here in Iowa," said Leon. "These folks ain't got many niggers so they need the practice."

Bingo scowled and didn't answer Leon. He would stop any lynching anybody tried on one of his boys. Even Earl. But first he had to see the rope tossed over the tree limb. Otherwise he wasn't going to run off at the mouth.

"How close we getting?" said Leon.

He hadn't got the words completely out when Bingo's headlights hit a house on the outskirts of town. Bingo hit the brakes and pulled up.

"Douse them lights," said Isaac.

Bingo hit the knob and they couldn't see a thing.

"Jesus, it's black as coal out here. Shit," he said.

"Turn them on enough for us to get off the road. Then we can walk," said Leon.

Bingo hit the lights and they spotted a trail leading up to a pair of corn sheds. He turned the wheel and parked the car behind them and doused the lights.

"Feel like I'm in some damn mine shaft," Bingo said as the three of them got out of the car.

They walked slowly in the direction of the road and gradually their eyes became accustomed to the light of the moon.

"We got to stay in these fields and make it around to the man's garage," Bingo said. "That's where Earl is right now, I bet, if he ain't off already."

"We didn't pass nobody on the road, did we?" said Isaac.

"Yeah, he at the garage like I said, so shut up," Bingo repeated.

Earl pulled the two ignition wires from their posts and let them dangle by the floor. With a penknife he scraped away the rubber insulation from the ends of each. Making sure they weren't close to one another, Earl let the wires hang and got out of the car.

He crept between cars and unscrewed the gas cap of the American Bantam business coupe on his right. Then he reached into his pockets, unwrapped a couple of Baby Ruths, and threw them into the hole. He could hear them splash in the puddle of gas still in the tank. He went to the two other cars on the lot and did the same, each time listening if the candy splashed or not. With a quick check of the farmer, he crawled out front and started unlatching hoods. In one motion he lifted a hood and leaned inside, unscrewed the crankcase cap, and shoved another bar home. He went from one car to the other, three in all, not counting Bingo's Auburn and a tractor, which got a bar each in the gas tanks. He laughed nervously when he finished, his pockets eleven candy bars lighter.

Then he turned again to the La Salle. It would take him longer to hot-wire it up front. He had to make sure the coast was clear before he started. The farmer groaned and turned over on his back. A tiny pinging sound came down the street from the saloon after one of the sitters hit a spittoon dead center. Earl jammed his toothpick one more time, tasted the blood, and made for the hood.

Suddenly Earl jerked around at shouting and commotion coming from the saloon. He turned to see a tangle of arms and legs rolling out onto the sidewalk and into the street as if someone had shaken them out like dice. Earl dove headfirst between the cars. A crowd followed the fight and bustled around shouting, "Clean his ass, Charley!" and pushing dollar bills at each other with closed fists. The sitters stopped spitting and threw shadow punches, rights, lefts, while the two in the street kicked and clawed at each other.

"I'll get those mothers now." Earl whistled with a wide smile and a quick switch of his pick from under his tongue to his teeth.

He jumped up to the left side of the La Salle, opened the hood and bent down over the engine, keeping an eye on the crowd. He could hear by the tone of the spectators how the fight was going. It was the best diversion Earl had had all night. Like stealing somebody's socks while he watches a trapeze act.

Earl's hands were loose and quick working over the wires. He had done a La Salle before and it was good to see one again. With his knife he pared the insulation and twisted the junction. He grounded the ignition and saw the spark jump. Everything was hot, waiting for him to pull it together underneath the dash.

The he heard the noise of the crowd shift and he ducked behind the La Salle's front fender. One of the men in the fight had broken free and was running from the crowd, straight down the street toward Leroy's garage. The crowd followed after him, waving their hands and cursing. Earl watched them come and a cold sweat broke out above his lip. He broke his toothpick between his teeth.

Bingo, Leon, and Isaac stumbled through the weeds behind the buildings on Main Street.

"Holy shit, hear that noise?" said Isaac. "They got him. Lord, those sounds! They got him!"

Isaac sprinted toward the street, caught his foot on a clod, and flipped headlong on the ground.

"Hold your ass, fool," said Bingo. "You kill yourself for nothing."

"They got him—you hear that shouting? Man, don't tell me. They got him treed!"

"Hold onto it, Isaac. We got to see them before they see us. I don't give a shit if Earl is swinging right now," Leon said.

"Yeah, we got to protect ourselves," said Bingo.

They inched closer to the side of the building which faced the street. The noise was as loud as ever.

"Stick your head around and see, Leon," said Bingo. "You darker than us two so they won't see you so fast."

Leon turned and sneered at him. "Shit," he growled.

The big pitcher stuck his head around the building, then Bingo and Isaac shot theirs around just below.

"Lord, they got him," said Isaac.

They could see the crowd pushing among themselves to get a look. "Kill him, make him eat it!" "Bite that dog, Bobby!"

"Get us the rod and rush them," said Bingo.

"Where the gun?" said Isaac.

"In the car. I took it," Bingo said.

"Hold it. How we know what's happening with those boys?" said Leon. "Can't see shit from here but pushing and yelling."

"I knows me a lynch mob when I sees one," said Isaac.

"Yeah, I'll get the rod. We can find out," said Bingo.

"Shit. Christ almighty," said Leon. "We got to go to the garage and see if Earl's there before we do shooting. When you going to start thinking, Bingo?"

"I say we rush them now," said Isaac. "Earl be getting killed in there."

"I'm with you, Isaac. You, Leon?" said Bingo.

The man tripped over his own boots and fell just fifty yards from where Earl crouched. The crowd jumped around him and pushed his opponent on his back and the two went at it again. The spectators clapped hands and screamed for blood.

Earl ran his tongue around his lips and started to breathe again. The crowd inched toward him, the two fighters rolling over on top of each other, those on the edge pushing to get a look. If the fight didn't break they'd be on him, he thought, going at it right in front of his headlights. He had to make his move.

He slid into the front seat and bent down below the dash. A quick twist of the hot wires and he had the car juiced. He pushed the starter button and it turned over. Then he hit the seat again in case anyone looked over. The fight kept on. Now three men were in the middle, swinging in a wild free-for-all at anybody close by. Earl spit out his toothpick and put it in gear. "Fuck 'em now. I'm coming," he grunted.

Just then the farmer rolled over and sat up, looking Earl straight in the eye. Earl shot him a grin and waved. The farmer raised his arm to wave back and lost his balance. As he rolled over and passed out again, Earl pulled the La Salle into the street.

He switched on the lights and drove straight for the fight. He gave it a little gas and pulled around near the sidewalk. Without glancing sideways, he drove right past the crowd, past the gamblers on the fringe exchanging bills with every punch, past the old sitters who were still throwing arthritic shadow punches at each other. He thought he spotted Leroy Hawkins in person.

He kept going, jamming the pedal to the floor, without so much as glancing in the rear-view mirror to see if anyone was chasing him. He was almost out of town when three men ran out from the side of a building right into his headlights. He ducked his head, then raised it just as fast. The three took no more than three strides before reversing themselves and diving like frogs back into the darkness beside the building.

"Those was colored," he said and went for the brake. But he

162

knew he couldn't stop and kept right on driving. Into the dark countryside as fast as the La Salle could travel.

"We're dead ass," shouted Bingo as the three of them sprinted across the fields toward the Lincoln. They ran through ditches and between rows of soybeans. Panting and stumbling, but not letting up.

Only Burt Burdlow, who ran parts for Leroy Hawkins, glanced up at the La Salle as it drove by the fight. Burdlow bet another fin and leaned over to see how his boy was doing before it hit him. He took another look down the road and saw the taillights fast disappearing.

"Criminitny," Burdlow sputtered. "That looked like Leroy's La Salle."

He ran over and spotted Hawkins near the center of the crowd and grabbed him, trying to shout in his ear. Leroy ignored him and threw a right uppercut. Burdlow screamed at him.

"Someone's stole one a your goddamn cars, Leroy!"

Leroy caught the tail end of it and leered at Burdlow. Burdlow moved his head up and down as fast as his jowls let him. Leroy turned and scrambled to get out of the crowd. He kicked someone in the ankle and lost his balance, taking two others to the ground with him. Struggling and kicking like a horse, Leroy pulled himself out of the pile, Burdlow panting behind him.

They ran over to the garage.

"Damn sight it's gone!" Leroy bellowed. He reached inside his pants pockets for the keys to the office. "Best car I got, Burdlow!"

Leroy poked a key at the lock but couldn't get it in. He looked at the key and tried it again. "Goddamn, what the hell!" he shouted.

"C'mon, Leroy, that car's getting away!" Burdlow whined.

Sweat oozed through Leroy's fingers as he fumbled with the key and the lock. He bent down. "Light me a match!"

Burdlow struck a kitchen match on his shoe and put it near the lock.

"Something's in there," Leroy said. He picked at a thin piece of wood lodged in the lock's opening, a piece of wood like the toothpicks Earl sucked.

"Let's go around back," Burdlow said. He and Leroy took off. They found the door opened without a key. "Goddamn it," Leroy growled as they fumbled for a light switch. Burdlow made his way to the storeroom.

"They're gone! The keys are gone!" he yelled.

Leroy thundered into the room and whipped the door around to take a look.

"Jesus Christ!" he said. "Fucker knew right where they're at. Jeez-us!"

He hurried off to the front office. Burdlow followed quickly behind.

Leroy pulled open the drawers of a single dust-covered filing cabinet. He rummaged through oil-stained bills and records and spare pages to parts catalogues. In the third drawer he pulled out a shoebox.

"About time!" he said, pulling out a pile of keys.

They hustled out the front door and jumped into a '33 Ford. Leroy churned the starting motor. The fight was still going and had moved about ten feet closer to the garage.

"Who's that?" Burdlow said, pointing at the old farmer lying just in front of them.

"Goddamn Cecil," shouted Leroy, stamping his foot on the accelerator. Finally the engine turned over. He jerked it into gear and it lurched forward. They drove past the farmer, the left wheel splatting his half-eaten peach into the dirt.

Wheeling around the fight crowd, Leroy pushed for as much as he could get out of the Ford. Burdlow leaned out as they went by and shouted with his hand cupped around his mouth.

"Car's stolen—Leroy's car! C'mon!" he yelled, but he couldn't be heard over the noise. No one paid any attention and they drove on by.

The Ford reached the saloon going thirty miles an hour and straining for more. Then it coughed once, twice, and backfired, jerking Leroy and Burdlow forward into the dash. Leroy pumped it but it coughed more, hit on a few cylinders, and sent them out of town just past Dan Nichols' hog pens. There the Ford sputtered and coughed, lurching in violent spasms and throwing Leroy and Burdlow back and forth in the front seat.

"Holy shit, what you done to this thing, Leroy?" Burdlow yelled, holding his hands up against the dash.

"Goddamn the thing," Leroy answered, searching the dash lights and kicking the pedals.

Leon looked over his shoulder as the three of them ran and saw nothing but darkness.

"Stop now one time," he gasped and reached out for Bingo's shoulder.

They pulled up behind a pile of uprooted stumps. They lay gasping and spitting. After a few minutes Leon spoke again.

"Know that car?" he said. His voice was hoarse from running. "That one going like hell?"

"So what?" said Bingo, breathing with his mouth wide open.

"That car saw us, it had to—we run right out in front of it like blind dogs," he said.

"Yeah, so let's keep on running," said Isaac.

"No, man. That some farmer he'd been stopped now. Right?"

"What you saying, Leon?" said Bingo.

Leon breathed deeply to get his voice. "Ain't one person could be going out of town that fast," he gasped. A smile snaked across his face.

"Damn!" Bingo bellowed. "Fucking Earl!"

"Lord high!" said Isaac. He laughed out loud. "Earl getting away!"

They took off for the Lincoln, stumbling, and laughing as they went. They hit the drainage ditch by the road and were about to cross when Isaac yelled.

"Get down!"

A second pair of headlights met them and they hit the ground.

"They chasing him!" said Isaac.

The car approached them but slowly. They could hear it coughing and choking. It barely lurched by.

"Car ain't doing shit," hissed Leon.

The car pulled up and stopped about fifty yards down the road. They watched as one of two men got out and pulled up the hood.

With a muffled burp the engine had cut out. The car coasted on the gravel and stones with only a slight whining from the transmission filling in the gaps between Leroy's profanities. Burdlow looked into the black of the road beyond their headlights. He couldn't see any taillights.

"Long gone," he said and pushed his door open. Leroy sat pounding his fists against the steering wheel. Burdlow lifted the hood of the Ford and looked at its grease-soaked engine, an engine that before his very eyes was choking on peanuts, caramel, and chocolate.

"C'mon," said Leon, and they made their way through the fields, past the stalled car, back to where the Lincoln was parked. They could see the second car's headlights slowly weakening about 150 yards down the road.

"Push it out," Isaac said. "We can up and go and those boys won't notice nothing."

They eased the car onto the road and pushed it until the road began an incline.

"Start it but no lights," Leon said.

Bingo turned the ignition and they slowly started off. He

drove by the light of the moon, watching the road with his door open and his eyes glued to the rocks passing by below. Slowly the headlights in back of them grew smaller and finally they disappeared behind a hill. Then Leon gave the word.

"What the hell." He laughed. Bingo flashed on his brights and gave it gas. He pushed the Lincoln flat out down the road, leaning close to the windshield to catch sight of Earl's taillights.

Leon raised a finger to point in the distance. They stared for a minute, squinting their eyes, but couldn't make out anything.

"Jump on it. We'll get him," said Isaac.

Bingo stepped to the floor and watched the needle rise. He had it over sixty-five; the tires winged over the gravel pinging rocks off the underside of the body.

"We got to be gaining now," said Leon. Bingo kept up the speed. He couldn't sit on it any harder.

"Now I know Earl's up there," Leon said finally.

"How you know?" said Bingo.

"Cause we ain't catching him. Any car up there is going like hell to beat us out," Leon said.

"Sure is," said Isaac.

"Good dog," said Bingo. "That Earl drive like a thief."

Earl was waiting for them in an alfalfa field just inside Dooley. The La Salle's lights were doused and its radiator was steaming over like a teakettle. Earl cracked a wide grin when Bingo drove up. He was chewing on a candy bar and a fresh toothpick.

"Hey, man. How you all doing?" He laughed. Rivulets of sweat ran from his chin into a damp triangle on his shirt. "Come show you my new car. Brand-new car from a man down the road."

Earl bent over laughing and clapped his hands.

Bingo met him with an open palm, and shook his arm off.

"We been hot-assing it down that road," Bingo said.

Earl's laugh cracked into a soprano. He pulled out his hand-kerchief and wiped his face.

"That was you boys I damn near run over back there in that town. Fuck all—never seen you dive like you did, Bingo," Earl crowed.

"Thought you was getting hung, Earl. We see that crowd—how you get out of there? Thought you was dead," Isaac said. His face wrinkled and went sour.

Earl wiped his nose, then pulled the cloth through his fingers. He spat out his toothpick. His gums glistened.

Chapter 12

They stayed in town long enough to roust the owner of a Stand-
ard Oil station out of bed to gas up the La Salle. He came to his
door with a shotgun, wearing nothing but a pair of gray long
underwear, and swearing under his breath. Bingo gave him two
dollars and told him to keep the change, a nickel.

On the road south toward Missouri the La Salle opened up
and cruised, carrying four passengers besides Earl, who drove
with one hand on the wheel and the other draped lazily across
the top of the seat. Fat Sam Popper and Donus Youngs
stretched out in the back seat, the first time in days they didn't
have to share a seat with two others, five satchels, and the bat
bag. In a half hour they were sound asleep, the bills of their hats
pulled over their faces like shades. Turkey Travis sat in front
with Earl, chewing bubble gum and working a crossword puz-
zle with the light of his cigarette lighter. He had to stay awake
in case Earl should doze and lose it. Raymond Mikes sat on the
end in back, looking at his notebook, his leg propped up next
to the door by Turkey's elbow. They were going to drive all
night, taking no chance of letting Leroy Hawkins get a motor-
driven posse together and hunt them down.

As he kept his eyes glued to the road ahead, the black night
air running cool past his face and down his neck, Earl grinned

and ran a thin whistle through his teeth, so small and silent it sounded like the air seeping through the side vent. He was thinking about how cool he'd been back there, punching the locks and moving like a thief. He couldn't wait to get on and find another job.

The wheel jerked in his hand from the tug and pull of the tires hopping over the stones. It was a lulling sensation, vibrating through his arms and shaking the flesh, and he set his head and tried to sleep with his eyes open. He looked over at Turkey sitting next to him and saw him slowly drift off, with his chin buried in his chest. Turkey had pulled on a heavy green sweater which had one arm cut off at the elbow and paint spattered on its front. He slept with his mouth partly open, and his lower lip hung limp. The long drives didn't bother him as long as he could sleep sitting down. Never complaining, never letting on if he was cold or hot or hungry or bored, Turkey kept things running loose. He could pitch every other day if needed, wouldn't complain, and gave what he had. He was twenty-seven, from Catawba, North Carolina, no woman or kids, a father who sold moonshine whiskey to the white moonshiners, and he had decided at sixteen he couldn't do very much very well except pitch. He slept without dreaming, his head shaking like a loose light bulb on a streetcar.

Fat Sam and Donus snored, heavy, rasping snores which would have bothered Earl if he could have heard them above the wind. Every few minutes Fat Sam inhaled and Donus exhaled exactly opposite one another, like a locomotive gaining speed. Fat Sam had always had trouble with his nose; because of it no woman could stand to sleep in the same room with him. It lay on his face like a mushroom flattened on a log, too flat, he claimed, to let in all the air he needed at one time. His 240 pounds slumped loosely on the seat, making him look more like a hustler or a barker than a left fielder who could pound stinging line drives as effortlessly as slapping crab apples off a tree.

For Donus the ride was never comfortable, and he jerked his

head awake every few minutes. His ankles swelled every night they spent on the road and he spent an hour in the morning soaking and wrapping them with elastic bandages. He'd joined the team after losing his job in an ice house in Louisville, and with every bad meal, every two-hundred-mile drive, every sprained finger he got off a bad hop, he wished he were back there with his wife, Loretta, and the three kids. He couldn't stand anything about barnstorming except the money, and he sent most of that back home. Fat Sam fell against his shoulder and Donus winced himself awake again.

In the Lincoln, cruising alongside the La Salle, Esquire Joe drove steadily through the night, gazing at the beams of the headlights as they cut through the darkness. Five of his six passengers were sleeping on him; only Big Juice Johnson, in the front seat, was awake and cleaning his nails with a pocket knife. Esquire Joe tried to talk to him, gave a few whistles out when something big splattered against the windshield, but Big Juice never even looked up. The new pitcher was lean and tall like Esquire Joe himself but he had something about him, something in the way his bones stuck out beneath his skin and the way he looked, that made Esquire Joe afraid of him. He lifted his head to shoot a stream of juice through his teeth and out the window. That was all; he seldom said much; on some days he could pitch like hell and no one could see him. And he kept that knife on him, the chaw inside his lip, and the hollow, hungry look.

Esquire tried to hum himself some blues, some Cab Calloway sounds to take his mind off Big Juice. He would send his mother a letter tomorrow, he would put in ten dollars for his sister. He would remember what his mother had told him before he left —to keep himself clean and think good thoughts and not let women turn his eye. He would remember to read his New Testament when he got by a lamp. Eighteen, skinny, with a head full of trash, nothing he could do but swing a bat and shag flies, been doing it since he was twelve and left the fifth grade to be a bat boy for nickels and fresh air, now driving a car better than he ever thought he'd drive, driving for the best colored ball players alive. He was still too nervous to know it was him, Joseph Abraham Calloway, with a wide smile across his face that mirrored itself in the windshield, and he thought of things he would do tomorrow.

In the back seat, Mungo Redd, Splinter Tommy Washington, and Isaac Nettles slept with their heads leaning straight back on the seat. Mungo and Tommy had come up together out of Atlanta's Sherman High School and had been snapped up by Sallie Potter as soon as he saw them. Mungo weighed 145 with his uniform on, Splinter Tommy 150. Mungo threw right, hit left with a fat bottle bat and his hands two inches apart. Tommy choked up on a skinny-handled bat with a big barrel and could foul off fifteen pitches in a row for a quarter. Tommy had three brothers back in Atlanta getting as good as he was, and one sister of the four who could field anything hit at her. He was determined to go back to Atlanta in a few years, pick up a right fielder, and turn his family into a complete outfit taking on all comers. Mungo hadn't been back to Atlanta since he last saw Sherman High School eight years ago. His mother died having him, his father was shot in the back five years later by the owner of a cotton farm. He would play ball with Splinter Tommy as long as they could get themselves to a field.

Isaac Nettles, thirty-eight and feeling it, knew this was his last year on the road. Had he not disliked Sallie Potter so much he wouldn't have come along. But he was still good, still a tough clutch hitter and as smart a player in the field as anybody could want. The hair over his temples was graying some, his legs took more time to loosen up, and he slept more nowadays than he ever had. Come October he would take his boy Charles down to Florida and live with his uncle who ran a tire shop. He could play a little ball, put on some weight, and forget about things. He wanted to stop worrying, to stop waking up at night and worrying about what he'd dreamed. He didn't need that.

The Lincoln slept better than the new La Salle, and much better than Bingo's Auburn. It rocked away the bumps and its smooth felt seats, though stained with sweat and dirt, were as comfortable as a barber chair on a hot afternoon. Esquire Joe held it steady, slowing once in a while on a curve or through a town, sometimes guiding the wheel with his knee and stretching his arms above his head. He kept himself awake spotting eyes in the fields, and humming.

Bingo pulled his knee up to his chest and slept heavily against the bag with his catcher's equipment in it. He had eaten a package of boiled ham and drunk a half pint of Old Forester before going under. His weight was down to 215 and he could feel himself straining to connect up at the plate. He slept with his mouth closed, a contented look on his face like he was stroking a dog and drinking a Dr Pepper. He would check with Raymond in the morning about money and things; he would call Lionel back in Pittsburgh when they got to Kansas City. This trip gave him too many responsibilities; he said that every day. Often he felt like chucking it and getting him a girl and a new car and getting on down to Saint Louis or New York City or Tampa. Didn't matter so long as he could hook up with somebody, somebody who knew his name and his price. Do some fishing, shoot some ducks in the fall, and forget about paying bills and buying food and making terms with the other man. All of the things he would have to think about tomorrow.

Leon Carter slept with his head against the window. He breathed heavily and slowly, shutting out the world, as the night covered over the hunters preying in the fields outside, with eyes glowing like coals and noses smelling out food.

In the La Salle Raymond Mikes, his cast-bound leg stretched out between the seat and the door ahead of him, was figuring, scratching numbers in a worn notebook which told him how everything stood and for how long. He raised his eyebrows, then frowned, then curled his lips as he calculated, then paged back to look for a sum of three days or three weeks ago. He had columns for spending money, for expenses, for salaries, for extras, and then a column for the leftover, the cream that went into Bingo's pocket if Raymond let him have it. There was a power in the figures, and Raymond had felt it from the first day he began his book, when Bingo made him manager in charge of finances. It eased the stiffness and the itching under his cast, it took his mind off not hitting a ball for over a month in the heart of the season. Every penny for laundry to spark plugs came out of his book with his permission. He could cut Bingo off or give him life, he could keep the team in one place or get it on the road. All with a few scratches from his pencil.

But now his figures were coming out bad and he knew it. The chunk of capital they had made in Chicago and Milwaukee had shrunk to almost nothing in the last two weeks and Raymond saw no way out unless they hooked up with something good in Kansas City. The car Earl had picked up was a help; it got the monkey off Bingo's back as far as his Auburn was concerned. Before too long the team would have quit rather than continue on in one car with twelve men. And Bingo didn't have the money to get another car because Raymond couldn't give it to him. Raymond smiled to himself as he thought of Bingo huddling with him a few days back and pleading with him not to tell the team and especially Leon how things were going. Raymond had nodded his head and played obedience, and savored the look in Bingo's eye. A look which told him he had the boss hanging on a window ledge ten stories up.

He hated the worries, and the reminders he wrote for himself of things that had to be done, he hated the bare truth of the figures when they were on the decline; but in the light of his flashlight, hearing the snoring of the team and feeling the approach of another day and maybe another dollar, Raymond felt good about what he had found for himself. And he had thoughts of doing some bookkeeping for somebody big back in Pittsburgh or Chicago, of handling those figures. His head bobbed and he felt himself drifting off. Then he shook himself awake and finished out his totals.

They kept on, through Charney and Burnham, Dubridge and Chariton, slowing to forty through the towns and speeding into the country again to hug the one-lane iron bridges. Earl pulled up to Esquire Joe and they jockeyed back and forth to pass the time until Big Juice Johnson was jolted awake and his scowl put Esquire Joe back on one steady speed. Raymond Mikes had drawn up a list of towns they would pass through on the way and Esquire Joe kept his eye on it. He never tried to read a map. A Kansas City mile marker flashed by every fifty miles, or every hour, depending on how Esquire Joe was keeping track. He switched feet on the accelerator pedal to keep up the circulation but it did little good and his muscles started to ache.

They stayed side by side, so as not to choke the motors with dust, looking like a giant four-eyed monster cutting a swath of light through the dark. Everyone was out but Earl and Joe, heads bobbing with the bumping monotony of the drive, legs and arms bent at odd angles. The four in Earl's car awoke suddenly when he thumped a coon against the underside, but their eyes slowly closed again like stage curtains and they slept on.

The sun shot its rays over the horizon at a quarter to five and Esquire Joe pulled into a Sinclair station to get some gas. He waited behind a tractor with its cultivators lifted three inches off the ground. When it was his turn he went into the station for a candy bar and pop and took a thirty-five-second piss in the outhouse. Isaac and Donus Youngs got up and followed him, Donus squatting over the hole and relieving himself of the baloney he had eaten the night before. Two swipes of page 322 of the Montgomery Ward catalogue, and he was in the back seat again, trying to get more sleep. Near the pump Esquire Joe drained his bottle of grape soda just after Earl finished his. Joe belched, finished his candy bar, and shook out his legs.

He asked the attendant if there was a diner down the road and the man looked back at him and shook his head. "Nothing?" Joe asked with a surprised look on his face. The man just nodded again and put Joe's dollar in his shirt pocket.

The cars had got a half mile down the road when Esquire Joe pulled over to the side of the road and jumped out. On his knees in a drainage ditch he vomited the candy bar and grape soda. Then he rolled over and held his stomach. Isaac pushed him in the back seat, gave him a handful of crackers to eat, and drove on himself. In ten minutes Joe was asleep, the crackers falling through his fingers as they lay limp on his stomach.

By six-thirty the sun was so bright no one but Esquire Joe and Bingo could stay asleep. They stretched and yawned and someone asked for breakfast. Fat Sam Popper took out a Thermos and drank the last of some cold black coffee. He spit the last mouthful out the window. He ran his tongue over his teeth and could taste the deadness of his mouth, the film on his teeth, a trace of dust from the ride. He wanted some cold water to splash himself awake, something to fill his stomach and make up for the bad night's sleep.

Earl turned into the drive of a clapboard diner. A pair of half-ton trucks were parked out front. He and three others walked slowly in, slamming the screen door against its frame. They were met by a thin woman wearing an apron who jerked her head in their direction and stared. Three customers lowered their coffee cups and turned around. Two of them were dressed in gray coveralls, the third was a leathery old farmer in blue jeans and plaid shirt. They watched Earl, Donus Youngs, Leon, and Mungo Redd as they walked in, not saying anything, not drinking their coffee.

The four Stars sat down at the counter, still trying to put some life into the morning, yawning. The woman didn't make a move. Then Leon looked up at her and waited.

"We ain't got nothing for colored in here," she said.

Leon looked away and exhaled heavily. He looked at the

others, then over to the three customers who hadn't moved, hadn't taken their eyes off the Stars.

"We got money. We just want something for breakfast," Earl said and stood up.

The two men in coveralls stood too, one of them knocking his fork to the floor.

Leon lifted his eyes to them without turning his head. His eyes were always bloodshot and sore in the morning. Then he rubbed his hands together in front of him.

"C'mon," he said and turned to walk out.

He tapped Earl on the shoulder and pulled him along.

At the door he turned to the woman. "Anyplace else round?"

"Kansas City's only sixty miles away," she said and shook her head. The two men sat down, one picking up his fork and jabbing it into the yolk of his fried egg.

Outside they calmed down Earl and tried to decide whether to try for Kansas City, or keep plugging at the diners on the road, or pull off and set up the Coleman stove.

Chapter 13

The telegram was waiting for Bingo when the Stars walked into the Hammond Hotel on Kansas City's north side. Lonnie Buttons, the little one-armed desk clerk, had it waiting next to the guest register, where he had written in the names of the Stars one by one in big black letters.

"Hey, the calls, the calls we been getting!" Lonnie Buttons wailed in his tinny soprano voice. "Knows you coming, knows it just because things start picking up."

Bingo grabbed Lonnie's arm and pumped it. "Meet this one-armed mother, Joe." He grinned at Esquire standing to his left. "This one hook here been in more shit than the both of us."

"Fugger, Bingo. Fugger you is. Here, take this thing before I got to pay the bill." Lonnie handed Bingo the telegram.

"Better be good news and money or it's your ass, Buttons," Bingo said and he tore it open. He read it slowly, pausing at the end and then reading it through again.

> TROUBLE. SALLIE COMING FOR BLOOD.
> LEAVE TOWN NOW. CALL ME. LIONEL.

Bingo looked up and scratched his head. Leon came over and read the telegram.

"From that man in Pittsburgh, I bet," Lonnie Buttons said. "Man been calling the phone off the wall."

Leon passed the telegram to the rest of the team.

"What you think's coming off?" Bingo asked.

Leon yawned. "Don't know and don't give a thin damn." He lifted his foot on a stool and tied his shoe. "Ain't no man on this team leaving town now anyway."

Bingo rubbed his hands over his face and sat down heavily in one of the lobby's overstuffed chairs.

"How you mean, Leon?" Splinter Tommy said. He had just passed the telegram on to Mungo.

"Well, Splinter, we here and the Monarchs is here—"

"And we need the cash now," Raymond broke in. "If we don't play them boys we dead—dead broke."

Bingo folded his arms in front of him and stared off across the lobby.

"What the shit's coming off?" he snarled.

Bingo dialed Lionel collect from the Hammond's lobby. The connection was bad so he had to press his ear to the receiver.

"Yeah, he's coming. Last time I checked he was on his way to where you is standing now," Lionel said on the other end.

"He was hot; I know because he called me just before he left and said I better forget about the Bingo Long Stars because he was on his way to collect some IOUs."

Lionel's voice cracked over the line. Bingo pulled the phone away from his ear and winced.

"What's he got up?" Bingo said. "What else he say?"

"Don't know, Bingo. Jimmy Riles told me he's losing money bad at the park back home. That's one thing."

"How about the blackball shit?"

"That's just what it is. The league boys they shook their heads when Sallie say put up a boycott—don't let them Stars ever play here no more, Sallie said—but they ain't never put nothing down on paper. And Sallie knows he ain't got shit for butter with them. Justice Grime, Raymond Dickey, Big Porter Jack— you know them boys would sign you up fast if they could. Everybody knows that."

"So what's he up to, Lionel?" Bingo asked.

There was silence on the other end. Bingo could hear Lionel clear his throat and something clinking like ice in a glass.

"My guess Sallie's going for the full house. Strong-arm shit, as I guess it," Lionel answered.

"Hell."

"Yessir. I think he got him some guns and some boys and he going to stick them on your ass and press."

"That why you said for us to skip KC in your wire?"

"You got it. I ain't sure but my cards smell awful from the way Sallie was talking. He ain't cool so you got to watch it."

"You think he got guns," Bingo said.

Lionel paused again. "He ain't got nothing else."

As Leon toweled off from his shower, Bingo told him what Lionel had said on the phone. Leon slapped himself with talcum.

"How much money you got in your wallet?" he finally said.

Bingo pulled a pants pocket inside out.

"That's what I thought," said Leon. "Ain't hard to make plans when we in the shape we in."

They had a game at five o'clock that night with the Monarchs, one the next night, a Saturday-afternoon game, and a Sunday doubleheader.

The Monarchs played at Franklin Park, a double-decked stadium built by their owner, A. C. Franklin, fifteen years ago. It was the best in the Central Colored League, with locker rooms, concrete grandstands, a major-league playing surface, and floodlights in clusters standing high over the stands. The Monarchs played in the Central League and toured California, Mexico, and Cuba in the off season, playing as many games as any team around. A. C. Franklin was a hustler the like of Lionel Foster and Sallie Potter, cigar-chomping and crafty. He had learned the game from his mother, Wilma, who brought the Monarchs from a sandlot outfit called the Watkins Street Boys to the franchise many people considered the best-run in the country. When Raymond Mikes wired from Milwaukee, Franklin dropped an out-of-town date and set up the series with the Stars. Four games, 70/30 his, and Bingo jumped at the offer.

The Stars were tired and stiff from the driving, yet one step inside the ball park started things flowing. Just the sight of mowed grass and chatter that could come from nowhere but from colored put them in the mood. They were back where people knew the language. Bingo took the first real batting practice he'd had in weeks, with the sweat pouring off his face and soaking his uniform down to his butt. The infield started warming the ball—shoveling it, skipping through—and Leon loosened his shoulder and reached back for the whip.

The Monarchs with their blue-and-gray suits stood on the edge of the dugout steps calling the Stars outlaws and gypsies and freight liners. They were good and full of spit, anxious to put the Stars through the wheel. They loved to take on a barnstorming outfit, a team with big heads from playing small time, and then watch it roast in its own grease. The fans were with them—old black hands in riding caps and bow ties who read the papers on Bingo and Leon, and the ladies who could quote averages and scream precise instructions on where to pitch Mungo and Sam Popper and Isaac Nettles. They sat with newspapers over their heads to keep off the sun, ready to roll them up into megaphones to boo the ump when he robbed them of a strike or a stolen base.

In game one the Stars were sluggish from the dead ball they had been playing. The Monarchs jumped on Leon for two quick runs in the first. They dug in on the high, hard fastballs and beat out bad throws. A hung slider was ripped between the outfielders for a stand-up double. They threw dust and spit in their gloves, chattering and whistling between their teeth at the Stars, who had yet to cock their hats on their heads and get into the game. Only a line shot Mungo turned into a double play at second kept the Monarchs from splitting the game wide open by the fourth inning. They were up on the Stars 4–1, and the crowd was hot on Bingo's back.

Leon sharpened up and found his stuff by the fifth and stunted the Monarchs' bats. He struck out Webbly Moore with a screwball on his fists and got Cephas Doyle, the six-foot-six-inch center fielder, to lunge after a change-up and fall on his butt. Leon glued a long, smug look on his face and walked off the mound. An old-timer behind the dugout chirped, "Chappy! Chappy! Chappy! Chappy!" and told Leon, since Chappy Dickson was the finest pitcher ever to throw for the Monarchs, that he was doing all right.

In the seventh Bingo slapped one. He had taken good looks at Eddie Smith's fastball in innings before. Hitting it was a matter of squeezing: his eye, his hands, his timing, to set them and compress them into the ball, though it didn't want to go, with a crack that jolted him to his teeth. He loped around the bases with a loose pride in his joints, knowing he could jam any bastard's fastball through the spaces between his teeth and out of sight.

The game went into the ninth, 4–2. Leon hadn't allowed a hit in the last four innings. Yet the Monarchs matched Smith's tough pitching with tight defense and a pick-off play that wiped Splinter Tommy off second in the eighth.

Then, in the Stars' last chance, a walk, a bloop single from Sam Popper, and a sacrifice put the tying All-Stars on second and third, with Mungo Redd at the plate. The skinny shortstop dug in, fluttered his fingers along the bat handle, and waited for his pitch. He would line it behind the runners into right, a slicing drive cracked just inches above the second baseman's glove, snaking for the line.

Then something caught Mungo's eye, breaking his concentration. He stepped out of the box. Isaac in the third-base coaching box had suddenly dropped his hands and was staring into the stands. Mungo took a look and saw it too. Three men were filing into the seats behind the backstop. Two he'd never seen before. The third was unmistakable, a white derby propped on the back of his head, a cigar, and a face full of sweat. No doubt about it, it was Sallie Potter.

Mungo screwed up his face as if he had jammed a thumb or bitten into something sour. In an instant he rethought the situation, that they'd been running like hell from that man, driving and eating crap just to get from under his fingers, far enough away to forget the smell of his breath, but now he was on them, no farther away than the box seats. Mungo replayed it: they were back where they started from, breaking themselves for him, bringing in the people so he could count up the receipts. Mungo wiped the bat off between his legs, picked up some dust. The bench had spotted Sallie, they craned their necks to get a glimpse. Mungo knew they were thinking what he was. Seeing the fat man again.

"Get in the box, boy!" the umpire growled, and Mungo jerked himself back into the ball game. Men on second and third, one out. Eddie Smith would pitch to him instead of putting him on as the lead run and face switch-hitting Donus Youngs.

The second pitch was his. A hard slider dipping away from him at his knees, and Mungo slashed at it. The crack and a streak —labeled two bases down the first-base line. Mungo knew it, kicked out of the box and looked up to see the Monarch first baseman Culsey Gipp dive headlong for the liner. In a snap of leather the ball was his. He hopped to his feet and threw in a single motion to second, where Sam Popper was sliding back in headfirst to avoid the double play. But the ball was there, Popper and Mungo were dead, and the crowd came thundering alive: stomping, cheering, shaking their heads. The Monarchs had taken Bingo Long's Stars and the great Leon Carter and had taken them good. They stood and applauded them home with noise enough to fill three blocks in all directions. All except the fat man behind the backstop, who sat and blew clouds of cigar smoke above him, smoke not quite thick enough to cover his satisfied smile.

Bingo kicked the ten-foot-long bench against the wall with a single swipe of his foot.

"Goddamn him! Burn his ass!" he cursed, slamming his fists together with a crack. The veins bulged out on his neck. "What the hell's he doing on my back?"

He kicked a towel and it flew up against a light bulb overhead.

"Fuck him, Bingo," Isaac said. "Calm your head and fuck him, that's all."

Isaac was the first of the Stars behind Bingo into the concrete block dressing room beneath the stands. The sudden loss to the Monarchs along with the sight of Sallie had numbed the team. They clustered around Bingo, eying him, their uniforms drenched from three hours in the heat.

Leon rubbed a pair of ice cubes over his shoulder. He had thrown nine tough innings. He looked over to Bingo, who had lit a cigarette and was dragging heavily on it.

"Test him, Bingo," he said. "Got to test him."

The ice melted tracks down Leon's arm.

"What you mean, Leon?" Isaac asked him.

The pitcher didn't look up. "See what the man doing here. Why he spend the money to come all the way over from Louisville all of a sudden. He could a got us in Cleveland or Chicago if he wanted to."

"Yeah, I'd kicked his ass full of holes," Bingo snarled. "He ain't got shit on me."

"Then why you so bothered?" Leon snapped back at him.

The rest of the team was quiet. Earl Sibley sat down and pulled out a pocket knife to clean off his nails.

184

"Maybe he got money," said Mungo.

"Shove his money!" Bingo said. He fired his cigarette against the wall. "I got the money around this team. I signed you boys up with money so don't be forgetting that!"

"Get your sense back, Bingo," Leon snorted. He eyed Bingo and Bingo stopped short. "Ain't no money brought Sallie here. Unless it's money he ain't got."

"Then what?" said Bingo.

"Test him, I say," Leon said.

"Maybe he got the law," said Isaac.

"Shit," said Bingo.

"Maybe he got a new contract for us," said Mungo.

"That's shit too," said Bingo.

"Bluff. Maybe just a bluff," said Leon. He flicked water off his hands and stripped his pants off.

Bingo shook his head, turning over the possibilities. He lit another cigarette. Then the door opened.

Two men in white suits and dark glasses walked in, the two with Sallie in the stands. They stood shoulder to shoulder, backs to the wall.

"Get the flies out," Bingo said, nodding to Esquire Joe.

The two men didn't move. Then one of them spoke.

"Boss just want to tell you he in town. Boss say he just want you to know that." The man had two teeth missing on the left side of his mouth.

"Boss can tie his ass in knots," Bingo said. He got up and took a step for the two and Isaac quickly stood in his way. Their spikes clacked on the concrete floor.

Leon got up from the bench. "You boys best got the wrong dressing room," he said.

The two turned to him, expressionless, eyes dark behind the shades. Then they left.

The room echoed with the slamming of the door. No one spoke until Earl swung his leg over the bench and clicked in the knife blade.

"The boys had rods on," Earl said. "Stick out on they legs like hards."

Bingo was so hot over the sight of Sallie he was late to settle with A. C. Franklin. As he toweled off, one of Franklin's boys ran into the locker room and whistled at him. The Kansas City owner had $585 for him sealed in an envelope an hour later. Thirty percent of the gate. Bingo grinned. "You sure can run the till, A.C." Franklin didn't crack a smile, said he would see Bingo on time the next afternoon. The money lay nicely in Bingo's inside lapel pocket, primed for the first night in Kansas City.

The lobby of the Hammond was lit with a giant cut-glass chandelier. It had come from the Sheppard-Chase down the street, at its auction after the hotel went under in '33. The chandelier went for thirty-five dollars despite the auctioneer's claim that it was a genuine Austrian piece, once having illumined the laps of presidents and princes. In the Hammond, at nine that night, with a bulb burned out on its left side and one flickering in the center, the thirty-five-dollar Austrian beauty shone on Sallie Potter, sitting beneath in a sofa wetting down a cigar with the tip of his tongue.

Most of the players were upstairs resettling themselves. They shook out clothes wrinkled beyond recognition. Suits that had been stuffed into satchels like wads of newspaper, and underwear yellow with sweat. Three solid weeks on the road left clothes with stains no woman alive could wash clean. That didn't bother the Stars, but they did agree the smell was too much, a stench so strong they could see it.

Bingo had his gear sent out to be cleaned, everything but a pair of boxer shorts and his driving cap, which he wore as he lounged on his bed and read the *Kansas City Star* and drank from a bottle of Old Fitzgerald. Lonnie Buttons had brought him up a pail of ice. What Bingo didn't use in his glass he put in a bag and wrapped around his knees, numbing the caps and tightening the tendons in the back. After a half hour of ice Bingo ran hot water over the knees for five minutes, a trick he said cleaned house inside the bones and made old juices pick up and travel on. When he finished, his knees glowed like lavender tomatoes.

In the lobby below, one of Sallie's boys flashed a ten-dollar bill in front of Lonnie Buttons. He told the one-armed clerk that he didn't want anyone upstairs to become aware of who was in the lobby. Lonnie grabbed the bill and folded it neatly with the fingers of his right hand.

"No, sir, no, sir, on my good arm, ain't no one upstairs is friends of mine," Lonnie said. He tucked the bill inside his shirt, in a pouch just above the knot tied in the shirt sleeve below the stump. "Nothing in the good Lord's heaven be making me make friends with those boys up there. Ain't no friends of mine. No, sir."

He patted the stump where the bill was and nodded his head up and down to Sallie's assistant. "Don't have no frets about Buttons here," he repeated.

Sallie sat and fingered his diamond pinkie ring, occasionally eying his boys for a nod or a signal. The Missouri night was hot but dry, and Sallie wasn't sweating like he would have been in Louisville. He felt at ease on the hotel's sofa, more comfortable than he'd felt since Bingo had taken the team and left. Now Sallie was back in their laps, facing them straight on, smugly mindful of all the corners he had talked them into when it had been necessary—slapping figures and clauses at them so fast their eyes swam. There was a sweetness about dealing. Sallie had tasted it long ago one night as he watched Lionel Foster squeeze a man to tears in the backroom of the Chop House, when Sallie was twenty-seven and just learning the ways to make a man sweat. Bingo, Leon, Louis Keystone, even Lionel —they all had their levels, all had a soft space in their heads just waiting to be taken with a well-placed dollar bill.

Just then Sallie caught a sign from his man. Donus Youngs entered the lobby, returning from the post office, where he had sent another fifteen dollars back to Louisville, another two weeks' groceries.

Sallie hopped up and called Donus over one on one. Donus stepped over casually. He eyed Sallie's pin stripes, the stickpin in his wide white tie, the white derby. Donus had never played for Potter, he had hitched with the Stars out of Lionel Foster's Elite Giants, but he had heard enough about Potter to have some opinions. And he didn't trust anyone who dressed like Sallie did.

Sallie moved in quickly, offering some small talk, feeling Donus out. He had done his homework on Youngs, established a buying point, and was about to pick his trump cards.

"Send the kids some pennies today, Donus?" Sallie said. He relit his cigar. "You got the money in the mail now, sure enough?"

Donus kept his distance. "No business to you," he said.

"But you said the word, boy—business. We here to talk business," Sallie said.

"I'm playing, get paid," Donus said. "Nothing more to talk about."

"C'mon with that bullshit, boy. I hears how you been making out. I been talking to the woman. Loretta, she tell me."

"You see her?" Donus said quickly. His face tightened. "You been down home?"

"Nice talk. I had a nice time with her. Saw the boys. Found out just the things you boys been going through on the road," Sallie said. He had counted on the rise he'd seen in Donus.

"Shit," said Donus. "You don't know shit."

Sallie slipped the cigar around to the left side of his mouth.

"I got money for you, Youngs. More than this birdshit Bingo giving out. And you won't have to suffer with them fat ankles you been writing your wife about. Hear me good, Youngs. I talking more sense than you heard since you left Pittsburgh," Sallie said. He leaned closer to Donus.

"If I want your dough I would be up to Louisville to knock on your door, Mr. Potter," Donus said. He rubbed his palm over his scalp. "Right now I ain't buying."

Sallie stepped back, turned his pinkie ring over and let it catch the light.

"Then we got to work other ways to make you listen," he said. "Like maybe you think the woman going to be all right back home. Maybe you think the boys going to be fine running around back there. Maybe somebody might step out and crack one a them ankles, make it big and fat like yours after you been riding."

Sallie smiled without breaking his lips apart.

"That's shit, man," Donus said. His face tightened again and he glared at Sallie. "Ain't nobody be messing over my kin. Ain't nobody be doing that."

Sallie rubbed his hands together slowly. "Think what you want, Youngs," he said. "You know what I said. We be talking later."

Donus took a step forward and pointed a finger in Sallie's face. He waved it slowly, his lips parted slightly. Then one of Sallie's boys walked up behind the owner, breaking into the light and eying Donus. Donus held back.

"Get on up now," Sallie said and turned his back.

Donus took a few steps backward then turned and stepped up to his room. It was time to soak his ankles again.

Sallie spoke briefly to his man and sent him over to Lonnie Buttons. Five more dollars in Lonnie's stump sent him up to Mungo Redd's room to tell Mungo he had a call waiting in the lobby. Mungo skipped down behind Lonnie. His eyes met Sallie's and he stopped dead. He gave a quick glance at Lonnie, who winced and rubbed his shoulder. Mungo turned and took a step up the stairs and he was grabbed by the arm by one of Sallie's men.

"Just want to talk over old times, Mungo, baby," Sallie said and led the shortstop over to the corner of the lobby where he had talked to Donus.

Mungo crossed his arms in front of him and breathed nervously.

"Thought you had the game with that drive today, huh, Mungo?" Sallie said. "Nice clean hit, that boy Gipp took it out of his asshole, took it right away from you."

Mungo didn't answer. His eyes flashed around the room; his knees twitched.

"Let go of the kid's arm so he can talk calm," Sallie said to his man.

Mungo swung his elbow away when the man stepped back. He kept silent.

Sallie eyed him. "You know what I'se here for, Mungo. You know me. I don't fool. I got a black book on you all over the league because of how you run out on me. And when I signed you out of school you know you didn't have a pair of socks to your name and I put you with some good ball players so you could learn your game. You know that, Mungo. . . ."

He started to twist his ring around his pinkie finger again.

Mungo hadn't moved, hadn't opened his mouth; he was nervous and wary of Sallie, aware of what the man would try to tell him.

"So I giving you a chance, Mungo. You can hit it with me and be the glove man around instead of some nigger gypsy playing cow teams and stepping in shit."

Mungo recrossed his arms, slapped at his ear, wiped his nose, and stood like a coach giving signals in the third-base box.

"No talk, huh, boy?" Sallie said. The loose skin beneath his jaw shivered as he said it. Mungo wasn't easy. "So hear this: I'se here to collect on those five bills you been owing me for some time now. I bet you ain't never told Bingo about that. No, sir! But that's what I want from you, Mungo, and I got my boys to be with me here to see you agree."

Mungo spit a cuticle from his thumb at the floor. Sallie didn't like it. The owner took out his white handkerchief and wiped his neck.

" 'Course you could come back to Louisville with me tomorrow and we be all even. That's right, Mungo. You got two ways to go."

Then Mungo shook himself; his head jumped as if he were taking a relay from Splinter and leaping in the air to avoid the spikes of the runner.

"Hey, Sallie," he said quickly, "you still driving the bus, you still got that hat and that getup you got for being a driver, huh, Sallie? You still driving that big fucker bus, huh, boss, the only boss driving the bus and feeling like he is where he ought to be? That still you, Sallie?" Mungo fired it at him, the words rapid and choppy, like infield chatter with something on it.

Sallie pushed his chest up to the shortstop. One of his men hopped up behind him.

"Five hundred on the lap or I'll carve you for that money, Mungo!" Sallie growled at him.

Mungo hopped back, bobbed away from the man who grabbed for his arm, and stepped up the stairs.

Sallie watched him then angrily turned and whipped the butt of his cigar into a tray of sand. He nodded to the two others and they walked swiftly out of the Hammond and into the street.

By the time Donus made up his mind to give Bingo the word, Mungo was halfway through his story. Bingo was still lying on the bed, feeling high from the Fitzgerald.

"Get Leon in here," he said to Donus when he came in the door. Donus left and returned moments later with Carter.

"You into him for that much?" Bingo screamed at Mungo.

"Yeah, I mean for the judge. Floated me the money for when they got me for cutting this boy. Long time ago. Sallie paid the judge and I walked away. Said it was five bills," Mungo explained.

"Cold shit," Bingo snarled. He looked up at Leon. "Sallie been putting the needle to Mungo about some money already. Says he got him for five hundred bucks unless Mungo go back home with him."

Leon shook his head. "So that's how the fat man is operating. I should have seen it coming."

"He say he bring his two boys along so Mungo don't have second thoughts," said Bingo.

"Yeah, they down there," Mungo said.

Leon grabbed a piece of ice out of the pail and sucked on it. "Mungo first. I wonder who he after next?"

"Mungo must a been second," said Donus. "Because he got me."

"What the hell, Donus?" Bingo said.

"Same stuff—he want me to come back and play for him. Otherwise he say he going to mess with my family," Donus said.

"Sure enough, he playing the game," said Bingo.

"We know we got his ass sticking on the wall if he came out here to strong-arm," Mungo said.

"You got it," said Leon. "But that don't make it no better right now. He got some thugs and guns and he putting things up front."

"Sallie with a gun is shit with a stick." Bingo laughed. "Fat man never did make it with no guns."

"But we got to play this smooth," said Leon. "Because Sallie ain't the one with the guns."

Bingo scowled and cracked a piece of ice between his teeth.

"Go get the boys in," Leon said to Mungo. "We got to fill in everybody about what's going on."

Mungo took off down the hall and started knocking on doors. He came back five minutes later with Splinter Tommy. "The rest is gone," he said.

On West Bedlow Street Sam Popper and Esquire Joe strutted beneath the street lights in their newly pressed suits and ties. Sam had promised Esquire Joe he'd fix him up with his cousin Jean Lynn and once in Kansas City it was a matter of a phone call to set the time for dinner and a show. Esquire Joe was game and had personally seen to it that his derby was put in shape for the evening.

"I is doing you a real deal of a favor, son," Sam repeated to Esquire as they walked. "Jean Lynn really my third cousin so she far enough away not to have my looks but still close enough for me to put my hand in with her when she feel up to it. You see I doing you a favor by cooling off just this night and letting you meet a real lady."

Sam's nostrils fluttered as he talked. His short squat legs took two steps to Esquire Joe's one as they went along. Sam had a way of turning his head and talking directly into Esquire Joe's chest and Joe had to look down at the top of his head to understand him.

"Yeah, yeah, I got it, I'm ready," Esquire Joe said over and over again.

They crossed Loft Street, only three blocks from Ballantine's, where Jean Lynn was to meet them, Fat Sam grilling Esquire Joe on the favor he was doing him, Esquire Joe nodding. They hadn't noticed the car that had turned on Bedlow and for a block and a half had slowly kept pace with them as they walked. It pulled up alongside suddenly and a man in the back seat jumped out and blocked the path in front of them.

"Hey, Sam, boy, how you been?" Sallie said from the front seat.

Sam and Esquire Joe pulled up short. Sallie's man stood square-shouldered in front of them. Sam smiled nervously at the owner.

"Say, if it ain't the boss cigar," he said slowly and a weak smile washed over his face. "Old Sallie in town, sure enough."

"That's my boy, Sam," Sallie said. He motioned him over to the car. "Bring your partner with you; we got to talk."

Sam ambled slowly over. Esquire Joe had no choice but to follow. They were joined by the man on the sidewalk, who slid into the back seat with them. The three of them sat shoulder to shoulder staring at Sallie, who turned and faced them with a wide smile and his ever-present cigar.

"Now, Sam, tell me who you got here," he said.

"You don't know him—this boy's a star! Esquire Joe Calloway right here."

Esquire Joe ducked his head and brushed his hand across his face.

"Wanted to hear you say it for me," Sallie said. "I been reading in the papers about Joe Calloway like he was on top of the heap."

Sallie ran his tongue down the length of his cigar. Then he leaned around and stared into Joe's face. "Listen up, Joe. Listen to what I tell Sam here so you knows how things is."

"Don't lean on him, Sallie. Don't do that," Sam broke in. He started to sweat from the heat the five of them generated inside the car. He could smell the liquor on Sallie.

"Okay now, Fat Sam. Here's the goods. We been friends, Sam, and I know we still is. No talk on why you left me. I just telling you to come back now. Got five hundred says you'll come."

"Aw, shit, Sallie," Sam droned. Esquire Joe turned his head to get a look at Fat Sam's expression.

"Five bills with no papers. I ain't going to shave your ass, you know that, Sam."

Sam squirmed and made a face. He ran his hands together.

"Give me a break, boss. I run with the team. I got to stay with them. If they decides to come back with you then count me in," Sam said. His eyes pulled together slightly and met Sallie's. His upper lip began to twitch, like the muscle was being tugged by a string.

Sallie motioned to his driver and a lighter suddenly appeared under his nose, kindling the cigar with a bright orange flame. The smoke billowed.

"Okay, I'll paint it for you, Sam. I ain't going to twist your arm; my boys would never lay a hand on you, you got my word. But I want you, Sam, back on the Ebony Aces where you got a home. I got money to put up if you want it even though I got your hand down on a contract. I could get the law on you just on that paper alone.

"It's straight cash I'm talking, Sam. Enough to make you and this kid friend of yours listen if you got the sense I know you got. Five bills. Right now. Another bill for the kid if he want in too. Yeah, Sam, him too. We all be in Louisville by the first of the week playing some ball and telling the people Fat Sam Popper is home to stay."

Sam looked at Sallie then glanced at Esquire Joe. Esquire had his eyes glued on Sam.

 Chapter 14

The crowd showed early at Franklin the next day, heckling the Stars as they went through batting practice for Friday's game, cheering when a Monarch hit one out or speared a line drive. The Monarchs were loose and having fun. The feel rubbed off on the Stars and they started to chatter and spit and get the nonchalance out of their moves. They bantered with the old-timers in the crowd and made eyes at the ladies. Posses of boys charged through the stands shagging foul flies. They dove under the stands like dogs after meat, only to emerge seconds later full of dust—one of their number clenching a ball with both hands, prize that it was, only to give it to the ball boy in exchange for a red slip good for an ice cream. Any kid running off with the ball never got into the park again. Jakie the ball boy saw to that, and he knew every kid in the park by his first name.

Big Juice Johnson was going for the Stars. He warmed up in silence, fixing a scowl on his face, trying to make his fastball as mean.

The Stars played the Monarchs even up through the first three innings. Big Juice shook off some control trouble and managed to face down the Monarch hitters with a good fastball and a tricky slider. The crowd sat back fanning themselves and appreciating the play. The stands were almost filled. A breeze blew in from the outfield and caught the shirts and fluttered the evening newspapers.

In the top of the fourth Sallie showed. His two men walked with him on each side, shuffling slowly between the rows of people until they reached an open spot behind the backstop. The Stars had a perfect view of him from the bench. They took notice.

"How he get those seats?" Isaac complained. He watched with the rest as Sallie smoothed himself and eyed the playing field.

"Franklin," came a reply from the end of the bench. Leon sat there with his jacket on.

"How you know?" Isaac asked.

"He an owner, ain't he? Just like Sallie." Leon snorted. "They all got feelings for each other."

"Yeah, like undertakers got feelings for stiffs," said Raymond.

Esquire Joe laughed then stopped short when he saw no one joined in.

Sallie kept his seat from inning to inning, an unmistakable site because of the constant cloud of cigar smoke trailing out over his head. His cohorts left then returned every so often with a hot dog or a cup of beer, but Sallie sat like a stone. The Stars watched him nervously, hardly able to take their eyes away, as if they were waiting for him to do something or make some move.

Donus saw him and wondered about things. He tried to keep his mind on the game then caught himself eying Sallie again and again. He wondered about Loretta and his boys. He wondered what Sallie had done, what he planned on doing; he watched the thin smoke as it rose from the fat man's cigar, and he went over in his head the discussion between Sallie and him in the lobby of the Hammond.

Mungo looked over when he had a chance. He thought of the money and laughed to himself. Sallie had nothing on him, he told himself.

Fat Sam Popper kept his eyes off his former boss. He didn't want to think about the money, about the threats or the messing, about the things he owed Bingo and the rest. He scraped his spikes against the concrete floor of the dugout and looked over to Esquire Joe. Esquire craned his neck like a goose looking at Sallie and his two friends. Then he shot a glance at Fat Sam and met his eyes again. The two of them winced at the contact.

Then Splinter Tommy flew out and the bench emptied in a flurry and the Stars took the field. Only Raymond and Leon stayed behind, sitting far enough toward the end of the bench so as not to have a good view of Sallie.

Out on the mound Big Juice Johnson had his stuff moving for him; he worked hitters in and out, jamming on the fists, then making them reach for sharp-breaking curve balls. The Monarchs touched him for a run in the fifth, and two more in the eighth when Jimmy Nixon rocked one out of the park with a man on. But Big Juice didn't let up. By the eighth the score was tied 3–3.

In the top of the ninth, as the Stars dug in for a rally, Sallie and his two escorts stood up, brushed themselves off and walked out. Esquire was up at the plate when the fat man left. Isaac, coaching at third, clapped his hands and asked for a liner. Esquire Joe gave it to him and was followed two hitters later by a triple from Fat Sam Popper which rattled against the top of the fence in left center and drove in two runs.

It was all Big Juice needed. The Stars slapped their gloves and whistled after the three Monarch outs. They smiled and felt it coming back. The people jabbered sour grapes at them, the talk the Stars liked to hear from an enemy crowd. Yet as they turned the corner from the dugout and headed into the dressing room, Bingo, Isaac, Fat Sam, Donus, and a lot of the others shot a quick glance at the place in the stands where Sallie had sat.

Leon cracked a towel against the wide butt of Fat Sam as he waddled into the shower. Sam yelped and rubbed the blotch of red, burning skin.

"Popper, you can sure pop the ball," Leon whined.

Sam scowled at him then flexed his arm and winked before losing himself in the steam of the shower.

Later, as the team toweled off and rubbed on deodorant and talcum, Mungo bent over a basin brushing his teeth, Bingo started in. He dragged on two cigarettes stuck in the corner of his mouth.

"We being threatened, you all know that now. The fat man here got into Donus with shit on his old lady and his boys. He been talking to Mungo and Popper and even been smelling money in front of Joe. Sure as shit he threatening us.

"So we got to keep peace with ourselves and see the snake for what he is. Don't let him shave our ass like he damn sure wants to. You new boys ain't seen the fat man at work so just take my word for it. This here team wouldn't be here if it wasn't for one man, the same man I'se talking about.

"Raymond, show everybody the plaster on that foot case we forgot. See, I ain't lying. Ain't lying!"

He took another drag from his cigarettes and wiped the perspiration which was starting to form on his forehead and neck.

"You getting nervous, Bingo?" Isaac asked from the corner.

"Shit!" Bingo barked, and with it his cigarettes flew out of his mouth and bounced crazily off the bench in front of him, causing him to dance a two-step to keep from landing on the hot coals. He breathed another "Shit" as he picked up the soggy smokes and tossed them in the can across the room.

Some minutes later he got the word from A. C. Franklin's runner that his money was waiting for him upstairs. Bingo started to hustle. He looked up at Leon, Donus, Raymond, and Splinter Tommy Washington, who were the last of the team still in the locker room.

"I give you a bet the boys will stay warm now that things is singing. We getting some money, a good town, and we playing some ball. You tell me how Sallie going to break into this."

He smiled and shook his head in agreement with himself.

Leon was about to reply when Bingo clapped his hands and skipped for the door.

"Damn, I got to get on up to that cash."

Friday night in Kansas City was like home for the Stars. It was Louisville, Pittsburgh and Lionel's Chop House, Cleveland or south side Chicago. The players drifted in twos and threes out of the Hammond and into the street. They were looking good and, money in hand, left trails of aftershave when they turned a corner. Donus and Isaac and Turkey Travis hit the movies and Gary Cooper. Splinter Tommy and Mungo found a steakhouse. Big Juice wandered off to look up a friend. Back in the Hammond, Bingo huddled with Raymond and Fat Sam over the telephone trying to get rid of the car Earl had picked up for them. Fat Sam's uncle had his fingers on connections that could take care of things, or so he said. The three of them worked out the details. The uncle would deliver the car to a junkyard, where it would get a paint job, a set of ownership papers, and some new numbers. In return he would give Fat Sam a car that he guaranteed was worth the same money, with no questions asked. Sam said it had probably been lifted from down south, but he wasn't sure.

They bickered price for twenty minutes until the deal was arranged. A time was set for the transfer.

"Hope we getting something as good as what we got," Bingo said.

Fat Sam shook his head. "The man's blood. He doing us a favor."

Bingo shook his head.

"Anyway, ain't no way you can pull off something like this without the uncle," Fat Sam said.

The three of them got up and went down to Leroy Hawkins' La Salle.

An hour later Bingo stood at the bar of Mel Jones' Pennant

Lounge. He had his charcoal pin stripe pressed and smooth. He drank beer with whiskey kickers. The Pennant Lounge had a jukebox and the people were talking through it. A few yallers sat at the bar looking thin and interested. Bingo patted his palm on the bar and eyed Raymond and Fat Sam talking shop with two Monarchs who had wandered in.

"You know, Leon, all them days on the road has made me quiet."

Leon gave a short laugh.

"Yeah, I mean I used to come in a place like this and turn on the lights. The people would come around and the words and trash would fly without me even thinking about it. Now look at me."

Bingo brushed at a lady in green who stepped by.

"You be all right with some more shots," Leon said. "Never was worth a shit sober anyway."

"No, sir, Leon. I think something's serious with me now. My nerves or something ain't falling in line. Maybe I got something, huh?" Bingo said.

"Like Sallie?"

"Piss on Sallie. He only makes me mean. Not nervous."

The juke dropped "Empty Bed Blues" and Bingo hummed into it.

"Dammit, where's Louis! He's the boy I need with me. He could pick up the ladies and make the music and do him some stepping. Why ain't we heard from Louis, Leon? He ought to be here now, he ought to be right here with us."

Leon drank from his beer. "He's probably into something illegal back in Louisville by this time."

Bingo took out his handkerchief. "They named that town after him."

He leaned over to the bartender and nodded for a refill. The beer was light and cold, better than the warm bottled beer they had been drinking on the road which sometimes lay in the car shaking and knocking around beneath the seats for days before they got to it. Bingo peeled off a bill then stopped and put the roll back into his pocket. He remembered he had a tab at this bar; he hadn't had one since they'd left Chicago.

The bartender came over again. "You got a game up later?" Bingo said to him.

"You in it," the bartender said and refilled his shot glass.

"How about the gumbo? About 4 A.M. going to be ready?"

Another nod from the bartender and a thumbs-up wave.

"Can smell the crabmeat now. Just sticking in my mouth," Bingo said.

Leon stood with his back against the bar, his long legs stretching out and crossed. He wore a light brown suit, a knitted shirt without a tie beneath his suit coat. He seldom wore a tie, never dressed to flash like Bingo. He was thirty-six years old, but with his close-cropped hair, tight brown skin, and the clean bone lines in his face, in the prime of his life.

"Dammit, Leon, it's when the times start coming back that I get the old feelings. A good town like K.C., playing some ball, hitting the music and the juice, the man say he got some cards ready to ruffle and the gumbo is steaming. That's my league, that's it.

"That's why Louis he ought to be around with his big-ass grin and his heels and all that shit he tries to throw at the women. I get in a place like this and I get to miss that boy like a brother."

Leon looked over his shoulder at Bingo and laughed. "You a sentimental old shithead, ain't you, Bingo?"

Bingo slapped his thigh and put his arm around a lady in a yellow dress with arms almost as big as his and giant breasts.

Saturday's game drew the biggest turnout yet, a loud, sarcastic crowd that jumped on Bingo and the rest from the first inning on. The Stars and the Monarchs started off at each other with big bats, towering drives, and liners that shot out from the plate and made the outfielders scramble. Turkey Travis threw for the Stars and could barely keep the lid on. But the Stars hit for him; by the fourth it was 7–6 Monarchs.

Raymond Mikes kept things alive on the bench. He screamed barbs and insults at the Monarchs as they dug in. Big Juice Johnson caught the drift of it and hurled some guttural insults at the third baseman or the third-base coach or anyone else close enough to hear him. He spat wads of juice from the lump in his cheek and they dotted the dirt in front of the dugout like oil spots.

"Your arm is limp dick, Mavis," he growled at the Monarch pitcher, and Raymond howled and the Stars chimed in with descriptions of their own.

Yet throughout the line drives and run-scoring rallies, between double takes at Big Juice and the back-slapping celebrations after Fat Sam Popper belted two out of the park, the Stars shot glances into the stands. Quick, furtive looks but noticeable to every player: they were looking for Sallie. Still the innings moved on and the seat Sallie and his friends had taken in the first two games remained occupied only by a thin, light-faced woman and an old man who wore a green poker-playing eyeshade and drank from a paper bag. There was no sign of Sallie Potter. Anywhere.

Turkey couldn't hold them in the eighth and a Star rally fell short when Donus fanned with the tying run on second. Monarchs 12–Stars 11. The crowd had seen what they had come for. Tomorrow the doubleheader would settle any doubts still on the line.

The locker room echoed with gripes and bad words from players scolding themselves for dropping the game. The Monarchs had pasted their ears back with barnyard slugging, the kind of game the Stars hated to lose. They showered and toweled off with little idle chatter. In less than half an hour the room was empty except for Bingo and Raymond.

"At least one thing," Raymond said. "The books is looking up."

Bingo nodded and belched. "What you say that crowd was today—three, four thousand folks?"

"I doubt it but they was thick," Raymond replied. He tossed towels in a pile and kicked at scraps of tape.

"Got me a fat roll up in the top office waiting. That's one thing sure. Makes three in a row," Bingo said. He knew Raymond had heard the same sentiments after the first two games.

"Makes you look good. Especially now when you needs it."

"Huh?" Bingo asked.

"I mean with Sallie being around," Raymond said.

"I got you. And you talking right, Raymond. That man with some money could a hit the boys in a tender spot after we come off the road looking like half-dead chickens. No money, no shit, no nothing."

"You know it, Bingo. My book said we was down."

"But that's done now. Don't think we got no worries now with the money coming and the boys playing ball like they is. See how hard we took this game today. We was sore losing like we did. Sore with them people laughing."

"Yeah, like losing to Lionel back with the Aces," said Raymond.

"Hell, even worse. Them boys is the Stars like the paper says and they know getting whupped by them Monarchs is bullshit."

"Yeah, that's how it is, Bingo," said Raymond.

"Can Sallie touch it? Huh? Can he flash his dudes and take my boys now that they eating and dressing and playing for the people?" Bingo said.

Raymond flashed him a grin and whipped a towel behind his back.

"Shit."

Sunday was picnic day at the park. The people spread the food out in the stands, the chicken and pork and beans, cold pork chops and homemade bread, and melons. They sipped beer and orange drink from paper cups or from the bottle. The kids scurried underfoot, some still wearing white shirts and bow ties left over from morning Sunday school. At twelve-thirty the umpire bellowed that it was time and the two teams started the day's doubleheader, the final two games of the series.

The afternoon would be long so the teams toyed with each other, relying on rhythm and cool to get through the plays, knowing enough not to be careless. The Stars wanted the first game. The crowd had been on them the last three days and there was only one way to get back. An opening win would even things out, a sweep of the header would settle things in the Stars' minds and give them a good push off into the West.

On the hill, twisting and kicking in the baggy green and white, Leon poured everything he had at the Monarchs. He turned the eighty-two-degree heat into sweat and steaming motion, pushing off the rubber, carving slashes into the dirt with his follow-through. He threw his fastball, his screwball, his hard slider which buzzed downward just before Bingo gloved it, his hesitation pitch, his grease ball which dropped into the hitter's ankles like a stone because Leon spun it off his fingers with a smear of toothpaste taken from the glob in his back pocket, his curves, three or four varieties depending on how much he wanted to break it off or at what speed he wanted to come in with it, and then he leaned back again and fired his pin-sized fastball. The papers seldom wrote up Leon for his stuff, the fact that he could throw almost any pitch known if he wanted, because they were fixated on his fastball, the way he challenged batters with it inning after inning. The Monarchs knew it well. They stepped in and swung viciously at it, the good hitters bearing down on the fastball, knowing the challenge of having to face it, spinning around in the box with a grunt and a flash of the bat. Leon showed it to them, put it on the line for that instant, and then took it back.

The game moved on with Leon in control. The people applauded lightly at first, then added to the response after each inning, knowing full well what they were seeing. Bingo chattered each pitch home, the Stars flipped the ball around the infield with shrill whistles and popping leather. In the fifth Mungo doubled on a liner through the middle which hit the base and bounced away from the outfielders. With two outs Earl Sibley singled him home and the Stars were up by one. Leon went out once again; Raymond flipped the score book to the Monarch side, which was clean and orderly. The sameness of Leon's perfection let Raymond's mind wander, and soon he found himself checking the stands for Sallie again. He didn't see him. As far as he knew the fat man hadn't showed yet.

In the Stars' half of the seventh Raymond spotted Bingo leaning over to get a look at the seats behind the backstop. But the blank look on Bingo's face gave Raymond the answer—still no Sallie. He didn't know whether to be glad about it or simply indifferent. It was his broken foot that had started things back in Louisville; the team had backed him like brothers and then taken him along and treated him like one of them. If they hadn't, he'd be back in Louisville living off what he could borrow, taking odd jobs not too difficult for his cast to take. So he looked up for Sallie, and when the others saw him do it they couldn't help but take a look themselves. Then they watched Leon, who seemed untouched by anything this day, go through the Monarchs' batting order.

In the eighth Bingo singled and was pushed home by a walk, a sacrifice, and an infield out. The Stars led 2–0. Leon had allowed but a lone single back in the third.

In the ninth inning the people perked up and called for the Monarchs to make some noise. Leon, drenched with sweat, his spikes caked with dust from the mound, tugged at his hat, which had a half-moon circle of sweat creeping out into the cardboard bill, and fired his last bunch of fastballs in the game. They followed one another in methodic but violent regularity, snapping Bingo's glove before the bark of the umpire. The final out was popped up into Donus Youngs' mitt and Leon had his one-hitter. The old men behind the dugout stood up and chattered and knocked their canes against the wooden benches. Leon took the handshakes from the Stars and from a few Monarchs; he smiled and stuck his glove in his pocket with the toothpaste.

In the fifteen minutes between games the Stars drank water and chewed on oranges and halves of sandwiches.

"Think that man Sallie left town," said Esquire Joe, breaking the silence about the owner.

"Don't give no shit if he want to live here," said Fat Sam Popper.

Bingo swallowed a slice of orange, the peel and all. "Yeah, you got it now, Sam," he said.

A minute later home plate came alive with Dixieland, the sounds of a six-man rag band brought in by A. C. Franklin for the between-game show. A trumpet leaned into the lead, backed by a clarinet, a sax, a trombone, a tuba, and the drummer with his pair of snares and a bass hollowed out and fitted with a homemade kicker. It was a hometown group which doubled for weddings and wakes and family reunions. They started in on "Sweet Georgia Brown" and in no time had the kids leaning up against the backstop jigging and whistling in their own versions. The trumpet wore the cap of an old marching uniform. It was lined with gold braid and crowned with a two-foot peacock feather that arched out from the crown. The others wore long-sleeved white shirts with bow ties and rhinestone cuff links. They flashed hankies over their faces and wiped the spit from their mouths; the music never stopped, just changed key and went into something new.

"These boys is in our league, ain't they now?" Bingo said as he admired the group. "The man A. C. Franklin knows what the people want."

"Just what we need, huh, Bingo?" Raymond yelled.

Bingo tapped a bat against the bench. "Take them along soon as they'd come—if I had me the means, that is."

"Oh, wouldn't we ramble?" Fat Sam added. "The people would hear us then they'd see us."

"I'd throw in a circus, maybe some girls off the back end of some trailer, get me some animal acts—that would be a touring group!" Bingo howled.

Then he turned his head to see a man hop out of the stands and saunter up to home plate. He wore a pair of baggy pants and dusty shoes, a suit coat with tails that were ripped up his back, and a moth-eaten top hat. He stepped and danced to the music, clicking his heels and jumping into the air, his arms flailing and cutting the sky like tree branches in a storm.

"Jump up now, Pink Meat!" someone from the crowd yelled, and the fans began to cheer him on.

"Pink Meat, you got it, you in heaven down there!" a lady yelled.

He twirled and tossed, he raised the dust then jumped out of it. His heavy shoes knocked together like weights then flew in the air in flying splits. No special dance, no routine; he just moved to the beat of the bass and cocked his head when the trumpet riffled.

"Hey now, didn't think old Pink Meat was around no more," Bingo said above the laughter of the Stars.

"Who that man?" Esquire Joe asked as he stared out at him.

"Pink Meat Purvins, boy. He the greatest dance man around," said Bingo.

"How he do all that?" said Esquire Joe.

"He just don't know no better," said Mungo. "You just play some ragtime and Pink Meat be on the floor dancing and kicking until he can hardly breathe."

The band didn't let up. Pink Meat stayed with it. One of the Monarchs came out of the dugout and began mimicking him. The crowd howled their approval.

"What's he do for a job?" Esquire Joe asked.

"Ain't nobody ever asked," said Bingo. "Most I ever seen him, he was either dancing for nickels or he was drunk. He probably be that when he gets through here."

When the band wound down Pink Meat went into a slow-foot shuffle and doffed his hat.

"There's the sign," said Bingo.

A minute later, as Pink Meat danced blindly, his eyes closed and his feet moving to the whisper of the snare, the coins started to come.

"Do us the high boy, Pink Meat," someone yelled.

The trumpet cracked his lip on a high F and Pink Meat leaped into the air. He jerked his head to the side at the top of his leap and reached out to touch his heels. He seemed to pause up there for a second before he came down. The coins flew at him like hailstones.

"Fucker's a kangaroo," said Mungo.

"He can jump too," said Esquire Joe.

As the band cleared off, Pink Meat scrambled around home plate tossing the coins into his top hat. The sweat poured off him and onto the dust of his shoulders. He flipped the coins like peanuts.

"Hey, Meat!" Bingo yelled out to him.

He kept at his work.

"You still on top, Meat!" Bingo went on.

Pink Meat flashed a grin at him and raised a big, sandy palm. Then he hustled off, hopped the fence without breaking stride, and was away down a corridor.

"The man going to be wet tonight." Bingo laughed.

In the second game the Monarchs decided to put it to the Stars in one deciding push. They came out after Big Juice Johnson's fastball on the first pitch, digging in and legging out hits as if each was the game-winning safety. The Monarchs were edgy after Leon's one-hitter: they hated to be shut out in Franklin Park, in front of the paying fans and the kids who thought they were the greatest. A sound thrashing of Big Juice in the second game would make memories of Leon short.

Bingo strapped on his pads around pant legs that were as damp as steamed towels and eyed the stands. After four days in K.C. he began to pick out some familiar faces: the girls who winked and smiled through the screen, the old sitters who jabbered and heckled him, even the kids who nagged him for a ball or the butt end of a Lucky. Yet at the beginning of the second game of the doubleheader, he still couldn't spot the one face he angrily expected. Sallie hadn't shown for the second day in a row.

Bingo plodded out to the catcher's box. The rest of the Stars, each with a quick glance in the stands and chatter to cover it up, ran ahead of him.

Big Juice had a glimmering of the stuff the fans saw Friday; he kept the Monarchs off balance and quelled rallies before they had a chance to erupt. The game fell into a go-ahead-catch-up routine: the Monarchs touched Big Juice for a run, the Stars would come back to tie by getting to the Monarchs' J. C. D. Jackson. By the fourth it was 5–4 Monarchs; by the sixth, 6–5 Stars.

In the bottom of the seventh Big Juice lost his steam and walked two men before giving up a tying single. Bingo walked out to talk with him on the mound and saw that his pitcher was fighting to stand up, to keep the exhaustion inside instead of letting it drain out with his sweat and heavy gasps. A day's rest had hardly been enough after the game Big Juice had thrown Friday. He stood on the mound with his arms hanging at his hips, his glove under his arm, pushing the chaw slowly around the hollow of his cheek.

"You got any stuff left in you, Juice?" Bingo asked him as he looked away at the Monarch runners on first and third.

Big Juice let fly with a wad of juice.

Bingo kicked at the dirt and turned to the bench. He didn't have to say anything, he didn't motion or nod. The man he wanted was already taking his jacket from his shoulder and tightening the laces on his spikes. Leon would come on in relief.

The arm hadn't cooled down, hadn't set long enough for the numbness to begin its slow, pervasive crawl. Leon could still feel his fingers; the joints were loose and the tendons stretched like the long rubber bands he wanted them to be. When his arm was ready he could feel each part of it: the wrist and its sound-less swivels, the forearm, the elbow that shot pinpricks of volt-age into the muscle, the upper muscle and shoulder, which growled and tightened when pushed. Together, every part alive and working, the arm talked to Leon, told him when to push or to let up, when to curve or knuckle. It hesitated, Leon shook it, scolded, the arm shot its answer, demanded heat, then ice, went numb, came alive.

Leon took the ball and went into his warm-up pitches.

Big Juice walked off and sat next to Raymond. He was sapped, the score tied, the five green stars on his uniform buried in the damp folds of his blouse, absorbing the drops of sweat that slid from Big Juice's chin.

On the mound the arm twitched and jangled, reached for the ball, went down back, up and over with the motion. The ball shot for the plate. Once again, as the Monarchs stood on base waiting to score, the arm came. Again. Up and over. Again. The arm twitched, got the feel, came over. Again. Leon kicked at the dirt, threw a hissing screwball that sunk at the batter's crotch. He swung. The inning over, score still tied.

In the top of the eighth Mungo hung a liner to the opposite field. It curved over the third baseman's head and went for the line. Mungo was out of the box at the crack and legging it around first as the left fielder swooped over to cut it off. The ball landed fair and twisted off into foul territory, taking the out-fielder with it. Then in an instant he slipped and careened into the retaining fence, the ball bouncing crazily past him into the corner. By the time the Monarch righted himself and gave chase, Mungo was into third and heading home. The throw was a token; Mungo had an inside-the-park homer. He grinned like a kid between gasps for breath. The Stars were all over him.

With one run up, Leon pushed everything up front to keep the Monarchs off the bases. The crowd hollered and kicked the wooden benches for a rally. They didn't want to lose the second one, hated to see their boys drop the series. The Monarchs chattered and clenched fists for an upsurge.

Leon mixed them up, placed them in and out, poured fastballs high and hard when he knew his man was off balance. Everything the arm had ever done in twenty-five years came out, then he reached for more. He took the signal from Bingo and nodded at the target. He had seen it, thrown at it for years, and when he was on he could tell it by the sound in the leather. He got through the eighth still in the lead.

At the plate Esquire Joe swung on the first pitch and popped up. Bingo pulled him over when he got to the bench.

"Dammit, Joe, you can't be hitting first pitches. Give the man a rest!" He nodded at Leon. "You got to learn how to use the time for ourselves."

Esquire Joe stumbled over next to Fat Sam. He hadn't thought the angles and knew he was wrong. He didn't look up at Sam.

A short time later they ran out again. The crowd clamored for the Monarchs to turn the game around. They could feel a win, could see the Monarchs stroking line drives through the infield.

Leon fidgeted, then he leaned and raised his arm. He threw fastballs, straight without any dressing, lifting his foot like a billboard in front of the batter's nose to tell him another was coming. He threw twelve of them. The arm twitched between each one, then straightened and fired. The Monarchs waited for them, dug in, swung viciously. Twelve fastballs sailed in, with every muscle in Leon's arm spinning on the seams. Like seconds they counted past, until three Monarchs had fanned and the game was home.

Leon walked off the mound. Another one-more-time. He draped his jacket over the shoulder.

Chapter 15

In their last night in Kansas City the Stars slept heavily, stretching their legs between the cool white sheets, smelling the overstuffed pillows. In the morning they would head out west, and start a string of miles that wouldn't lead to a hotel like the Hammond for days, maybe weeks. Bingo lay flat on his back, with one leg sticking out from beneath the covers. A bottle of Old Fitzgerald lay dead in the bucket of half-melted ice Lonnie Buttons had brought up. Next to it lay the peels of half a dozen oranges. Bingo snored like a horse.

It was 2 A.M. when the car pulled up in the alley, doused its headlights, and parked beneath the iron fire escape which zigzagged up the rear of the Hammond. A tall, heavy-set man got out. He grabbed hold of the railing of the fire escape and swung it down to him. A dull, groaning vibration ran up the iron, the only noise in the dead quiet of the night. The man slowly climbed the stairs, reversed at the second floor, turned again at the third, once more at the fourth until he reached the sill of a window. He stopped, glanced down at the car, and saw the orange glow of coals on the end of a cigar. A door swung open and a second man got out and followed the same route up the escape until he was at the side of the first. They both crouched in their dark suits and dark driving caps. From the ground they were almost invisible against the sooty brick of the Hammond.

They tapped twice on the window. Inside the room Earl Sibley hopped out of bed. He was fully clothed except for his shoes, which he slid into and laced. Big Juice Johnson had turned in early that night and was sleeping soundly. Earl crept over to the window and slid it open. Sallie's two men slipped in the room. They motioned with their hands to Earl, who made sure the window was closed again. The room was pitch black save for the light from outside, but the three of them seemed sure of their movements.

One of Sallie's men stepped over to the closet and took out a paper bag stashed in its corner. He took out a roll of adhesive tape and some thin, tightly wound rope. He pulled out a five-inch strip of tape and ripped it from the roll. Flipping the cord to his partner, he gave the sign to Earl. Earl went over to Big Juice and jostled him lightly. The big pitcher grunted and rolled over. With that the first man moved in and slapped the tape over Big Juice's mouth. Big Juice jumped with surprise and swung out his arms, but the second man grabbed them by the wrists and in a quick move that took the semiconscious pitcher unaware, the man flipped him over in the bed and tied the cord quickly around his wrists. The third man pulled the covers down and did the same to Big Juice's struggling feet. In a minute he was completely bound and gagged, and he squirmed and fought against his ropes like a fish caught in a net. Earl pressed down on his shoulders and whispered loudly into his ear.

"Cool down, Juice! You coming with us."

Earl scrambled out of the window and waited for the two others to lift Big Juice out to him. The pitcher had only his T-shirt and a pair of green boxer shorts on, so Earl grabbed a pair of pants and a shirt. Like a special-delivery package, they lifted the squirming Big Juice out the window to Earl on the fire escape, who held him until the two others could carry him down the rest of the way. Big Juice tried to bang his hips and legs against the railings of the escape but stopped when one of the men kicked him solidly in the small of the back. Once they were down, the door of the car opened and Big Juice was pushed into the back seat. Earl winked to no one but himself at the landing and slipped back inside the room.

He went into the closet again and took out a second bag. Waiting until the two men made it up to the window, he fidgeted in his pockets and found a toothpick. It was that time again, and he jammed it into his teeth, stinging the gums. In his back pocket he felt for his homemade pick. Everything in place.

The three of them edged along the escape until they reached a window three over from Earl's. The room, like all the rest at this time of the night, was completely dark. Earl slowly pushed up the window, which gave without resistance. The two windows had been opened and their frames soaped two days before while the Stars played over at Franklin Park and Lonnie Buttons napped in the lobby below. Earl crept stealthily inside, eying the dark shadows of the room where Mungo and Leon slept in their beds. Once inside, he paused and waited for the silence to take hold. He listened for either Mungo or Leon to stir, but heard not a sound from either of them. He motioned for one of the other two to come inside. The man slowly and awkwardly stepped through the sill, knocked his head on the frame, stopped short, then came all the way in. To Earl, he had made enough noise for three men. The second man soon followed, and the three of them crouched together for an instant. They let their eyes condition themselves to the room's darkness. Then Earl motioned the others over to Leon's bed.

Sallie's men closed in, one at the head of the bed with a strip of tape ready, one at the foot with a piece of rope. Earl tensed himself, pulling out his ice pick and readying his right hand for a clamp over Mungo's mouth should he jump awake. The two men inched closer to Leon's bed, not making a sound, ready to pounce.

Then they stopped. A nervous silence followed, and one of the men turned quickly back to Earl. "He's gone. He ain't in the bed," he whispered hoarsely. Earl slipped over and ran a hand over the sheets. They were rumpled but empty. Earl paused for a moment to try to figure out what had gone wrong. He got to his feet and bumped the first man's elbow. The ice pick fell from his hand and bumped on the wooden floor. It squibbed crazily under the bed.

"Shit!" Earl hissed in a half whisper. He hit his knees and reached blindly under the bed.

"Who's there?" came a voice from the bathroom.

The two men froze. Then one reached for his revolver. Earl scrambled under the bed.

"Who's out there?" the voice said again in a low growl.

It was Leon, sitting on the toilet seat in the dark, rubbing his arm with cubes from a bucket of ice at his feet. He hadn't slept all night.

He got to his feet and poked his head out of the bathroom door. The two saw his silhouette, exchanged glances, and stumbled backward for the window.

"Hey, what the hell!" Leon bellowed.

Mungo turned over hurriedly in his bed. He sat up and clunked his elbow soundly against the wall. The two turned toward him, one of them pointing the gun. Leon came toward them from the bathroom.

"Leon, what's coming—" Mungo blurted.

"Hold it, mother, just hold it now," the man with the gun said. "You get hurt if you come closer!"

The two of them braced themselves with their backs to the window. Mungo froze against the bed's head bar. Leon leaned up against the wall, still in plain view of the two.

"If you is thieves we ain't got nothing," Leon finally said. "Get the hell out where you come in."

The two stood for a second, breathing quickly. "We give the orders—" one of them started, when Mungo suddenly leaped from his bed headlong into the man's outstretched gun. He hit with his full force and knocked it to the floor, at the same time pulling the man down on top of him. They hit the floor with a loud thunk and struggled with each other. The second man quickly turned and lunged out the window. He slammed his back into the sill as he scrambled through it and brought the window crashing down. Once outside, he stumbled down the fire escape like an elephant, shaking the iron against the building with a racket that reverberated through the rear wall. The Stars in the other rooms bounded out of their beds at the noise.

Back in the room, Leon dove on top of Mungo and joined in the swirling of arms and legs. Mungo caught a hard knee in the jaw and fell backward against his bed. Earl slid farther under Leon's bed, determined to stay out of sight. Out in the hall Isaac and Splinter Tommy banged on the door; finally they lunged against it and stumbled into the room. Leon couldn't keep the man from scrambling over to his revolver. He was about to put his hand on it when Mungo spotted him and went headfirst after it once agai . He got there just ahead of the beefy hand of the man and flipped the gun up to Splinter Tommy just as he would to start the first leg of a double play. Tommy instantly pivoted and tossed it underhand to Isaac, who lifted the cover of the toilet and dropped it in. Then they hustled on top of the scuffle and pinned the intruder. They rolled him over on his back and Splinter Tommy and Isaac sat on him.

Just then Bingo came running into the room with Raymond hobbling behind him and Fat Sam Popper and Esquire Joe bringing up the rear.

"What's happening! What's happening!" Bingo shouted.

"Got a man what's been trying to break in the room," said Mungo. "The other one got away out that window there!"

Bingo lifted the frame and leaned out but the alley was dark.

"Hey!" Fat Sam yelled out. "That boy one of Sallie's. He sure is!"

"Goddamn," Bingo said and lifted up the man's head by his hair. He grunted with pain. "What you doing in here?" Bingo shouted in his face.

"Nothing—ain't doing nothing," the man mumbled. He could hardly draw his breath because of Splinter Tommy's and Isaac's weight.

By this time the rest of the Stars had stumbled into the room, some of them in pajamas, most in their underwear.

"Shit, if he's Sallie's boy that mean Sallie's around here somewhere," Isaac said.

"Yeah, sir, and this boy is hot for a chase to skin the fat man's balls once and for good," Bingo said. The rest of the Stars nodded with him.

"I got the car running already," said Esquire Joe.

"Get your pants on and open the doors," said Bingo with a grin on his face. The team spread out down the halls back to their rooms. Mungo and Leon stayed behind and tied up their guest with his own rope. As they worked Earl lay huddled against the wall popping the toothpick into his gums.

Mungo and Leon finished tying and gagging the man and lifted him into the bathroom and into the tub. They were about to hurry off with Bingo when Raymond yelled down the hallway.

"Earl and Big Juice is both gone!"

"They must a been took!" Bingo said and motioned for Raymond to hurry on. He and the Stars pedaled down the stairs for the Lincoln.

Earl heard them go, popped his head from under the bed to check things out, and scrambled for the window. He raced down the escape, hardly touching the steps. He reached the alley at the same time the Stars hit the street out front.

"Where's the other car?" yelled Raymond when he spotted the empty parking spot behind the Lincoln.

Earl bounded down the alley and turned into a loading dock. He had moved the team's second car, a De Soto, in case he needed it.

"Shit! Where in hell—" said Raymond. He stopped short with Donus and Mungo while the others piled into the Lincoln.

"They must a stole our other car, Bingo!" Raymond said.

Earl slid into the front seat of the De Soto, turned the key he had left in the ignition, and screeched out and away. He kept his headlights off, and in the dark of the night he was nothing but a blur. He turned left away from the Hammond and stepped on it. The toothpick was in bits in his mouth, one part wedged between two molars, the gums shiny red with blood.

"Fuck the other car," yelled Bingo as the Lincoln lurched ahead. Raymond made a leap for the side, grabbed onto it, and swung his cast inside. Mungo and Donus followed him and the Lincoln flew off.

"Where we going?" shouted Esquire Joe.

"The hotel—hit Sallie's hotel!" Bingo yelled back.

"Where's that?"

"Turn left!" yelled Bingo, and Esquire Joe jerked the Lincoln across an intersection, leaning like an overloaded truck, and down a cross street.

"Yeah, where you going, Bingo?" said Leon.

Bingo shrugged his shoulders and with a big empty look on his face yelled back, "Don't know, Leon."

The Lincoln roared on for two more blocks.

"Try the Franklin Elite, how about that," Leon finally said. "The bosses always stay with the bosses."

"Yeah, hit it down there," said Bingo.

Esquire Joe looked at him excitedly, waiting for directions.

"Turn here," yelled Bingo, and Esquire Joe whipped the wheel and they turned.

The Lincoln sailed on past three blocks, took a left, and Esquire Joe sat on it down a main street. Bingo punched him in the ribs to slow him down. Esquire Joe exhaled with the blow and dropped the speed quickly down below the limit. In five minutes they neared the Franklin Elite.

Then they spotted it.

Sallie's car was parked out front. The boss himself and his

bagman stood on the street in front of it. They were talking into the chest of a Kansas City policeman.

Esquire Joe pulled the Lincoln up short a half block away. For a second they watched.

"Goddamn—the law got him first," said Mungo.

"Look at him fry," Bingo crowed. "Look at the cigar pop up and down like he was choking on it."

"He got to be. That policeman knows he ain't clean," said Mungo.

They watched awhile longer, when Leon spoke up.

"Shit. We watching him get away from us."

"Huh?" said Bingo. Then it hit him. "Yeah. Hot damn, we got to get to the fat man. Ain't going to let no po-liceman take the fun. Hit it over, Joe."

The Lincoln drove up next to Sallie and the officer. Bingo and the Stars piled out on the street.

"What all you boys doing here?" the officer said, turning to Bingo. He had his hat pushed back on his head and a red ring ran around his forehead.

"Just looking for our boss here, boss," said Bingo.

"At three in the morning?"

"Sure enough, we was worried," said Bingo. "You just let him go with us, Mr. Police, and we'll keep him home."

"He's got a citation coming for the way he was traveling," said the officer.

"Just happy because we won the games today, officer," said Bingo. "We play them Monarchs, you know, and this here boy is our boss. You got it?"

The cop wiped his forehead with his handkerchief. "You that colored team, play down by the yards? That you?"

"You got it." Bingo grinned. "And our bossman here just got his head in the dithers. He so happy about it."

"Yeah, shit," the officer said. He looked up at the Franklin Elite. "You boys staying here?"

"You got it one more time, chief," said Bingo. The Stars standing behind him shook their heads in agreement.

Sallie and his man stood on the other side of the car. Sallie bit the soggy end of his cigar and fumed. Finally he spoke up.

"Look, Mr. Officer, you just let me go on my way and cut this talk with these guys. I weren't doing nothing," he said.

"Swallow it, boy," the officer said. "Or I'll take you in."

Bingo smiled. "He needed that, Mr. Policeman. Yessir, you done said the right thing for him."

The officer exhaled loudly. "Look, I got to get some food now and I ain't got time to jaw like you coloreds got. So you take the fat boy and his friend with you and get the hell off the street."

Bingo shook his head up and down. "You got us, boss. We don't give you no trouble on that."

"Yeah, just get the hell to bed, why don't you," the officer said.

He ambled slowly back to his car, turning his head to the Stars with a look of resignation. Bingo and the rest looked back at him with wide-eyed, pleased faces.

"You have a good night now, Mr. Officer, and we'll be talking to you," Bingo said as the policeman drove away.

Sallie and his man moved for their car. Bingo and Isaac stepped in front of Sallie; Splinter Tommy, Donus, and Leon met the other. A slow grin oozed over Bingo's face. Then Mungo interrupted.

"Right here in the back seat," Mungo yelled out as he opened the door to Sallie's car. He pulled Big Juice up for the rest of the team to see. "Our man here tied up like he was in the post office."

Big Juice shook his head and muffled a cry from under the tape. Mungo ripped the tape from his face. Big Juice spat on the pavement.

"Shit! I'll kill him! I'll split him up," he cursed at Sallie. He struggled viciously with his bindings. "Get me out, Mungo! C'mon!"

222

"Cool down now, Big Juice. We all going to take care of the bossman. All together like friends," Bingo said. He flicked a piece of lint from Sallie's shoulder and smoothed the fat man's lapels. Sallie eyed him coolly but didn't say a word.

"No Earl?" Bingo asked Mungo.

"Earl? Shit!" hissed Big Juice as Mungo untied him. "That mother the cat that let these assholes in the room! He in charge here!"

"Knew it—damn! I knew it," said Isaac. "A thug is a thug. Knew it when he joined us, Bingo. No good."

"Where's he now?" said Leon. He looked at Big Juice, then at Sallie.

"Seen him last putting me out the window," said Big Juice. "I'll kill him too, you watch."

Bingo laughed out loud and clapped his hands. "Can you take that fool! Can you take him?" he cackled.

"Three shots at where he is right now," said Isaac.

"Long gone," said Bingo. "Ooo-wah, he's long gone."

With a look from Leon, Bingo ushered Sallie into his car, took the wheel himself. The rest of the Stars split up in the two cars and headed back for the Hammond. As they parked, the first rays of the sun shot out over the trees. Six in the morning. They trouped past the night clerk, who slept under a newspaper at the desk. Sallie and his man marched out of the pack like convicts being pushed to the chair. In Leon's room, Bingo sat on a chair while Leon locked the door; the Stars stood around Sallie and his man in the center of the room. They could hear the dull kicking noises from the man tied in the bathtub.

Bingo looked up at Sallie and motioned to Mungo. Mungo stepped around and jerked the cigar out of the owner's mouth. Sallie's lips popped shut.

"What we going to do with you, Sallie?" Bingo said. "First you try to scare my boys, then you try to buy them, then you just up and take them. And if we hadn't stepped in while you had your pants down with that policeman you'd be in the jug now trying to explain what Big Juice was doing in your back seat looking like some damn mummy. Then you got Earl to working for you and he's cool so when things mess up he ain't around and we ain't never going to see that cat again. Done took our car too."

Leon sat down on the bed. "Figure all of us got a hunk coming out of you, boss," he said.

"Yeah, that's it. We'll just let Big Juice take you in the bathroom with him and he'll pay you back for all of us."

"Okay, Bingo, all of you—" Sallie began.

"We ain't told you you could talk," Bingo interrupted. Then he smiled and sat back. "But go ahead. My ears is anxious."

"I got friends around," Sallie said. "I got people who look out for me if I ain't around. People who got money, you know that."

"You ain't got shit, Sallie," Leon boomed. "You standing in front of us with your nuts in the cooker."

"Just a matter of how done we wants them," said Bingo.

Sallie put his hands on his hips and looked up at the ceiling.

Leon motioned to Bingo. "C'mon into the other room, Bingo."

They went into Isaac's room with Raymond and Fat Sam and Donus.

"What you want out of him, Bingo?" said Leon. "We got to figure out things."

They talked it over for a few minutes. Raymond threw in a few figures and Leon warned Bingo about getting the law into it. Then they went back to Leon's room, where Sallie was getting razzed by Mungo. Mungo did a perfect imitation of how Sallie had baited him three nights before. The Stars ate it up.

"We figure you was out to bust us, Sallie," Bingo started in. "Leave us out here with a team and one car while you got fat with the boys back in Louisville. You really think they would a played for you after all this? Shit, you been figuring for years that cats is just dying to play for you. Yeah, that's it. And now you here standing there looking dumb."

224

"I ain't going to let you rile me, Bingo," Sallie answered. "My boys messed up and you got lucky. So that's that and now we call it even and we don't mess no more."

"You ain't learned yet, Sallie," Bingo answered. "I ought to let Big Juice have you for what you just said."

He looked over at Big Juice. The pitcher was leaning against the wall with his eyes half closed.

"Hey, Juice," Bingo yelled to him. "What was you thinking when you was tied up in that car?"

Big Juice jerked his head up. "I'll kill him. Do it right now. Split him up to down."

"C'mon, Bingo, cut the trash and get me out of here," Sallie said. "I go back east and never see you and the boys again. I'll give you that."

Bingo looked to the doorway. "You got it yet, Raymond?"

Raymond came over with a sheet of paper in his hand. He gave it to Bingo with a pen. He looked at Sallie.

"You can sign with the same writing pen the boys used to sign my cast here, boss," Raymond said. "You remember the foot I broke, huh, boss?"

Bingo held the paper out for Sallie. He handed him the pen.

"Sign your name to this here. Every part of it and then put in 'I agree' in back of it," Bingo said.

"What the hell," said Sallie. He read the paper.

"Just something to help us for all our trouble, Sallie," Bingo said. "A little deal for you."

"I got to have the car! It's my car, dammit," said Sallie. He grabbed the paper and let it sail to the floor.

"Was your car," said Bingo. "Big Juice. Get here to see that the fat man signs this thing. And put a smile on your face when you does it."

Mungo held the paper up to Sallie. He scribbled his name across the bottom.

"And 'I agree' goes in there too," Bingo demanded. "Lawyer told me if you got that in there it's for keeps."

Sallie slashed at the paper. Mungo handed it to Bingo and Bingo blew lightly over the signature.

"You done it sweet, Sallie. I knows you would." Bingo grinned.

Then he motioned to Mungo and Splinter Tommy and they grabbed Sallie and his man and began ripping their clothes off. They stripped Sallie down to his white boxer shorts. The fat owner cursed and threatened Bingo as they worked him over, and Mungo got out the rope. With a strip of tape to shut him up, and the lengths of rope tied securely around his hands and feet, Sallie writhed on the floor like a walrus. The Stars stood around laughing and pointing. Mungo stooped over Sallie and tickled him in the ribs. The fat man shook and flopped and turned livid with rage.

Ten minutes later they picked up Sallie by his hands and feet and put him in the tub with his two friends. The three of them lay there packed together and looking like a great bowl of pudding.

"Ain't that three fools in the tub for you," said Bingo.

Then Mungo finished off the celebration by turning on the cold water. In no time the three were up to their necks. When the Stars stopped laughing they slowly filed out of the bathroom. Raymond returned a moment later. He waved one of Sallie's cigars he had taken from the owner's coat pocket in front of Sallie's face. Raymond smiled slightly, put the cigar lengthwise between his fingers, and slowly broke it in two. Then he left. The only sound in the room was the methodical dripping from the tap into the tub.

They stood in Bingo's room wondering if they should hit the sack or the road. Kansas City was behind them as far as the Monarchs were concerned. The road west was wide and empty, with plenty of teams ready to take them on for one last time before fall harvest, when there would be no time for ball. Bingo checked his watch. Seven o'clock in the morning. His eyes were wide open though he was tired from sleeping only half the night. The rest of the players stared at him with tired but wide eyes.

"I say we get that car Sallie just signed over to us gassed up and head on out," Raymond suggested. "Get us a good start."

"Take me couple of hours to fall back to sleep anyway," Bingo said. "How about you boys?"

Fat Sam, who was napping in a chair, and Big Juice, who was sore from his hour and a half in ropes, wanted to stay and sleep until noon. The rest of the Stars decided to pack up and take off.

"I got us a breakfast about an hour out," Leon said. And with that they began to get things together.

It took thirty minutes of riding in the Lincoln and Sallie's Oldsmobile before they began to doze off. The lulling vibrations and bumps were still ingrained into their joints, despite the four-day respite on soft, stationary hotel beds, and one by one the Stars leaned their heads against a window or an armrest and slept. Esquire Joe and Splinter Tommy, the new driver in Earl's place, aimed the cars down a two-lane blacktop road into the Kansas farmlands. No one said anything about Earl or the car. They knew he was probably traveling in the other direction for Chicago or back to Detroit. They left what they couldn't use of his belongings with Lonnie Buttons at the Hammond.

After a little more than an hour on the road Leon told Esquire Joe to watch for his diner. A few minutes later they pulled in by a small white frame building which had a leaning and faded Phillips 66 sign out front. Leon got out and walked over to the front door. He wiped a circle of dust from the window and looked in. Moments later he came back to the Lincoln.

"Must a closed up for good," he said slowly. "Nothing in there but dust."

Bingo leaned up to look out at Leon.

"Mean this is your place?"

"Was," Leon replied.

He slammed his door and Esquire Joe pulled out onto the road.

By nine o'clock Fat Sam awoke and complained that he was hungry. Donus added similar sentiments, then Isaac, and finally Mungo. Bingo turned and glared at them.

"What ain't in your stomachs ain't in mine too," he shot back.

The five of them looked on down the narrow, flat road and tasted the sourness in their mouths. They were hot and hungry again.

Chapter 16

He awoke that morning thinking about it, flexing it, gently touching the muscles to see if he could feel anything different, something sore or pulled. But there was nothing. The arm wasn't tight, nor particularly loose or agile, nothing felt strained or twisted in any movement, and that bothered him. Since they had left Kansas City he knew something was wrong, but the arm wouldn't tell him what. It worried him when his arm didn't respond, didn't go through its usual aches and then return to him. Since they had moved on into Kansas, four days away from the Monarchs, three uneventful games with semipro teams, the arm hadn't been there. It hung like a side of beef in a butcher's cooler despite hot packs, liniment, and massages. When he picked up a ball to throw to Bingo or Fat Sam, there was no sharp twinge or deep grating in the shoulder, there was no distinctive pain whatsoever, only a motion and follow-through that produced no more than a soft toss as gentle as that of an umpire throwing out an old ball to the bat boy.

Leon didn't say anything about it; he didn't fret or rant at the arm. He simply went through the motions. He worked out with the team, played his right field, traveled and slept at hour-long intervals, then awoke the following morning and wondered if it had come back. He went through his ritual of flexing and massaging it—perhaps he could feel if it had recovered—and he dressed and went through the day's routine with the team. He had known every kind of sore arm in the book in twenty-five years of pitching. His arm had been so sore that he bit his lip with the pain, didn't sleep as he hadn't the night following the doubleheader in Kansas City, but then it had smoothed itself out and come back as strong as ever. In the last ten years, with the Ebony Aces and the winter touring teams, he had pitched once every three days, more if he was needed, and the arm came through as if it had a mind of its own and would go about throwing strikes whether or not he was in the mood. It had always come back; balked some, shot some pain to the bone to let Leon know what it thought, but it had always come back.

In Topeka they played two close games with the Owls, a white team that traveled around the state and learned its black ball from a pair of three-game series with the Monarchs. Leon passed up both games, preferring to roam right field, communicating such to Bingo with a shake of his head. In the hotel that night, the first one they'd stayed in since the Hammond, Leon called Bingo aside and the two of them talked in Leon's room.

"Bet you thinking we got to find out what happened to Sallie, huh, Leon?" Bingo said as he draped himself over a creaking wicker lounge chair in the corner.

"That ain't it," Leon said. He put one foot on the bed and leaned on his upright knee. He was wearing just a T-shirt and the pleated pants from his everyday black driving suit.

"So what you got for me?" Bingo said to him.

"One thing, Bingo. And you got to know it first," he said. He stared right at his catcher as if he were ready to pitch to him. "I'm going home. Going to leave the team."

"What you mean?" Bingo said.

"You heard it right."

"What now? We going good, got money and plenty of games. . . ." Bingo sat up straight in the chair.

"That ain't it. I ain't got no complaints about the team."

"What then?"

"My arm is done. Arm is just done. That's all there is to say."

"C'mon now, Leon, that wing of yours got more in it than both of us got."

"No more. Last four days since K.C. I been bringing it along, thinking nothing was different. But it's gone. Can't do no more than lift a satchel."

"It'll come back, always comes back. Ain't no such thing as a arm just dying," Bingo said. Then the expression sunk from his face. "What you saying, Leon?"

"I know this time. She won't come back for cold or hot or oil or rubs. Don't hurt, don't ache, just nothing. Like it was asleep."

"There you got it. The arm is sleeping like mine does sometimes. Takes days, sometimes two weeks before they come back smiling and saying, 'Bingo, we going to work for you some more like always.'"

"Yeah, Bingo, but that ain't it. This time it's gone. I know it and just today got the guts to tell myself. Been telling myself lies all week."

"How come you so sure?"

"Shit, I been living with this thing for twenty-five years. Waking up every morning and listening to what it tells me like we was two persons. And what it been saying so far is plain to me like when we saw that bone sticking out of Raymond's foot."

Bingo stood up and walked over to the window. He flipped up the shade and stared out without seeing anything. Then he turned and snapped at Leon. "Can't leave. We got to have you."

"Got to leave. Going to."

"Why?"

"Shit."

"Yeah, why? Why you got to leave the team?"

Leon made a face. "What else is I going to do?"

"Ain't no trouble there, Leon. Lots of things you can be doing besides pitching."

"Just hold that—"

"No. Leon, I got it now. You just be sticking with us and keeping your name on our papers like always and ain't nothing going to be different. We going to have Louis back here just a while and get things cooking. All you got to do is dress up in your uniform and let Esquire Joe say, 'There he is, Leon Carter, the greatest pitcher the world ever saw,' and let us boys do the rest. That's it, Leon, that's it."

"And the Monarchs and the Bays and the Colored Giants and all them teams going to lay down like they was a bowl of grits while we blow by?"

"Shit, I ain't worried about them teams, Leon. I is talking about these here touring teams we play. They just wants to see you; they don't have to get beat by you."

"I see what you thinking about, Bingo. But you is talking to the wrong man—"

"C'mon now, Leon," Bingo interrupted.

"Listen here now. I said I was going home and I got to mean it. I ain't going to stick around and be no Pink Meat Purvins for you that you can point to and say, 'Look, he's the man, folks, you just throw in your nickels and dimes now and keep him going.' I ain't going to slide with you boys with a dead arm and fool the folks by saying I thrown yesterday or just giving them some warm-ups or what you think they want."

"Won't be like that, Leon. We won't be using you for the clown. We just be showing you off like we advertise on them papers so the people won't think they being cheated. We could hook on with some damn preacher like that Father Divine or we could get us a white team to travel with us and work some routines. We could get us some clowns or them animals and have us a traveling show, get us a band, man, we'd be running five miles down the road and the people still wouldn't see the end of us. Think of them possibilities."

Bingo pounded his fist into his palm with every new thought, his voice thumping out the words.

232

Leon nodded his head slowly back and forth until Bingo stopped.

"Hold it now, Bingo."

Leon looked directly into Bingo's eyes. Bingo didn't try to avoid him. He saw the rings of sweat growing beneath the pitcher's collarbone. He remained silent and put his hands limply into his pockets.

"It's the choice I got to make," Leon went on. "I been getting by all these years on what my arm does for me and now that it's quit I can't be playing it for a fool.

"We been playing this game all our lives, Bingo. Hustling and scrambling for every little bit of meat been dangled out front of our noses. If we got a chance to see a base with just a slice of daylight we slip through that sliver and take the base if it takes us a goddamn broken finger or a cut leg to get it. 'Cause if we don't, you know there's some fool out there dying to take it from us because he ain't had a meal since week before last.

"Twenty-five years since I first picked up a crab apple and threw it at my little brother I been going like that. Now I ain't got it no more. And you can't expect an old man like me to fake it. Can't expect me to smile like them stage boys with their big white grins just to fool the folks."

Bingo didn't interrupt him. He turned and paced across the room, shaking his head and pushing his hands in and out of his pants pockets.

"Got to think of something, got to get something up," he murmured.

Leon moved his leg from the bed and sat down on it. "Anyway, I been thinking about the woman and the kids and how it's high time I get back there and do some fathering."

"Best fathering you can do is to keep sending back that money," Bingo said. "Like you been doing."

"Wouldn't work, Bingo, any way you cut it. You ain't the one that's got to be living with me and I is. My arm been my life,

Bingo. When I ain't got that I ain't alive. You can't be telling me to fake it out."

Leon stopped short. The room seemed to echo with the words, then fell silent in the void of Bingo's pacing, the rhythmic thumping of his fist into his palm. He looked up at Leon.

"You just want to hop a train on out?"

"Yeah."

"Just right off without hanging on for a while to try things out?"

"Yeah."

"Got your mind made up, don't you?"

"Set on it, Bingo."

Bingo stopped in the middle of the room and put his hands on his hips.

"You is an old-country son-of-a-bitch, Leon."

"You got it, boss," Leon said. He eyed the slow smile on Bingo's face and returned it with one of his own.

Then Bingo's face went sour. "But what in hell we going to do now?" He scowled. "Goddamn, just get started good and now this. Beats my ass."

Leon looked up at him without having anything to offer. And unconsciously, his arm twitched.

Leon wanted to slip away, quietly, without an elaborate farewell. He would tell the team what had happened to his arm because he said he owed them that much, but he would do so in small, unceremonious meetings with two or three Stars at a time. He had nothing to hide, nothing to leave out from what he had told Bingo. Then he would pack his satchel and get on a bus for the trip back to Louisville. The team would keep on, through Kansas and wherever they planned on going, only with another space open in the back seat, and a little more leg room.

Bingo racked his brain back in his hotel room. Without Leon he would be down to nine men and Raymond. His pitchers would have to throw almost every other day unless he got help. The only man on the bench would be wearing a cast. He tossed down the last of a bottle of Old Fitzgerald he had picked up that afternoon. His watch read 2 A.M. He paced slowly around the room, scratching himself through a yellowed T-shirt that had been soaked with sweat earlier in the night but now had dried. Raymond sat on Bingo's bed flipping through his records notebook, pushing a snub-nosed pencil into a page then stopping to check his figures. He was the only Star Bingo had talked to about Leon.

"What you got in mind for Leon's going home pay?" Raymond said.

"Shit! How I supposed to figure that when I can't even think of ways to get us some goddamn players," Bingo snapped.

"Going to give him anything?"

"What you mean! Course I got something in mind!"

"How much?"

Bingo sat down in the room's lone chair. "Give me time on that."

Raymond worked some figures for a minute then looked over to Bingo. "Figure we can pay him out for what he played this month. Up to you on what you want on top of that."

"You think we could land us some boys from Franklin in K.C., huh, Raymond? I mean I got to be thinking about that before I'm thinking on how to make Leon rich."

"Yeah, sure," Raymond answered. He bit the end of the pencil and let out a long, slow breath. "I been thinking, that's all."

"On what?"

"Just remembering how you all jumped up for me when Sallie put me on that bus when my foot got broke."

"Son-of-a-bitch." Bingo scowled. He sat up and looked angrily at Raymond. "Thinking I'm up to do some Sallie shit after all I been through for this team. Son-of-a-bitch."

"Hang on to yourself, Bingo. I ain't making no accusings on

you. I just bringing things up so you remember how things can fall when they fall. You wearing different shoes now than you was wearing back home."

"Yeah, Raymond, goddamn it. I knows what shoes I is wearing and who's still running things. Don't need you to keep me from messing up."

"Just bringing things up, Bingo. Can't let you be forgetting them figures," he said. He looked at the notebook, pretending not to notice Bingo's cold stare.

The Stars sat around the lobby of the hotel the next morning saying little, engaging in short, unstimulating conversations that started slowly, then ended. Isaac tried to read a newspaper but brushed the pages past his face without paying much attention. Leon's bus would be by at ten to take him to Kansas City, where he would hop a train back to Louisville. Some of the Stars had lingered earlier with Leon, questioning him about his arm, trying to talk out their surprise and shock over learning of his abrupt departure. Bingo settled with him on money after only a few minutes. Leon said he didn't want but what he had coming in salary; the rest, he said, could be put back into the tour. Before Bingo gave Raymond the word, Raymond had an envelope ready. Raymond had settled with Leon the night before after filling him in on how the team stood.

Bingo shuttled from a chair to the telephone. He had been trying to get in touch with A. C. Franklin all morning. "If A.C. got some stringers laying somewhere that ain't signed no papers with him we in luck," Bingo said to Raymond.

"Why not some Monarchs?" Raymond said.

"Jesus! Franklin would want my ass for his own boys. Right here in his country he got his people tied up by the balls."

"All the good owners do," Raymond said and he added a quick smile when he saw one of Bingo's scowls on its way.

"First we lose Louis because of some damn thing. Then that asshole Earl Sibley runs off like a thief—"

"That's what he was," Raymond broke in.

"Now this thing happens to Leon. And I never thought that man would lose his wing like that."

Bingo got up to try another call to Kansas City. He stepped over Raymond's outstretched foot and Raymond jerked the cast out of the way. "Get that damn thing healed up," Bingo barked.

A short time later Leon came down the steps with Fat Sam Popper and Esquire Joe. The three of them walked over to Bingo's chair and waited for him to get off the phone.

"Sit yourself down, Bingo. We got something to lay on you," Leon said.

Bingo looked at him strangely and slid slowly into the chair, his eyes raised in suspicion. "Yeah, so what in hell is coming off now?"

Leon looked at Fat Sam, who stood next to him. Esquire Joe stood at their shoulders a step back. Joe bobbed his head, looking first at the scowling Bingo then down at his shoes. He waited for Leon or Fat Sam to break the ice.

"Got some news from back east about Joe here," Fat Sam said. He smiled and nodded back at Joe.

"Yeah, yeah, so what's the news?" Bingo answered impatiently.

Fat Sam looked at Leon to give him the floor.

"The boy gone and got papers to sign. Got him a good offer," Leon said.

"Offer! What in hell! He playing for me. Who's making offers?" Bingo shouted. "Who I got to tell that boy ain't for sale?"

Bingo's shouts drew the rest of the team around the four of them. They crowded in on Esquire Joe and Leon, forming an impromptu team meeting. Esquire Joe eyed the rest of the Stars self-consciously; he rubbed the back of his neck.

"You got to tell the white leagues," Leon answered.

"Huh?" Bingo said and sat up straight in his chair.

"You got it, Bingo. Esquire here been asked to sign on with the Canton Reds—that minor-league team. Plain as you is sitting there," Leon said. He plopped his arm around Esquire Joe's shoulders.

"Holy damn, you telling lies?" Isaac hollered. "That the honest-to-God truth?"

The rest of the Stars followed, jabbering questions and pumping Leon for the straight story. Esquire Joe stood in the middle of the confusion, shaking his head, not knowing exactly how to react.

Bingo stood up and pushed his way through to Leon. "Can't be true! First your arm goes and now this on top. This all smells like shit, Leon. Pile of shit!"

"Calm it all down and let me talk," Leon said, raising his hands into the air like a preacher. The Stars finally muffled themselves. "Now give it to them like you did me, Sam."

Fat Sam cleared his throat. "It was me the one who got the call. First thing we got into Topeka, coming long-distance from Pittsburgh and from Mr. Foster."

"Lionel!" Bingo shouted. "Goddamn Lionel!"

"And he says, 'Sam, I got something in the fire for Joe Calloway.' Something he say he been working on for a good while. And I says, 'What you got up, Mr. Foster?' and he say, 'Don't know all the details, Sam. But looks like them white owners up there is ready to crack.' And he don't say no more except for me not to tell nobody, not even Esquire, and he would get back in touch. So he does just yesterday and he say he done it. He gone and made a deal with this Canton team who tell him they got contracts with the big leagues. All done up with the ink dried on the papers."

"That's shit. He giving you shit, Sam," Bingo argued. "Ain't no big-league team around ever going to sign colored for no money. I know that for sure."

"That's what I told him, Bingo. But Mr. Foster he say they been dickering with them for a long while just looking for the right time. And Mr. Foster say Esquire Joe just the right boy for them," Sam said.

238

"Don't believe one word of it. Not one," Bingo answered.

"Well, he say to get Esquire on a bus back to Pittsburgh 'cause he want to get things set for Esquire to play with some winter team. And he say do it quick," Sam said.

A short silence hung over the team. Then Mungo turned to Esquire Joe and punched him in the arm. "You mean the kid here, the white teams is going to take the kid?" Mungo squealed. And the Stars crowded in on Esquire and good-naturedly jostled him about. Esquire Joe uncovered a wide, nervous smile which betrayed his enthusiasm, as if he had just hit a game-winning home run and was being greeted at home plate.

"Don't know what there is to make a damn celebration about." Bingo scowled. "It's shit as far as I see it."

He pushed his way through the Stars and over to the phone. "Got to make me some calls and find out what in hell's going on."

He screamed at the operator through the thin, round table phone. Then he waited, drumming his fist on the counter of the reservation desk. "C'mon, c'mon," he mumbled.

The Stars remained grouped around Fat Sam and Esquire Joe, pumping them for more details. Then Bingo walked over to them.

"Ain't no one at the Chop House. No one around to pick up the phone," he fumed to Leon.

"What you going to say if Lionel do answer?" said Leon.

"Leave that to me," Bingo said. "Up until then ain't nobody going nowhere to join no damn white-league outfit."

"Could be wrong about that," Leon said slowly.

"Don't count on it," Bingo said.

"Ain't never seen you talk to yourself so hard," Leon said as Bingo stared straight out into the hotel's lobby.

"You ain't never seen my team being cut up so fast either," Bingo retorted quickly. "And you ain't no damn help."

"Shit, be glad for the kid," Leon said. "If those boys think the

239

big leagues is finally signing up colored, then who could you better like to see go first but Joe?"

"I don't have to be glad about nothing. You know they been talking for years and nothing come of it," Bingo said. He got up and went to the phone again. "I know who I'll call. I'll ring up Louis back home. He'll be on to this."

He connected himself with Chessie Joy's place and left word for Louis to call him when he came in. Chessie told Bingo that he wouldn't have to wait long because Louis hung out in his place daily while he mended. Bingo hadn't hung up but ten minutes when Louis returned the call.

"Been trying to catch you, Bingo, for two days now," Louis yelled over the phone. "What in hell you doing in Topeka?"

"Never you mind, Louis. Just fill me in on what's happening with Lionel," Bingo thundered. He pressed the receiver against his ear.

"Just what I going to do, Bingo. Man, things is jumping here, what with Lionel setting things up."

"What he doing?"

"Man, he got through to them white owners. Got us some contracts. Ain't he told you? He signed me and Joe Calloway with the Canton Reds. The minor leagues. Done it last Thursday," Louis said.

"You too, Louis? You signed with the minor leagues, you sure?" Bingo said. Again he drew a crowd as he talked. Leon and Isaac walked over to the phone, followed by Sam and Esquire Joe.

"I thought Lionel worked this all out with you, Bingo. He told me things was all straight between you two. He been working on this thing for a month, he told me. Said me and Joe was just the boys to sign because we so young and got lots of time to break in, if the big leagues come around," Louis said.

Bingo didn't answer.

"You still with me, Bingo, huh? Lionel he told me them owners been playing with him for years just waiting for the right time to sign us up. Said he could made himself a bundle could he signed you and Leon up when you was still young. That's what he said, Bingo. I ain't lying."

Bingo spat into the phone. "Good thing you ain't here, Louis. I'd kick your ass across the room."

"Have a hard time, boss. I is fat and lazy from sitting around with these damn wrappings on me."

Bingo didn't hear him. "Going to kick some Lionel ass when I catches up with him. . . ."

Bingo kept the receiver to his ear but didn't hear Louis ramble on, then he hung up.

"Louis too, huh, Bingo?" Leon said.

"Can't believe it," Bingo said. "Been fighting Sallie all these times and trying to keep everything going so we can make some money and burn Sallie's ass in the meantime. And then who do I find out been working behind my back all these times? Goddamn Lionel Foster. Big sugar daddy. He say, 'Yeah, Bingo, you take these boys and I give you the starting money and you be off down the road. Don't worry about nothing back here, Bingo.' That's what he says. And now he sticks it to me."

"He must a had them white owners talking for some time," said Raymond. "If they is really serious this time they been some miracles pulled."

"You tell me," Bingo growled. "How many times ain't we seen them boys come around and dangle that money in front of us? 'Oh, if you just wasn't so dark, Bingo Long, you could make a hundred grand for my ball team tomorrow,' or 'Bingo, if we could only prove you was one of them Puerto Ricans we could sign you up.' How many times ain't we heard that shit?"

"Maybe this is for real," Raymond said.

"Until I see us colored boys roaming that Comiskey Park the same time as those White Sox then I say it's not for real."

"What's Louis say?"

241

"Louis don't say shit. He gone and signed some papers and he thinks he going to be hitting off Dizzy Dean tomorrow," Bingo fumed.

Leon, Raymond, and the others eased up and talked among themselves. They left Bingo to stew in his chair, stepped aside when he began to pace. In a half hour Leon's bus would arrive. A few minutes later Raymond got up and talked quietly with the pitcher. Then they both approached Bingo.

"Getting about time, Bingo," Leon said. "Got to make us some decisions."

Bingo stood up and rubbed his hands along his thighs. The tour flashed quickly before him: the head of steam he had when he took off from Louisville into Cleveland and Chicago, the money they made, the crowds, then dumping Sallie for good. He looked quickly over what he had left—at Raymond and his notebook wedged in his back pocket, at the players, Fat Sam, Mungo, and the rest, who would probably dog it on with him as long as he asked them to, whether they were making it big or eating from tins and sleeping next to the road. He thought of what it would be like without Leon, without the old man putting on his exhibitions and pumping home strikes day after day. His mouth suddenly felt dry and he longed for a glass of beer and a shot. He reached in his pockets and found he was out of cigarettes.

"Team decided they would do what you wanted them to," Raymond broke in. "I took us a vote."

Bingo jerked his head up and saw the players standing around.

"If you wants to call it a head then we could ride it back to Louisville and hook up for the rest of the season before winter ball," Fat Sam said.

Bingo shook his head. "When these things goes, they goes fast."

"Make you think all the time," said Leon.

"I figure ain't nothing I can do if Esquire Joe want to take his

242

chance back east," Bingo said. "Figure he learned about everything we could tell him and a lot we never should."

Esquire smiled. "That the truth," he said.

"Okay," said Bingo. "Okay to you, Esquire, if you think you onto something."

"How about us?" said Raymond.

"We got to play them two teams we got lined up today and tomorrow," Bingo said. "Ain't no cause to throw away money we got."

"I buy that," said Raymond.

"Hope they ain't got much better than some girls' team or we got our asses whipped," Bingo said.

Just then the bus pulled in and swung open its doors. Leon grabbed his satchel and the Stars followed him and Esquire Joe out of the lobby. The sun was high in the sky and getting hot. It reflected harshly off the dark paint of the bus.

"Figure the team will follow you up before too long," Bingo said to Leon as they paused alongside the bus. "No point in keeping us out here."

"You probably doing the right thing," Leon answered. "A touring group got to last just so long before you wise to tie things up."

"The boys can go back and play for Sallie if they wants. Just so they don't lay in with that Lionel bastard."

"Yeah, Sallie, he weren't so bad," Leon said with a grin.

"Just a big old fat man smoking that cigar," said Bingo.

The driver came back to the bus from the hotel lobby and hopped up to his seat. He shot a waiting glance at the Stars.

They grouped around Leon and Esquire Joe, offering handshakes and slaps.

"How about you, Bingo?" Leon said. "What you got in mind?"

"Figure on Mexico maybe. Or down to Cuba if I feel like it. Do me some fishing, find me one of them little girls and play some ball with them boys. They been inviting me since I was down there last," Bingo said.

"Knew you'd think of something," Leon said. He stepped onto the bus, stopped, and flipped his head back. "Catch you all later."

The Stars stepped away from the exhaust fumes of the bus as it started off. Then they hopped into the Lincoln and Sallie's Oldsmobile. The cars drove off in the opposite direction, to Velma and Sellersville and the three more games they had to play.

Minutes later Bingo looked over to Fat Sam, who was driving the Lincoln in place of Esquire Joe. "With all this shit we been through, only thing makes any difference is that I was born too quick."

"How you get that?" said Fat Sam.

"If them white owners is for real, think of what them dudes would a put up if I was young and skinny like Louis and Esquire. Could you picture that?"

Fat Sam nodded.

Bingo clapped his hands together. "Could you picture that?"

He drummed his fingers against the dash of the Lincoln. Then he felt again for his cigarettes and realized he hadn't bought any.

"Just ten years is all I would a needed, Sam."

He realized he hadn't bought anything to sip on either.

"Maybe eight," he said.

He leaned back and found a comfortable position to ride out the miles.

73 74 10 9 8 7 6 5 4 3 2 1